THE DEVIL'S AGENDA

A STORY OF FAITH, REDEMPTION, AND PURPOSE

A NOVEL

SCOTT K. WILSON

THE DEVIL'S AGENDA

Published by
GRANITE MOUNTAIN BOOKS, LLC.
Smyrna, Georgia 30082
GraniteMountainBooks.co
TheDevilsAgendaBook.com
TheDevilsAgendaBook@outlook.com

First paperback edition, Granite Mountain Books, LLC, December 2025
Printed in the United States of America.
Printing version: v2.0
File build: 2026-05-22
Design by Scott K. Wilson
ISBN 979-8-218-87361-5

Artificial-intelligence tools were used in the editorial process of this manuscript. All creative content, including storyline, characters, settings, and themes, is solely the author's original work.

Special thanks to the U.S. Library of Congress for the public-domain photographs of the Chicago & North Western Proviso Yard, Proviso Roundhouse, and Chicago Union Station featured on the covers and closing pages of this book.

In loving memory of:

Aunt Ronnie, Aunt Lucy, Aunt Joan, Uncle Larry, and Keena

To my wife Christine,

Not a day goes by where I don't think about how much I love you.

God set a course for your life long before you drew breath. A purpose. A calling. But don't fool yourself—there is an enemy who burns to wreck it.

– Pastor Hills, *First Cavalry Church, 1977*

Prologue

Fear hit Eddie like a hammer swung by God Himself—hot, raw, and mean. It filled every inch of him, crowding out thought until all that was left was pulse and panic. A minute ago, he'd been standing easy in the quiet, cigarette glowing between his fingers, watching the snow drift lazy and slow through the locomotive's headlight beam. He'd even been counting the inches piling on the deck, the way a man counts seconds just to prove the world's still turning.

Now, Eddie trembled against the control panel, the walkie-talkie groaning in his grip as the plastic began to buckle. His breath came short and sharp, fogging the air in frantic bursts. Somewhere behind the static in his head a thought screamed through... *Who screwed up? Was it him? Was it the damn system?*

He pressed a shaking hand against his chest, his heart pounding like a trapped bird—fast, frantic, dying to get free.

Each thud rattled through his ribs, echoing in his ears until it felt like the sound was coming from everywhere.

Locked wheels screamed against the frozen rail, a sound so sharp it split the air clean in two. It drilled into Eddie's skull like a spike through a drum, a pure note of chaos that made the bones in his face vibrate. The ringing was unbearable—high, endless—and for a heartbeat he actually thought about jumping. One last try for freedom before steel and momentum finished the job.

Bobby had jumped, after all. Eddie had watched him go—just a blur of movement and a shout swallowed by the wind. Bobby was young, quick, stupidly brave. But even then, Eddie knew the odds. Hitting the ground at fifty miles an hour wasn't falling—it was getting erased. For all Eddie knew, Bobby was a smear of blood and denim in white forest.

He swallowed hard, his throat raw. The world outside had turned to a storm of sparks—bright gold fury slicing through the dark, spitting from the rails as the train tore down the line. The trees blurred by, black and skeletal, their branches rattling like bones in a tin drum.

Then—silence.

Seconds before impact, everything froze. Time folded in on itself. Eddie's mind stilled, perfectly calm, smooth as a lake before dawn.

And with a flash, white and absolute, like a camera's bulb going off in a dark room, Eddie Ross took his final picture.

Chicago Union Station (1978)

The taxi shuddered to a stop like it was trying to shake something loose—maybe its last breath. I fumbled through my wallet with fingers gone stiff from the cold.

"This should be good," the driver said without looking back, just his hand poking through the slot in the scratched safety glass. His nails were chewed down to the quick.

"That'll be six bucks."

I handed over a small fistful of crumpled singles. He counted them like he didn't trust me—fast, eyes flicking with the kind of speed you only get from habit or nerves—and then slipped out of the car without another word.

"Turned out to be a nice day after all," he said, almost cheerfully, popping the trunk.

He hefted my suitcase and started to lower it to the pavement. The asphalt was dark with cold moisture, the kind that soaked in and stayed. I grabbed the handle before it could touch down. He paused a beat longer than necessary.

The trunk lid slammed shut with a metal groan. He turned, handed me a business card worn soft at the corners, and then froze, just slightly—just long enough to notice his breath hanging in the air like smoke.

"Cold for November," he said, half to himself, like the weather had snuck up on him.

I flipped my collar up against the wind and met his eyes. "That's okay," I said. "I came prepared."

When I step into the Great Hall, it hits me all at once: the low murmur of voices, the sharp scent of floor polish, and a tide of businessmen swirling like a school of fish in ties and overcoats. They loop the floor in restless patterns, briefcases in hand, watching the seated passengers like circling dogs eyeing a bone.

The benches are massive—thrones for the tired—and the travelers slump on them like offerings. Overhead, a shaft of light slants through a high window, and I watch the dust twist in it, lazy and golden, like ash drifting from something long dead.

The scent of fresh coffee pulls me around the corner just as the intercom stutters to life.

Train three thirty-two from Nebraska now arriving.

The words echo through the vaulted corridor with a crackle that scrapes the air. I glance at my watch—old and stubborn, still ticking—and cut through the crowd toward the ticket counter.

"Morning, Mack. I'll take the usual."

Mack's behind the glass, same as ever. He's got the look of a man who's been clocking in since the Hoover administration, and maybe he has. His jacket's older than me, and there's something permanent about the creases on his face—like time just gave up trying to smooth them out.

We met in June, right after the heat wave. I was wandering the halls looking for the men's room, still new to the station, when Mack came clacking down the corridor in polished shoes, fresh from a shine. He'd looked me over, eyes sharp under bushy gray brows, and said, "You look to be lost." Just like that.

Ever since then, we've been on a first-name basis.

"It's good to see you, Scott. One round-trip to Omaha, comin' right up."

"Thanks, Mack." I pass him the bills. "I'll see you in a month."

I descend the stairs into the underbelly of the station, where the air turns dense and metallic, like it's been trapped too long. Rows of train cars rest in their berths, motionless but humming faintly, like sleeping animals.

As I head toward the Omaha line, something flickers at the edge of my vision. I stop. A glint on the ground, small and sharp, like an eye just opened.

I crouch down. It's a Zippo—chrome, smooth, almost warm to the touch. The light overhead flickers across it in a way that makes my skin crawl, though I'm not sure why.

I flip it open and strike the flint. The flame whooshes up with a soft roar, steady and too bright for the dim platform. It dances—a little too eagerly—and I see an engraving on the side.

The design is... strange. Ornate, almost sacred, like something that belongs on an altar or a tomb. The script is foreign—not foreign like French or Latin, but foreign like not meant for mouths to speak.

I don't smoke. Never have. But I snap the lid shut and tuck the lighter deep into my jacket pocket anyway.

Somewhere ahead, I hear a voice—Melvin, maybe—calling through the mist. It echoes off the tiles and comes back thinner.

Melvin's voice rolled out from beside the car like warm thunder, rich and gravelly. He was one of the longtime conductors—black, late sixties, maybe older, with a laugh big enough to rattle rafters and a smile bright as snow under a floodlight. He always called me "Mr. Scott," though my last name's Walker. I told him once—just once—but he stuck with Scott, and I never corrected him again. It felt right, somehow. Like he knew something I didn't.

"It's great to see you, Mr. Scott," he said, eyes shining beneath his cap like he knew a secret he couldn't quite tell.

"You too, Melvin," I said, reaching to shake his hand. His grip was firm but soft, like an old leather glove.

He peered over his glasses, his expression shifting like clouds crossing the sun. "How's your grandmother?" he asked, careful.

I hesitated. "Not great. Actually… the situation with Comet's gotten worse."

Melvin flinched, a flicker behind the eyes. "I'm sorry to intrude."

"No, it's alright. It's just… some mornings he can't even stand. He'll lie there for hours. Every now and then he tries, but it's like his body's forgotten how."

Melvin shook his head slowly, as if the sorrow was familiar. "That's awful, Mr. Scott. You were giving him painkillers, right?"

"Yeah. They help, but not enough. That's why I'm heading back. The vet's coming out. I've got this feeling she's going to suggest we put him down."

He winced. "God have mercy. That'll break your grandmother's heart."

"Comet was the first horse she and Pop bought—1918. He's more than a horse. He's a memory."

"I'll say a prayer for her. Abigail, right?"

I nodded. "Yes. Thank you, Melvin."

I reached into my jacket. "Hey—look what I found. Just outside, a few cars back." I held up the Zippo. Its metal caught the light like it was made for it.

Melvin's eyes narrowed just a hair. "Can't say I've seen anyone looking for it."

"Alright. Just thought I'd ask." I smiled. "It's always good seeing you, Melvin."

"You tell Abigail I'm sending my blessings," he said, nodding slowly. "Tell her I remember her in my prayers."

"I will."

The car groaned as I climbed the steps. Heat slapped me in the face like an open palm. It smelled like dust, mold, and old cowboy boots—like a forgotten attic that used to be someone's favorite room.

I made my way down the aisle, brushing past other passengers stuffing bags overhead, when a mass blocked the way—a squat, grumbling hill of a man crawling on the floor.

"Where is it? It must be here somewhere," he muttered. "Dammit!"

"Excuse me, sir," I said. "Are you looking for this?"

I held up the Zippo.

The man twisted up like a puppet on a short string. "Yes!" he barked, wide-eyed. "Thank God. Where was it?"

"Back by the terminal. On the ground."

He snatched it from my hand like it was holy. "I thought it was gone forever." His eyes glistened as he crushed my hand in a two-pump shake. "Eddie. Name's Eddie."

"Scott. Scott Walker. Good to meet you."

"Well, Mr. Walker," he said, still breathless, "you just saved an old man's soul. This little lighter here?" He held it up like an offering. "Looks ordinary. But this thing's got history, you understand? History with a capital H. If you hadn't come along,

I'd have torn that station apart looking for it. Hell, I was ready to crawl under the damn train."

He flipped his pocket inside out, revealing a tear. "Slipped right down my pant leg while I was walking. I always pat my side to make sure it's there, and when I boarded—gone."

"Well, I'm glad I found it," I said, and meant it, even if I couldn't explain why.

He squinted. "You traveling alone?"

"Yeah. Once a month. Omaha. My grandmother needs help running her ranch."

I hoisted my suitcase into the rack and sat beside him. Eddie didn't hesitate.

"Last August, my grandfather passed. Now it's just her. Hundred acres, a handful of old animals, and a barn that could fall any day. She won't sell, though. Says the city's too noisy. Says it messes with her sleep."

Eddie nodded. "I get that. I'm no city man, myself. I'd rather hear frogs in the pond than horns on the street. And for your grandmother... well, that land's not just land. It's her life. Selling it would be like burning the family Bible."

He leaned back and wiped his glasses with a handkerchief.

"Where you headed?" I asked.

Eddie let out a belly laugh—deep and sudden. "Now that's a hell of a question."

"Try me."

He glanced around the car, then leaned in, voice lowering. "West. Far west. As far as the tracks go. Can't say what I'm gonna find there, but I know I'll find it."

His fingers brushed the scar on his forehead—a jagged, pink line, not more than a few months old. He flinched, realizing I'd noticed, and dropped his hand.

"That probably sounds strange," he said, "coming from a man just over 60."

"Maybe a little," I said. "But interesting."

Eddie stared forward, eyes glassy. "Took a lifetime, but I see it now. There's a plan for me. Always was. Took near-death to figure it out."

Something about the way he said it made me think of the engraving on the Zippo. The strange writing that felt like it knew me.

"You almost died?"

He nodded, slow as dusk. "Train wreck. Nine months ago. Dead for forty minutes."

My skin prickled. The air suddenly felt too close.

"I was in darkness. And I met the Devil."

I waited for the smile. For the wink. The chuckle that says just kidding. It never came.

"I'm sorry—what?" I said, half-laughing.

Eddie just looked at me. And through me.

"I met him," he said. "Not a metaphor. Not a symbol. Him. And believe me, son, he's real. He doesn't come with horns and a pitchfork. He comes wearing your regrets. Smiling like someone you trust."

I swallowed.

"This world, Mr. Walker—it's a battleground. You can't see it, but it's there. Invisible. Constant. The reason so many never find the life they were meant to live? It's because something's working real hard to stop them."

I didn't answer. Couldn't.

Eddie turned the Zippo over in his hand, slow and reverent.

"I was given a second chance. Now I know what I'm supposed to do. And I'm not afraid anymore."

He looked at me with eyes that had been somewhere I hadn't.

"I want to hear it," I said, quieter than I meant to. "All of it."

Eddie leaned in again, voice like gravel in a storm.

"Then let me tell you what happened in the dark."

The Roundhouse (1932)

Eddie lay still, listening. The sounds were back again—scraping, crunching, that dry, papery rustle like something dragging bones through insulation. It was the same damn thing that showed up most nights, some squat little critter nesting in the walls, but tonight it had turned up the volume. It started clawing around just after two—he'd checked the green glow of the clock with one gummy eye—and now it was a quarter to five.

The dreams had been better than real life—dark places, industrial and vast, full of steam and humming machinery and a blackness thick enough to drink. He didn't know why he wanted to go back there, but he did. God help him, he did.

He rolled over and tried to claw his way back to sleep. But it was no use. His throat was raw, like he'd been chewing dust, and the creature in the wall wouldn't shut up.

With a grunt, Eddie sat up and drove a fist into the wall,

the old plaster giving just a bit under the punch like stale bread. "Wish me luck today," he muttered, more to himself than to the thing inside the wall. It didn't answer, of course. It never did.

He yanked his robe off the bedpost, dragged his tired feet into the cold embrace of his slippers, and slid across the floor toward the kitchen, each step catching slightly on the warped hardwood. Passing the living room, he paused. There she was again—his mother—sitting in the same battered armchair like she'd grown into the upholstery.

Third morning in a row now.

Her head hunched down into her shoulders like it wanted to hide from the day, facing the window, her wiry silhouette framed in the pale, tired light filtering through the drapes. It stretched out across the floor and up the far wall like some kind of specter—thin and trembling.

The whole room smelled like old cigar smoke, stale and ghostly. Eddie stood there for a moment, his nose twitching, heart doing something slow and mean in his chest. The smell shouldn't be there. But it was.

He didn't speak. Just watched her—watched the way she didn't move—and the way her shadow did.

"Morning, dear," his mother sighed, like the breath was too tired to carry the words. "You're up early again."

She reached over with arms thin as broom handles and pulled him in, resting her chin on his shoulder for a moment longer than she usually did. He could smell the night on her—old tears, dried powder, and a hint of aged perfume.

"Any more dreams?" she asked.

Eddie hesitated. Thought about lying. Thought about telling her it was just the usual junk, a dream where his math teacher turned into a dog or something equally harmless. But no.

"Well," he said, "I was sleepin' good, Momma, until the scratching started again."

She didn't need him to say more. Her shoulders twitched at the word scratching, like she heard it too, even now, in the bones of the walls.

"This time it was loud, and it started early. But before that…" He smiled faintly and stepped to the standing lamp, yanking the chain with a click.

The light bloomed and peeled back the shadows.

That's when he saw her face.

Her eyes were puffy and raw, lids wet and trembling like she hadn't quite finished crying yet. In her lap sat an envelope—a little yellowed, a little crumpled—with FINAL NOTICE screaming red through the creases. She tried to cover it with her arm, but not fast enough.

Eddie pretended not to notice.

"I had the dream again," he said quickly, voice light, hopeful, even though the tension in the room was thick enough to stir with a spoon.

Her voice, when it came, was quieter now. "Which one?"

"The rail yard," Eddie said. "With the steam engines. Only this time I wasn't just watchin'. I was inside the roundhouse. There were sparks flying through the air like it was the Fourth of July—red and orange and white, all mixed up, like lightning had crawled into the rafters."

She sat up straighter, wiped her cheek with the back of her hand. She tried to smile. The lines at the corners of her mouth cracked like paper.

"You've been havin' this one a lot lately."

"Yeah," he said, more to himself now. "And it's weird, Momma. Each time it's clearer. Like I'm gettin' closer to something. Like it's waitin' for me."

She nodded, slowly. There was something fragile in the way she looked at him—like she saw more in his dreams than he did.

"And tonight..." he paused, nervous now. "Tonight, I was working there. I had a job. You were there too—and you looked proud of me. Real proud. I gave you money to pay Mr. Dunn—"

Her hand came down like a gavel on the arm of the chair.

"Eddie," she snapped. "I don't want you worryin' about Mr. Dunn."

She crossed her arms, hard, like she was trying to fold herself into something smaller. Her heel tapped the hardwood once, sharply.

Eddie didn't answer. He just moved to the window like something was pulling him—some magnetic hum that buzzed behind the glass. He threw up the sash with both hands and leaned out, the dank air slapping his cheeks. A flock of pigeons exploded from the fire escape like feathers from a ruptured pillow.

The city beyond was gray and soft, cradled in fog. Somewhere far off, a train wailed—a long, low sound, mournful as a church organ on a funeral morning.

"I'm going there today," Eddie said, nodding once. "To see if I can get a job."

"No you're not," she said, fast. "It's too dangerous. You know what kind of men work down there? And besides, no one's gonna hire a thirteen-year-old boy. Not now. Not with the way things are."

"I've got a good feeling," Eddie said. His fingers curled on the window sill. "I'm going."

Her voice came harder now. "Eddie! I mean it! Don't even think about goin' down—"

But the click of the lock stopped everything.

They both turned toward the door.

The sound of keys—jangling, clumsy, hesitant—and then the dull metal clack of the front latch twisting open. The old oak door creaked on its hinges like it hated being disturbed.

Catherine stepped through, dragging last night in behind her.

Her hair looked like it had been styled by a windstorm, makeup smudged, and there was a streak of lipstick on her cheek like a child's crayon drawing. Her eyes were sunk into dark hollows, and she smelled faintly of gin and city smog.

"Where've you been, young lady?" Momma asked, voice brittle as glass.

Catherine didn't stop.

"I said stop!" she shouted.

Catherine halted in the hallway, her shadow long and crooked under the single hallway bulb. She turned slowly, her expression flat and cold, like a wax doll left too close to the fire.

"Margaret told me you've been spendin' time with Ray. Is it true?"

"Don't worry," Catherine said, her voice tired. "I was just out with friends."

"Liar." The word wasn't shouted, but it cut sharper than anything else in the room. "Ray's no good. He's like your father. You want that? A man who drinks more than he talks? Who runs when things get hard?"

Catherine's mouth curled. "He treats me good. He's got a job. When I'm with him, we eat more than just..." she hesitated, but her anger pushed it through—"bread."

The blanket fell from their mother's lap as she stood.

"You think this is my fault?" she asked. "Why we got no money? Why we've gotta skip dinner some nights just to make it through the week?"

Eddie stood frozen, the train horn still echoing in the back of his skull.

"You think I like standin' in that breadline while you're out with Ray gettin' lit at some clip joint? You want to end up like me? Like your father made me?"

Then the tears came—ugly, real, and raw. She turned toward the wall and stared at the old photo of Luke. The sailor hat, the fresh-pressed uniform, the American flag. All lies now.

Eddie walked over and wrapped his arms around her neck. She didn't move.

He looked to Catherine. Gave her a little nod.

She turned, eyes glassy, and stomped off down the hallway. The door slammed behind her, rattling the frame.

Margaret poked her head around the kitchen door. "Why's everyone up?" she asked. "What happened?"

Eddie handed his mother a handkerchief. "I'll talk to her. She might listen to me."

Eddie tiptoed down the hallway, feet making soft sounds against the warped wood floor, the kind of floor that remembered every step. Princess, the white cat with one eye half-shut from age or suspicion—nobody really knew—was curled like a comma outside Catherine's bedroom door. She flicked her tail as Eddie stepped over her, not so much annoyed as vaguely judgmental.

He knocked—not too hard, just a few tight raps with his knuckles.

"Can I come in?" he asked, and his voice sounded younger than he wanted it to.

"Sure," Catherine muttered, with the fatigue of someone who'd been arguing with ghosts all night.

Eddie slipped inside and sat at the edge of the bed, where the blanket was half-on, half-off, like it had given up trying to comfort anyone. The bedspread was layered in fine, white cat hair that glittered in the shaft of sunlight sneaking through the curtains. Dust and dander floated in slow motion—suspended like particles in amber. One caught in his nose. He stifled a sneeze.

Catherine let out a breath through her nose, eyes half-lidded. "What is it, Eddie? I've been up all damn night."

"Mom's worried," he said, fiddling with a loose thread on the quilt. It came out easier than expected, like unraveling wasn't that hard after all.

"She always is. She needs to stop poking her nose where it don't belong. Stress she carries ain't all mine, but she wears it like my name's stitched into the lining."

Eddie didn't argue. He knew better. He just sniffled, nodded a little. "She says things because she cares. Doesn't want to see you mess up like... well, like she did."

That landed like a pebble in a still pond. Catherine blinked. Just once.

Then: "You didn't come in here just to scold me, did you?"

Eddie hesitated. Twice. "Can I ask you something?"

"You're already doing it."

"It's kinda important."

She rolled her eyes. "Spit it out."

Eddie glanced at the door like someone might be listening, then leaned forward, voice low. "It's about Ray."

Catherine groaned, a long, theatrical thing. "Jesus, Eddie. Really?"

"One of the kids—Stevie Wityak—he said he saw Ray with a gun."

Catherine sat up straighter, her mouth a line drawn tight.

"Other day, when Ray was dropping you off," Eddie continued, "the wind kicked up and blew open his coat. Stevie said he saw a holster. On his hip. And there's more—someone said he was seen near that bank, the one the mob knocked over a few weeks ago. People are talking. They think Ray's connected."

Catherine hissed through her teeth. "Eddie, what you're saying is crazy. You hear me? Crazy."

"I'm just telling you what I heard."

"Well, you can tell Stevie Wityak and anyone else flapping their gums that they're full of crap. Ray ain't in the mob. He's not some gangster with a tommy gun in his violin case. He works late. That's all. And if anyone says different, I swear, you better shut them up—use your fists if you have to."

Eddie glanced down at his hands—knuckles still scabbed over from a fight behind the dumpster the week before. That had been about marbles. This... this felt bigger.

"Just don't get into trouble," he said. "That's all."

She groaned again and rolled over. "You done? Because I need sleep."

"Almost. One more thing."

Catherine yanked the covers back up to her chin. "Make it fast."

"Can I use your bike today?"

"What's wrong with yours?"

"Chain snapped. Rusted clean through."

Catherine peeled back the covers just enough to glare at him. "Why?"

"I wanna go to the roundhouse. Proviso."

She sat up all the way now, hair spilling around her like smoke. "The roundhouse?" Her voice lifted in that mocking lilt she saved for dumb questions and family drama. "What are you gonna do, Eddie, fix the engines with your bare hands?"

"I wanna work," he said, puffing out his chest. "I'm strong enough. I can sweep. I can organize tools. I ain't afraid to get dirty."

"Eddie, they don't hire kids. Especially not ones that just turned thirteen."

"You don't think I'm tough enough?" His jaw tightened like it had been wound with baling wire.

Catherine sighed, long and slow. The kind of sigh that comes from watching too many people try and fail. "It ain't about tough. You're tough, all right. You've had to be. But those guys down there—they're different. They're not just working. They're surviving. Drinking coffee that's more grounds than water. Losing fingers to machinery. Going home to one-room apartments that smell like mildew and mustard gas."

Eddie swallowed hard. "I keep having these dreams," he said. "Three nights in a row now. I'm there, in the roundhouse. Cleaning. Just sweeping, organizing. But it feels... right. Like I'm supposed to be there."

Catherine looked at him—really looked this time. Not like a big sister tolerating her little brother's fantasy, but like a person trying to read something carved into wood, faded by time.

Finally, she nodded.

"Alright. But don't mess it up. The bike's chained to the stoop with the others. And Eddie?"

"Yeah?"

"Don't get yourself killed."

He grinned, hoped from the bed, and ducked out the door.

Princess watched him go with one eye still squinting, as if she already knew what awaited.

Eddie stood at the edge of the yard like a boy staring down the throat of a sleeping dragon. Above him, the sky churned in unnatural hues—crimson and mustard-gas yellow, with bruises of purple rolling like smoke across a dirty ceiling. The clouds moved slow but angry, swollen with heat and something else Eddie couldn't name. Below, the world mirrored that ugly sky: hundreds of railroad tracks ran out like ribs from a rotted carcass, gleaming with rust and light, their silver lines wiggling in the summer shimmer as if alive, as if breathing.

In the distance, the roundhouse waited. Just like in the dream. Exactly like it.

It loomed on the edge of the rail yard like a structure that didn't just exist in space—but in memory, in some half-buried corner of Eddie's mind he couldn't fully unlock. A wide, circular beast of brick and shadow, its rows of bay windows looked like crooked teeth, or dominoes punched into its middle like someone built a castle from jagged smiles. The smokestack belched long black clouds into the sky, unbothered, eternal, like a signal fire from some dark age.

Eddie swallowed.

Something tickled his leg—real enough—and he slapped it without looking. A squashed bug, maybe, or a burr. But when he straightened up, the world tilted.

Pressure bloomed behind his eyes like a migraine blooming in time-lapse. His temples throbbed, a pulsing like twin engines ramping to full speed. Darkness licked the corners of his vision, curling inward. Lights—streaks of them—zipped across his field of view, like tiny bolts of lightning breaking formation and running off in crooked squiggles. The heat pressed on him, thick as wool, sour with the tang of creosote and hot steel.

He stood still. Tried to breathe.

A tunnel opened in his mind—not the kind you walk through, but the kind you fall into, headfirst, helpless. And through that tunnel he saw it all again: the way the tracks gleamed, the humming silence of the yard, the ghost of motion behind the warehouse windows. It was déjà vu turned inside out. Every sense screamed that he'd been here before. Not just visited—but lived it. Worked it. Dreamed it. And not in some foggy, flickering way, but with clarity. This place was his, once.

Then, just like that, it snapped.

The feeling vanished. Cut clean. As if someone had yanked the filmstrip from the projector mid-frame. The tunnel was gone. The pressure in his skull eased, though not completely. He was back in his body. In his skin. But something had passed through him.

He stood there blinking in the new light, a little sweatier, a little more afraid.

He wasn't sure if he'd had a vision or a memory. He wasn't sure there was a difference.

But the roundhouse was still there, huffing smoke like a dragon curled in a nest of iron and ash—and Eddie knew he was going in.

The wind kicked up sudden, sharp—a dusty slap across Eddie's cheeks that tasted like iron and soot. He squinted up at the sky and saw the clouds twisting above him like something alive, folding into themselves with the lazy rhythm of bread dough kneaded by invisible, furious hands. The whole sky looked sick. Not stormy—wrong.

To the right, a huddle of boxcars sat in a long line, stacked shoulder to shoulder like livestock crammed into a pen. Their colors had long since faded—rust red, bruised yellow, moldy green—but still they stood out against the iron-gray field of track and sky. They stretched on and on, a hundred of them at least, all stinking of heat and metal.

To the left, he spotted movement: three steam engines, each on its own rail, creeping forward like sleeping giants shaking off their dreams. One puffed a cloud of steam so thick it swallowed a dozen boxcars behind it. The engines weren't moving fast, but they didn't need to. There was a menace to their size, to their momentum. Slow things crush just as hard.

Eddie glanced behind him—nothing but tall grass, brush in the distance, and time. Circling around would tack another hour on the trip. Maybe two. That meant the direct route was the only route. Over the rails.

He gripped the handlebars of Catherine's bike until his fingers went bone-white. The rubber squeaked under the pressure. His palms were clammy, his heart hammering like it was trying to punch through his ribs and run off on its own.

"Okay," he whispered. "Okay, just ride."

He pushed forward, easing down the embankment, the slope slick with gravel and cigarette butts and little bits of broken glass that winked in the sun like tiny razors. The bike creaked beneath him, the chain clicking with every half-turn of the pedals. For a moment, the descent held—smooth, manageable—but gravity had other plans.

The tires hit the bottom and the frame kicked up like a mule. A jolt slammed into Eddie's thighs hard enough to punch the air from his lungs. He gritted his teeth and fought to keep straight, but the gravel beneath the tires had the traction of marbles. Each pop and crunch under his wheels was a warning shot from the ground itself.

His arms burned. His legs screamed. The bike swerved like it had a mind of its own, a drunk and vengeful one at that. Eddie cursed and leaned back, muscles quaking, and yanked up just in time to clear the first rail.

Yes! The front wheel hopped over.

But the back didn't follow.

The tire caught—locked like a trap—and in the space between one heartbeat and the next, Eddie was airborne.

He flew, just for a second, weightless and quiet, as if the yard had swallowed every sound in the world. Then gravity remembered him.

He landed face-first in the gravel with a crunch and a wet scrape that turned the inside of his mouth into fire and pennies. Pain lit up his face like a bonfire. The world tilted. Something sharp cracked inside his jaw.

When he sat up, his vision throbbed at the edges. He spat—and with it came a small, white fragment of something that hadn't been loose before. Tooth. He knew it before he looked. His knees screamed at him, torn open and glistening. Blood trickled down his shins, hot and sticky and redder than it should've been.

The bike lay a few feet away, wheels spinning like they were still trying to run.

Eddie didn't cry. He didn't even curse.

He just stared at the gravel, the rail ahead, and the roundhouse in the distance. That dark, wheezing monster still pumping smoke into the sky. Waiting.

He wiped his mouth with the back of his hand and stood up. His knees shook but held.

"Still going," he muttered. "Still going."

Eddie slung his backpack across one shoulder, grabbed the handlebars of the bike with both hands, and took off—

running like the devil himself had crawled up out of the gravel and decided Eddie was next on his list. The tires rattled and shrieked against the rails, the frame bouncing wildly behind him like it wanted loose, like it hated him for dragging it into this mess.

Boxcars rose ahead like a rusted maze, hulking metal beasts parked in a slow-motion snarl across the yard. Eddie didn't stop. He ducked under the belly of one—a cattle car, stinking like old manure and engine grease—then shimmied between two others, catching his elbow on a rivet that tore a flap of skin loose. He didn't feel it. Not yet.

Far off, maybe a hundred yards, a rust-pitted pickup truck with mismatched green fenders shot down the dirt road, kicking up a snake of dust and gravel in its wake. The headlights glared like angry eyes, and the windshield wipers slapped back and forth with frantic urgency, even though the rain was just getting started—a weird detail that stuck in Eddie's head, even as his lungs started to burn.

Then came the sound. Not thunder. Not quite. It was sharper, cleaner, meaner.

A *screeeee*—high and thin like a bottle rocket slicing the sky—and then the sky itself broke.

Lightning slammed down so close that the air itself seemed to split in half. The light was blinding. The boom that followed was worse—like a bomb going off behind his ribs. Eddie's knees buckled and he hit the ground, face scraped raw by gravel already slick with water.

Somewhere ahead, a tree screamed and cracked, and Eddie saw it go down in a spray of branches—right at the edge of the yard, near the fence. It hit with a thud so deep it seemed to rearrange his insides. The boom rolled through the city like God pounding his fists on the rooftops.

Rain came in sheets now. Fat, cold drops that slapped his skin and turned the gravel into sludge. Eddie ducked his head, letting the bill of his cap shield his eyes, and kept going. Every step was harder than the last. The ground sucked at his shoes. The wheels of the bike snagged and spun. But he didn't stop.

Then he felt it.

A vibration in the soles of his shoes. Not imagined—real. He looked back.

The trains.

They were close now. Too close.

Three of them, crawling like mechanical dinosaurs, their steel bellies rumbling deep and low. The ground trembled with their hunger. Headlights cut through the steam and rain like fire through wax, and Eddie knew—knew—he didn't have time to fall again.

He gritted his teeth, hissed out a breath through the pain, and ran harder.

"Don't look back," he muttered. "Don't you dare look back."

The roundhouse loomed ahead now, huge and dark and billowing smoke like something that was alive. Like a mouth waiting to be fed.

And Eddie ran straight toward it.

CHOOOO, CHOOOOOOO!

The sound ripped through Eddie's skull like a hot nail. It wasn't a whistle—it was a warning. A judgment. A beast's scream.

"Oh no!" he gasped, stumbling sideways, nearly dropping the bike again.

They were blowing their horns. At him.

His heart pounded, a jackhammer in his chest, out of rhythm, out of time. His legs were rubber. Sweat poured off his forehead and ran into his eyes, burning, blinding. Everything turned into a squirming blur, like the world was made of snakes and smoke.

Should he run?

Should he freeze?

The question hung there in his chest like an anchor.

The ground shook so hard it seemed to jump beneath his shoes. The rails shivered, clattered, hissed. Birds shot from the trees like an explosion of black feathers, their wings flapping in a panic that felt contagious. The air thickened—hot, greasy, choking with smoke and steam. It oozed up from the train's underbelly like something alive.

One engine thundered past, then another, and another still—black iron monsters dragging breath and fury behind them. Their stacks coughed out smoke that boiled into the sky, where it tangled with the clouds. Wind lashed out and snatched Eddie's cap right off his head, sending it cartwheeling into the ditch like a shot bird.

He reached for it—instinct—but stopped short.

A face stared at him from the nearest engine's cab. A man—hard, sharp-featured, smudged in soot. The kind of face carved from stone and fired in coal. His eyes—charcoal pits—locked onto Eddie's and burned. His mouth moved. Eddie couldn't hear over the thunder of the steel leviathan, but he could read the lips:

"GET OFF THE TRACKS, YOU TWIT!"

The man pumped his fist, furious. Maybe scared. Maybe both.

Eddie snapped back to life. He hurled the bike off the tracks with all the strength he had left—watched it bounce and land in a mess of mud and weeds—and then he kicked the ground in frustration, hard enough to sting his toes.

The engines roared on, vanishing into the horizon, taking their fury with them.

Eddie stood there, chest heaving, hair plastered to his forehead with sweat and rain. He looked down at his scraped knees, the blood mixing with mud, trickling down into his socks. The world felt too big now. Like it had teeth.

But he was still standing.

And the roundhouse was just ahead.

When Eddie reached the roundhouse, he stopped dead in his tracks. The building loomed like something out of a nightmare—monolithic, hunched against the sky, breathing smoke and heat like some ancient metal dragon. From a yawning mouth carved into its brick flank spilled a glow the color of firelight seen through whiskey. Inside, machines clanked with mechanical violence, men barked at each other like dogs in a junkyard, and somewhere, a jet of steam screamed out into the summer air like a soul being exorcised.

Eddie swallowed hard. *Maybe I'm not tough enough*, he thought, gripping the strap of his backpack until his knuckles popped. *Maybe I should turn around*. The silhouette of the building, black as coal and twice as foreboding, loomed over him like a warning. *Maybe I won't stand a chance in this place.*

But he didn't turn. He couldn't. Not with the notice on his mom's lap and the taste of blood still faint on his gums from that fall across the tracks. So he puffed out his chest, the way he'd seen the older boys do, and rounded the corner.

What met him wasn't just noise and fire—it was a different world entirely.

Inside, the roundhouse was alive in the strangest, most terrible sense of the word. Everything moved. Everything groaned. Everything sweated.

On both sides of the massive circular hall, locomotives sat like giants at rest—hulking metal beasts with bellies full of fire, their sides twitching with heat. They didn't sleep; they waited. Their open maws coughed ash into the air, which drifted up to the rafters in lazy spirals before coating the ceiling's ancient beams in another layer of soot as thick as cake frosting. Welders sent arcs of blue light into the gloom. Sparks sailed like tiny comets, hissing when they landed on grease-slick concrete.

Eddie stepped inside, crouching low behind a stack of old shipping crates that reeked of oil and mildew and the ghosts of cargo long gone. He didn't want to be seen—not yet. Not until he knew what kind of men haunted this place.

Through the sweltering haze, he spotted one.

The man moved like he belonged here—stocky, thick in the shoulders, dressed in denim overalls that were more patch than fabric and a striped hat pulled low over a round, weathered face. He walked with the slow swagger of someone who knew the weight of things—tools, time, regret. He flipped a silver lighter through his fingers like a cardsharp, lit a cigarette with a calm flick, then tapped the lighter back into his pocket with three soft pats.

Next to him stood a different breed—a wiry redhead with a twitch in his jaw and something rodent-like about the eyes. He stuffed a plug of chewing tobacco into his cheek and spat a dark stream between his boots without looking where it landed.

The two men laughed about something—Eddie couldn't make out the words, but the tone was the same one men used in the alley behind the bar, the kind of laugh that came with dirty jokes and stories about scars you couldn't show in daylight.

Then they turned toward the biggest engine of the bunch.

It wasn't just large—it was monstrous. Jet black and wet with sweat, its side shimmered in the firelight like the flank of a bull ready to charge. It gave off heat in waves. Steam curled from its rivets and seams like breath from a nose. If the other engines were sleeping bears, this one was awake.

The men approached it like priests to a god.

And Eddie, crouched in the shadows with grit on his palms and a nervous twitch in his knee, realized something he hadn't known until now.

He *wanted* to be part of this.

He needed it.

"WHO THE HELL ARE YOU?!"

The voice came low and mean, like a rock dropped down a dry well. Eddie barely had time to turn before he was shoved hard from behind. He fell forward, catching himself against the crates—splinters raking across his arms like a cat's claws. The sting came fast. Hot. Real.

He turned, teeth clenched, blood starting to run in thin rivulets down his forearms.

Behind him stood a kid—no, a boy, but big like a corn-fed linebacker, maybe sixteen, with a buzz cut and muscles that looked carved from scrap iron. His grin split his face like a wound.

"You're on the wrong side of the tracks, runt."

Eddie bristled. "Who you callin' runt?"

The boy took a step forward, shadow stretching out across the floor. Eddie didn't back up. Didn't blink. Just lifted his fists a little higher. The boy noticed—the pause in his step betrayed him—and something behind his eyes shifted, like he'd just realized this wasn't going to be a one-swing fight. Eddie had danced before.

"I can take ya," Eddie muttered.

The boy smirked and turned half away, like he'd had enough. Eddie knew the move before it happened. The kid spun back fast, arm cocked like a sledgehammer ready to drop.

But Eddie was faster.

He dipped left, felt the wind of the missed punch graze his cheek, and drove a fist into the boy's ribs with a crack that echoed like a snapped broom handle. The kid staggered, clutching his side, and raised one hand. "You win."

Eddie didn't drop his guard.

"Alright, alright..." the boy laughed, now rubbing his side with a wince. "Not bad. Not a lotta kids your size know how to fight."

Eddie stayed silent, still buzzing with adrenaline.

"What're you here for?" the boy asked, the grin returning, this time less tooth and more curiosity.

"I need a job," Eddie said, voice shaky from the adrenaline drop. "Cleaning."

The boy scratched his head and looked around like maybe the answer was hiding behind one of the locomotives. "Damn. Shoulda come yesterday. Some other kid showed up and snagged the last spot. I'd know—I help manage the crew. There's eight of us that clean."

Eddie's shoulders sank. "But—"

"But what?" the boy cut in.

"I really need it." Eddie dropped his eyes to the floor, scuffing a boot in the dirt.

The older boy looked at him a long second. "Cheer up. I'll take you to Fleming. He runs Maintenance. Who knows? Maybe the old bastard's in a generous mood."

Eddie nodded, hopeful despite himself. "Thanks. What's your name?"

"I'm Arthur," the boy said, brushing sweat-damp bangs from his eyes. "But most folks call me Horse."

Eddie raised a brow.

Arthur pulled up his sleeve. On his forearm, a crude tattoo of an American Quarter Horse pawed the air mid-gallop.

"You did that yourself?"

"Damn right. All you need's a needle, some ink, a mirror, and more pain tolerance than sense." He cracked his knuckles and drove a fist into his palm with a grin—*Wham*!

Then, out of nowhere, came a flash—blue-white, like lightning without thunder—and a crash that shook the rafters. Dust and soot rained down from the ceiling like ash from a bombed-out church. Eddie turned toward the gaping doors.

The rain was coming down in sheets now. The sky gone to iron.

"My dad had tattoos," Eddie said, his voice half-lost in the roar. "He got them in the Navy. One for every place he went. Women. Ships. Ports."

Arthur nodded, impressed. "He sounds like my kind of guy. I've been thinking about the Army. Least I'd get to see the land. Navy's too much water. Don't trust anything that doesn't have solid ground under it."

He leapt onto a nearby crate and pointed through the haze. A rusty metal sign barely clung to the far wall, letters flaking like old scabs: MAINTENANCE.

"C'mon," Arthur said. "Let's go see if the troll's in."

They crossed through the steam and noise, past rows of dormant metal giants exhaling heat. Eddie couldn't help staring—at the welders slicing light from steel, the grizzled men bolting iron together, the grease-streaked artists painting numbers across the faces of monstrous engines. It was like watching a cathedral being built—but louder, hotter, alive.

Finally, they reached the office—a door that looked like it belonged on a haunted treehouse. Warped, knotted wood. Cracked hinges. Ready to give up the ghost.

Arthur knocked.

"Who is it?" came a voice—gravel mixed with phlegm.

"Mr. Fleming, someone's here to see you."

"Tell them to piss off. I'm busy."

Arthur gave Eddie a look. "Hold on."

"It's about a cleaning job. I told him he's late, but figured I'd check."

"You're pressing your luck, boy. I said I'm busy. And yeah,

they're all taken. Now beat it—"

Before he could finish, a tiny, red-faced kid burst into the office from the side. He was even smaller than Eddie. His face was streaked with tears and soot.

The boy choked out his story—about the older workers shoving him, calling him names, throwing tools his way. Fleming just leaned back in his chair and laughed. A joyless, wheezing bark. The kind of laugh you'd expect from a man who liked to watch things break.

"I quit," the kid said softly. He shoved past Eddie without a second glance.

"Arthur!" Fleming barked. "Tell that boy to come here."

"He's gone, sir."

"Not that one. The *other* one."

Eddie stepped in.

Fleming looked like he'd been aged in a barrel of sweat and tobacco. Cheeks sagged like wet leather, a dozen cracks lined his face. He lit a cigarette with yellow fingers and pointed at the chair.

"Sit."

Eddie sat. Hard.

"Hello, s'sir—"

"Wipe that smirk off your face. And cut the stammer."

"Yes sir."

Fleming blew smoke toward the ceiling. "You're lucky, kid. Most don't last. That last one didn't even make it to lunch. Crybaby."

He leaned in. His breath smelled like ashes and vinegar. "Why should I believe you're any different?"

Eddie's hands clenched in his lap. He remembered his father, the way he used to raise his voice just before the bruises started. But he swallowed it down.

"I might look small," Eddie said. "But I'm tough."

"Ohhh?" Fleming sneered. "Prove it."

Eddie scanned the room. His eyes landed on the cigarette in the ashtray.

He reached forward, picked it up, and snuffed it out with his bare fingers. Held Fleming's gaze. Didn't flinch.

The man rose, walked around Eddie's chair, and kicked it—hard.

"Brazen little bastard!" he growled, then clamped a hand on Eddie's shoulder. It felt like being gripped by a mechanical vice. "You've got guts. I'll give you a try."

He leaned down, whisper-hot.

"Here's how it works. You clean. That's it. No chit-chat. No screwing around. No laughing. No smiling. You get a break at noon. Until then, I own your hands."

"Yes, sir," Eddie said, breath hitching in his throat. His heart was pounding from being yanked forward like that—more from the stare than the grip.

Fleming's eyes, pale and colorless like wet gravel, didn't blink. "Pay's twenty-five cents an hour," he growled. "You slack? I dock you half a day. No warnings. No do-overs. Clear?"

Eddie swallowed hard, jaw clenched tight enough to ache.

"Crystal."

Fleming held the stare for another second, then let go of Eddie's shirt with a grunt. The old man turned and jabbed a thick, grease-blackened finger toward a broom leaning against the wall. Its wooden handle was splintered and broken halfway up, its straw head frayed like it'd lost a bar fight.

"There's your scepter, Prince Charming."

Eddie blinked. "Are there… are there any others?"

Fleming's look was a mixture of disbelief and disgust, like Eddie had just suggested trading in a wrench for a lace handkerchief. He didn't answer, just curled his lip in a way that made the silence feel louder.

"I'll take it," Eddie said quickly, lunging for the broom like it might run away.

"Arthur!" Fleming barked, voice echoing off the steel beams overhead.

Arthur's head popped around the doorway, his cap crooked and his grin already forming. "Yeah?"

"Show this punk around."

Arthur stepped inside fully, leaning on the doorframe like he'd been waiting for this all morning. "Gladly."

Once they'd backed away from Fleming's door, he reached out his hand, palm open and waiting. "Slip me five."

Eddie raised his own and gave Arthur a firm smack, their palms clapping together with a satisfying pop.

Arthur grinned like a man about to tell a great joke, spun on his heel, and threw his arms wide like he was unveiling a grand exhibit. "Welcome to the Chicago & North Western Railway," he said, dramatically. "Your new home away from home."

Jack

Eddie's bones had settled into the grind like old rails easing into their ties. A few weeks on the job, and his mornings felt more like muscle memory than choice. Up at five, always five, to the static-buzz drone of his alarm clock—it didn't beep so much as it chittered, like a bug burrowed in his brain. Breakfast was a sad joke: stale bread with a texture like cardboard and a slug of warm, metallic-tasting tap water that always left his throat dry. Then it was jeans from yesterday, still caked with soot and something that smelled vaguely like scorched pennies, and a t-shirt stiff from sweat and steam.

He moved like a ghost through the apartment, keeping quiet as he climbed out the window and down the fire escape, his sneakers whispering against the rusted metal rungs until reaching the ground. Then it was onto Catherine's bike, head down, gears grinding, the morning air lapping his skin. He pedaled through the city, then through the brush to the roundhouse, the bike rattling beneath him as the smell of oil and hot metal drifted in on the wind.

He never arrived later than six-fifteen. Not once. Word was, a single slip—a sleepy eye or a missed streetcar—and you were out. No second chances. Rail yard law.

At the shed, the bikes were collapsed into one another in a heap of twisted spokes, slumped chains, and bent frames. They looked like casualties of some mechanical war. Eddie ducked inside, swatting away cobwebs that clung to his forehead like a curse. He parked Catherine's bike in the back—carefully, like laying a baby in a cradle—and wiped a smudge from her seat.

Then came Keena.

She was always there on Mondays and Wednesdays, tethered to a stake near the gravel path, a wiry German Shepherd with eyes like amber marbles and a tongue that lolled from her jaws like a strip of bacon. Eddie had studied her tag the first week: Keena, Owner: Jack Luken. The other workers gave her space. So had Eddie—at first. But on the fourth morning, he brought a peace offering.

Now, she wagged hard when she saw him, whipping the ground with her tail.

"Hey, girl." He scratched her thick neck, fingers pressing into the ropes of muscle. "Got something for you." From his backpack he pulled a wad of newspaper and unwrapped it to reveal a sad slice of white bread. Keena took it with a polite nip, then plopped her butt in the dirt and stared up at him, eyes glinting with something like discipline.

"Drop," Eddie commanded, pointing to the ground. Keena belly-flopped immediately, tongue lolling in a sloppy grin.

He knelt, lifted her tag again.

"Hmmm... Jack Luk—"

"Eddie!" Arthur's voice came like a whip crack from behind the corner. He was hauling a burlap sack, face as black as chimney soot, blond hair greasy and flopped over his eyes.

"That dog's vicious! Are you tryin' to get bit?"

But Keena's stance changed. In an instant, she was up—legs splayed, hackles bristling, a low growl pulsing from her ribs like an idling engine. Her lip peeled back to reveal teeth so clean they seemed to glow.

"Easy, girl." Eddie soothed her spine with slow, confident strokes. She crumpled to the ground with a huff and flopped onto her side, tongue unrolling like a party streamer.

Arthur blinked. "Damn! I've never seen her act like that with anyone. Except Jack. And Red."

"Jack? The owner?"

Arthur nodded. "Big guy, ink on his forearm—train with tracks, smoke, and everything. That's my work." He thumped his chest proudly. "Always flippin' that damn lighter like a street magician. He runs with Red, the beanpole with firetruck hair and a 'stache you could rake leaves with. Odd pair." Keena gave a sharp growl.

"Relax, lady," Arthur said, holding up his hands. "Just messin.'"

He dropped the sack at his feet, which landed with a dull whump and burped out a puff of sawdust. "Someone spilled a gallon of oil in Bay Seven. I got volunteered. You busy?"

"What about Fleming?" Eddie asked. "Won't he be mad?"

"Fleming's blind until sweat's involved. Come on. You look like you could use a grime makeover." Arthur pulled a rag from his back pocket—brown and greasy like it had mopped a garage floor for a decade. "Wipe this on your face."

Eddie grimaced. "Why?"

"Because you look like a damn schoolboy. This place will chew you up if you keep shining like a Christmas bulb."

With a sigh, Eddie scrubbed his face until the rag came back darker.

"Good?"

"More," Arthur said, eyes narrowed. Eddie went at it again.

"Better. But now you're dirtier than me—give me that." Arthur took the rag and smeared it across his own forehead until he looked like he'd crawled through a coal chute.

The supply room groaned as the warped door scraped open. Inside, eight-foot chicken wire fences boxed in a jungle of junk—coils of tubing, rusted tool chests, a wall of keys nobody dared touch. Wind moved through the rafters, making the bell lamps sway overhead like the last seconds of a hanging.

Eddie froze, staring upward.

"Don't worry," Arthur said. "They do that."

They grabbed spades and found an oil drum with a broken wheel in the back. Together, they rolled it to Bay Seven, which was ghost-empty except for a few scurrying rats. Eddie mistook them for cats until one turned and flashed a pale, naked tail like a worm.

Arthur dropped the sack and sliced it open with a knife, splitting it like a trout belly. Together, they shoveled the sawdust over the oil slick, creating a sludgy carpet that smelled like burned toast and axle grease.

"Can I ask you something?" Eddie said, wiping his forehead with his sleeve.

Arthur shoveled. "Shoot."

"When we first met... why'd you have it out for me?"

Arthur chuckled. "Had to see if you had a spine. Around here, if you can't stand up for yourself, you're toast. Trust me—I learned the hard way."

"You got in a fight?"

Arthur paused. "Robbie Hitch. When I first showed up, he got right in my face. I cleaned his clock so bad. He never came to work again."

"Why?"

"Because he caught me on the wrong day."

Eddie looked up. "What happened?"

Arthur planted his shovel in the dirt and leaned on it.

"I used to live in Minnesota. Mom, Dad, little brother. One night... a fire. No one knows how it started. Smoke thick as tar, filled the house in minutes. I got out. They didn't."

He didn't look at Eddie. Just stared past him, toward the dusty yellow windows where a flock of birds suddenly shifted midair, all at once, like they were being steered by a ghost.

"Next morning, nothing left but embers. I walked to the tracks and hopped the first train out. Been here since."

Arthur looked down. "Maybe I'll see 'em again someday. Maybe in heaven." He smiled and chuckled.

Just then, Richie Ritter stormed in, cheeks bulging like a squirrel's.

"What's goin' on, Horse? Hey Eddie." He grinned, fingers deep in his pockets. "And who gave you two special privileges? Ol' Fleming sign off on this little date?"

Arthur didn't miss a beat. He flung a shovelful of sawdust in Richie's face. The boy exploded into a coughing, spitting fit.

"Pffffft! Puh! What the hell was that for?!"

"You talk too much."

Richie brushed flakes from his greasy bowl-cut and popped a handful of nuts into his mouth. "Anyway," he said through the crunching, "don't wear yourselves out. I'll see you at the ties."

They finished their task in silence, dumping the barrel into the yard's fire pit—a rusted graveyard of tires and drums. Arthur lit a cigarette, the flare of the match casting long shadows.

"Alright, kid," he said, smoke snaking from his nose. "Let's not push our luck. I'll see you out back in a bit."

Richie was the first to make it to the stack of railroad ties, and no one was surprised. He climbed it like a squirrel with a purpose, peanut butter sandwich clenched in one fist, the other helping him perch like a king surveying his domain. The sandwich was a rare treasure—peanut butter was a luxury around here, like fresh socks or a night without nightmares.

The rest of the boys were slower, slogging through the waist-high grass, lunch pails swinging from tired hands. They grinned like fools freed from prison, glad for the break, but even gladder to be out of Mr. Fleming's reach. For a few stolen minutes, they could just be boys—wild and loud and stupid. And they made damn sure to enjoy it.

"Look at me!" Kenny Coleman crowed, one of the older ones with acne scars and a mean streak. His face twisted like a kicked beehive. "I'm Mr. Fleming! Get to work, you filthy rodent!" he bellowed, pointing a gnarled finger at Jimmy Fresco.

Jimmy, younger and smaller and Italian, flinched, then grinned. He sat at the base of the ties, chewing slowly like he'd seen it all before.

"Oh no, it's Phlegming!" the kids chorused. They hocked and spat into the dirt.

"Me next, me next!" yelled Mark Tillerman, eager to play the villain.

Arthur, leaning back with a cigarette pinched between two fingers, squinted at him through the smoke. "Sit down, greenhorn. You've only been here, what, two weeks? You don't know Fleming. You don't know hell."

"I'll go," Nick Pino said, pushing forward. Fourteen, lean

as a whittled stick, and already a two-year veteran of the roundhouse. He strutted down the ties like a stage actor and squared up to Billy Baker—Eddie's age, with ears that flared out like they were trying to escape his head.

Nick's voice dripped with fake authority. "Well, well, well… Look what we got here. Not working again, Baker? That'll cost you…" He tapped his chin theatrically. "Half a day's pay!"

The boys howled. "It's Phlegming!" they yelled. Spit flew like confetti.

Jimmy raised a hand, serious now. "Hey, did any of you see those Dicks this morning? Tan overcoats. Asking questions like buzzards on a gutpile."

Eddie's stomach tightened. Ray.

Arthur exhaled smoke and waved a hand. "You're paranoid. They were probably railroad men. Inspectors or pencil-pushers."

"Nope." Jimmy shook his head. "They had buzzers. I saw one flash it. They're cops. Real ones. Looking for someone... or someone who knows something."

Before anyone could reply, Richie snapped his pocket watch open and let out a rooster's crow. "Lunch is over, boys. We're late!"

"How late?" Billy chirped.

"12:32," Richie said, eyes wide. "By the time we're back, we'll be five over!"

That did it. The boys scattered like firecrackers. They leapt from the ties, sprinting through the brush, crickets bouncing from their shins as they cut paths through the grass. Eddie ran with them, but the older boys pulled ahead—stronger, faster, more desperate. He broke from the younger pack, making for the far end of the roundhouse.

That's when he saw it again.

The rusty pickup truck with the mismatched green fenders—same one he'd seen on his first day.

He slowed. The area was quieter here, like something had sucked the sound out of the air. He reached for the iron handle of a side door—then froze.

Then—*BAM!*

The door burst open like it had been kicked. Eddie jumped back.

There were two men, and Eddie knew them instantly, their faces burned into his memory from his first day at the roundhouse. The first was mid-stature with broad shoulders, with the hardened look of someone who'd spent decades in the sun. His leathery skin was peppered with white stubble that crept down his neck, and his face had the calm wear of someone who'd spent a lifetime outdoors. The second was taller and wiry, with flaming red hair the color of a Macintosh apple, and a waxed orange mustache curled skillfully at the tips. After that day, Eddie'd seen them once more—from the window of an engine parked inside the roundhouse, and again outside on the turntable. He was sure they ran locomotives.

The men laughed as they push through the doorway but stopped short when they noticed Eddie. The door started to swing shut, but Eddie grabbed it.

"Pardon me," he said to the man in back.

The man gave Eddie a nod and casually spit into a tin cup.

Eddie stepped inside and peered into the dim light, hoping Mr. Fleming wasn't there—but half-expecting him to be. The lanterns on the walls and a thin stream of sunlight through the grime-streaked windows offered just enough glow to make out shapes in the haze. The floor felt soft beneath his boots—dirt, he thinks, though it could just as easily be ash, grease, or something worse.

He crept forward. A loud hiss echoed from around the corner, and Eddie flinched. Up ahead, he spotted a broom leaning against the far wall, caught in a shaft of sunlight pouring through a hole in the ceiling. It stood like a weapon waiting for its knight. Eddie smiled, imagining how much safer he'd feel with it in his hands. He scanned the shadows, inching forward.

Suddenly, a hand clamped down on his shoulder. Bony. Ice-cold. Like a claw.

Oh no. Mr. Fleming.

"Well, well, well… what do we have here?" Fleming purred behind him.

Eddie turned and sees that familiar cadaverous face—skin pulled tight over sharp cheekbones like a sheet over furniture in a forgotten parlor. His pale eyes gleamed as his lips peeled into a grin, exposing a mouthful of rotted teeth like rusted sawblades.

"I didn't think it'd take long," he sneered. "Caught you slacking already, did I? I warned you, didn't I?"

Fleming jabbed a finger toward Eddie's face and leaned in close. Too close. His breath hit Eddie like a slap: a rank blend of whiskey, rot, and something even fouler. Eddie's eyes watered, and his stomach turned.

"That'll cost you half a day's pay!" Fleming barked, spraying spit as he did.

"But sir…" Eddie started.

"Quiet!" Fleming snapped. He tilted his head up, eyeing the rafters above—beams of iron crisscrossing the ceiling like the undercarriage of a giant machine.

"You see those up there?" he asked. "They look awwfully dusty."

He looked down at Eddie again and grinned wider. "Been needing someone small to climb up and clean them." He chuckled, then broke into a full cackle.

"Fleming!" a voice boomed from behind. Deep. Rough. Unmistakably powerful.

Fleming's smile faltered. "Oh, perfect," he muttered. "It's Jack Luken."

Jack stepped forward. Broad as a bear, with arms like tree trunks and a calm fire in his eyes.

"Why don't you pick on someone else?" Jack said, adjusting the straps of his overalls, looking around. He smiled. "Looks like I'm the only one here. So I guess it's me."

Fleming raised his hands in mock innocence. "Now Jack," he said lightly. "This is between me and one of my employees. Surely it's no concern of yours."

Jack's right eye twitched. "Any time I see someone bullying a kid half their size, it is my concern."

"But Ja—"

"Shut it, Fleming."

Fleming's face tightened. He lifted his cane and jabbed it at Jack's chest. "You're not as tough as they say."

In one motion, Jack snatched the cane, snapped it over his knee, and tossed the pieces aside. He dusted his hands and narrowed his eyes.

"You got any more?" he asked, his tone smooth as oiled wood.

Fleming gasped, his hand fluttering to his chest. He took a shaky step back.

Jack towered over him. "If I catch you mistreating this boy—or any of the boys—again, we'll have a bigger problem."

Fleming gulped, took a swig from his flask, and wiped his mouth on his sleeve. "You'll never save the world, Jack," he grumbled. Then he turned to Eddie. His eyes burned with a promise. "I'll remember this." He limped off, cane-less, smaller than when he came.

Jack turned to Eddie. "What's your name, son?"

Eddie looked up, stunned. "Um… I'm Eddie."

Jack offered a hand. "Put 'er there, Eddie."

Eddie shook it. The man's grip is dry, rough, strong enough to crush a brick. Eddie's hand nearly shattered.

"I'm Jack," he says. "I've seen you around—and I heard about that scrap with Horse the other week."

Jack looked him over, impressed. "Word is you won."

Eddie shrugged, uneasy. "I guess."

Jack smiled. "When did you start?"

"Couple weeks ago."

Jack cocked his head. "Why here? Why this grimy old place?"

Eddie flushed. "I dunno… Just had a feeling it might work out."

Jack nodded. "Glad you followed your gut. Not many do." He squinted out toward the railyard. "You like trains?"

"Oh yeah—and westerns too. Always a train in a good western."

Jack grinned. "Ever ridden a steam engine?"

Eddie's eyes lit up. "No, sir—but I've dreamed about it. Closest I've ever been is watching from the ground."

"Well, tomorrow that changes. Red and I have a run. You're welcome to ride along."

Eddie hesitated, thinking of Mr. Fleming. But that fear faded fast. Fleming wouldn't dare cross Jack again—at least, not soon. And the idea of riding a real steam engine? Unbelievable.

Jack noticed his silence and added with a wink, "Think it over. If you're in, meet me here tomorrow. Seven sharp."

Eddie nodded. "Okay."

The brakes screeched on Catherine's bike as Eddie swung under the fire escape, his tires skidding over a puddle like a kid slipping on ice. He hopped off, nearly tripping on a rogue shoelace, then bolted up the rickety stairwell, taking two, sometimes three steps at a time. Eight floors up and breathless, he slammed open the apartment door.

His mother stood in the middle of the living room like a warden, arms crossed, toe tapping. Her glare could melt granite.

"Didn't think you'd make it in time for dinner," she said flatly. "And tonight we've got something special."

Eddie dropped into his chair like a bag of bricks and skidded it forward, legs still twitching from the run. Margaret was already seated at the table, her face unreadable. Her eyes flicked to the empty spot where Catherine usually sat.

"What is it?" Margaret asked.

Their mother grinned, the corners of her mouth tugging upward like a magician hiding a trick. "Well now... I don't want to ruin the surprise."

And that's when Eddie smelled it—faint at first, a ghost of flavor floating through the apartment. Then it hit him like a truck.

"I smell food!" he shouted. "Real food!"

The scent wrapped around his brain and squeezed. It was savory, rich. A whisper of beef.

"Is it roast beef?" Eddie asked, nearly climbing onto the table.

His mother said nothing. Just shuffled into the kitchen with a grin, grabbed an oven mitt, and reached into the cavernous mouth of the oven. She pulled out a cast iron skillet the size of a manhole cover. Steam billowed. Eddie practically levitated.

She moved slowly to the counter, careful not to spill, then stirred the bubbling center with a whisk. Without a word, she opened the breadbox—an act normally met with disappointment. But not tonight. Inside was a small stack of bread, and she laid out three modest piles onto plates, then ladled the gravy over each like it was molten gold.

"Well," she said, placing a plate in front of each child, "it's not beef. But it's the next best thing."

She beamed. "I was walking down a back alley off Clark Street and came across a fellow from the bistro about to toss a pot of beef drippings. I asked if I could have it. He said yes. I brought it home, reduced it down, added flour and spices, and voilà!"

Eddie took a bite and nearly wept. But before anyone could say another word—*slam, slam, slam*—the front door rattled like it might break off the hinges.

Eddie dropped his fork. It clattered against the plate, bounced to the floor, and spattered gravy across Princess' fur. She yelped.

His mother stood, uneasy. "It's alright," she said, dabbing her lips. The chair legs scraped across the tile with a screech that raised goosebumps on Eddie's arms. She leaned into the peephole.

"That's what I was afraid of," she whispered.

She undid the lock and opened the door with slow, reluctant fingers.

On the other side stood Mr. Dunn.

A squat man with shoulders like a toad, he wore a weather-beaten coat and a once-black top hat stained gray by the years. His sagging jowls were peppered with coarse stubble, and in one hand he brandished a stubby cigar that trailed a wicked line of smoke. His breath reeked of tobacco and bitterness.

"That's it!" he barked, pointing the cigar like a weapon. "I gave you your final notice last week. Rent's due today. No more extensions. No more sob stories. You're out!"

Eddie's mother straightened her spine but kept her voice gentle. "Mr. Dunn, please. I lost my job at the bakery. We just need a little more time."

"Do I look like I give a damn?" he sneered, stepping closer. "All tenants at Carriage House Apartments pay on time. That's the rule. You don't follow the rules, you don't stay."

"But we've lived here almost eight years," she said. "You know us. We're not trying to cheat anyone."

"And I know people who lived here longer and got tossed out just the same," he snapped. "Your time's up."

He drew in on the cigar, cheeks hollowing, then leaned forward and exhaled a dense puff of smoke straight into her face.

She staggered back, coughing, a hand pressed to her chest.

Eddie shot out of his chair so fast it cracked against the

floor. He planted himself at the edge of the living room, fists balled tight, blood roaring in his ears. He tried to look past her, but she filled the doorway completely.

"Is everything okay?" he called out, voice low and firm.

"Yes, hon," his mother said, but it lacked conviction.

Eddie moved beside her, placing a protective hand on her back. Then he turned to Mr. Dunn, stare sharp enough to cut.

"How much is owed?" Eddie asked.

Mr. Dunn blinked, momentarily caught off guard by the boy's boldness. "Eighteen dollars."

Eddie reached into his coat pocket and pulled out a small wad of cash—three five-dollar bills, soft and wrinkled. One was stained with a black swipe of coal dust, picked up somewhere between the roundhouse and here.

He pressed the money into the old man's hand. "Come back next week for the rest."

Mr. Dunn squinted at the bills, then at Eddie. "You're on thin ice, kid. But you just bought yourself a few more days." He adjusted his crooked top hat, gave a dismissive grunt, and turned to disappear into the evening gloom.

Back at the table, the room was quiet.

Eddie's mother glanced over at him, searching his face.

"Eddie," she said. "I think you have some explaining to do."

He didn't look up. Just kept eating, slowly.

"Where did you get that money? And why do you always come home dirty? I see smudges on your cheeks, your forehead, even your clothes smell like iron and ash. What's going on, Eddie?"

Eddie swallowed hard. He'd been rinsing off in the stream behind the railyard on his way home, but water alone couldn't clean everything. He could lie. Or he could stretch the truth.

"I got a job at the paper mill," he said, not meeting her eyes.

"The paper mill?" She didn't buy it.

"You didn't want me working at Proviso, so I found something else. It's messy work. I try to clean up first, but I guess I miss spots. We need the money. I'm the man of the house now."

She nodded slowly. "Just promise me you won't do anything dangerous. If they ever ask you to do something that feels wrong, don't do it. It's not worth it."

"Yes, Mamma."

She gave a soft smile and wiped the corner of her eye with the heel of her hand. "Your father would be proud," she said. "You're stepping up."

Her voice was low, almost reverent. For a moment, she just looked at him—really looked—like she was seeing someone new at the table.

"You're doing more than your share," she added. "I hope you know that."

Eddie nodded, his throat tight. He didn't trust his voice, so he just went back to his plate, pretending the gravy hadn't gone cold.

Suddenly, raised voices echoed from the street below—sharp, cutting through the stillness like glass shattering in a quiet room. Eddie froze. Through the cracked living room window, the sound of a girl crying out in distress roze above the din.

Heart hammering, Eddie rushed to the window and threw up the sash with both hands. The hinges groaned as it lifted. He leaned out, squinting into the dark, early evening. A single gas lamp cast a flickering halo on the street corner. In its glow, Eddie spotted two figures. One tall, one slight. The man wore a fedora and a long black overcoat that brushed his boots. He loomed over her, all shadow and sharp edges, like something hunting.

The girl's voice—thin, trembling—carried upward in uneven bursts. She spoke, pleading maybe, but Eddie couldn't make out the words. There was something about her posture, the curve of her shoulders, the set of her jaw. Then it hit him.

It's Catherine.

Before the thought even settled, the man raised his arm—slow and deliberate, like he was drawing back a slingshot—and slapped her. The crack of it echoed against the brick buildings. Catherine stumbled sideways, catching herself against the wall.

Eddie's blood went cold, then hot. He didn't think.
He bolted.

He sprinted from the living room, down the narrow hallway, throwing open the front door so hard it bounced off the frame. Down the stairwell two steps at a time. Out into the humid street air, thick with smoke and the scent of coal.

He finds her on the sidewalk, standing half in shadow, one

hand pressed to her cheek. Tears streaked her face, and her lower lip quivered. The man was gone. Just her now, trying not to crumble.

"Don't judge," Catherine said quietly, without looking at him. Her voice was brittle, a whisper strung tight with shame.

Eddie stepped closer, hands open, palms up. "Catherine…"

She turned on him sharply, eyes flashing. "I don't need your pity, Edward." Her voice cracked on his name.

He stopped, hurt flickering across his face.

"Catherine," he said, softer this time, the anger drained from his voice. "I'm going to get justice for what Ray did to you."

She turned her face away, wiping her cheek with the back of her sleeve. For a second, she said nothing. The gaslight flickered behind her, casting her shadow long across the pavement.

Then she whispered, almost too soft to hear: "There's no such thing as justice for girls like me."

Eddie looked at her, and his heart broke. But he didn't look away.

The next morning, Eddie was already pacing when the yard's first horn blew. He waited at the spot where Jack had told him to meet, just outside the roundhouse's gaping doorway, where sunbeams stabbed through the opening and lit up the grime on the floor like flecks of gold. The air smelled like coal smoke, motor oil, and sweat—all of it familiar now, like the scent of home. He shaded his eyes with one hand, peering into the haze of the early sun. The rail yard shimmered in heat and fog, the boxcars lined up like soldiers.

By twenty past seven, Eddie's nerves were fraying. He checked his pocket watch again—even though he knew damn well it had only been two minutes since the last time. Maybe Jack had been pulling his leg. Maybe it was a joke, a test, and Eddie was failing. The thought made his stomach churn.

"Mornin', Eddie." The voice came from behind, rough as gravel. Eddie spun around.

Jack stood there, already grinning, a brown sack slung over his shoulder like Santa Claus if Santa hauled iron for a living. "Glad you came."

Eddie exhaled in relief. "Good morning, sir."

"You ready to ride the biggest damn engine North Western's got?"

Eddie nodded so fast his cap nearly flew off.

"C'mon then. Let me introduce you to Red. He and I operate the engine together. I drive it, he keeps her heart beating. He might be a little surprised to see you, but I gave him fair warning yesterday." Jack laughed, then coughed into his fist.

They walked toward the engine. Eddie's jaw slackened. It was massive—a black-and-silver monster crouched on the rails like it was waiting to pounce. Its boiler stretched the length of one and a half boxcars, studded with thick iron bolts like scars on skin. A single headlight glowed dully on the front like a sleepy eye. Above it, a bronze bell hung heavy, with a cord trailing back toward the cab. From the smokestack belched a plume of black smoke that twisted up to the vents in the ceiling.

"That's why it gets so dirty in here," Jack yelled over the noise, pointing to the stack and laughing.

Two iron staircases flanked the engine, each leading to narrow walkways that ran along the boiler. A handrail was bolted right into the side, worn smooth from years of sweaty palms. Atop the boiler, leaning against it like it was a barroom wall, stood a skinny redheaded man. His arms were crossed. His denim overalls were patched and faded, and his little blue eyes squinted down at them through a curtain of red bangs. He smiled and waved.

Jack pointed up with a soot-smudged finger. "That there is Red."

Jack climbed the stairs two at a time, glancing over his shoulder to make sure Eddie was following. Eddie scrambled after him. They walked down the narrow deck, the metal warm underfoot.

"Red, this here's Eddie. He'll be joining us today."

Red grinned. "Hello."

Inside the cab, the heat hit like a furnace door flung open. Jack and Red got to work without fanfare, shoveling coal into the gaping mouth of the firebox. The clang of metal echoed like gunshots. Sweat poured from them in rivers. Eddie squeezed himself into a corner near the front door, wedged between the wall and the boiler.

When the firebox blazed and the gauges started to twitch, Jack and Red leaned back in their seats, their faces flushed.

Jack stood again, trotted down the deck and stairs, and disappeared. Red kept fiddling with valves and dials, tapping them like they were misbehaving.

Eddie murmured, "Thanks for letting me join."

Red just nodded, one corner of his mouth twitching into a grin.

Then came the jangle of metal on metal. Something was running toward them.

A blur shot through the front door—a German Shepherd, lean and wild-eyed. It leapt onto Eddie, licking his face like he was a long-lost littermate.

"Keena!" Eddie laughed, shoving the dog gently back.

Jack reappeared and chuckled, wide eyed. "Not sure how she got loose. I guess she's comin' with us."

Outside, a man shouted. "Okay boys, you're ready to roll!"

Jack rang the bell. The bay door groaned open.

He gave two short pulls of the whistle, then shoved the throttle forward. Steam hissed from the pistons. The engine bucked and groaned, then surged ahead like it had been punched in the gut.

It was one of those spring mornings that felt like a reward. The kind of day that whispered you made it—through winter, through darkness, through whatever ugly business had tried to snuff you out before the thaw. The rail yard was waking up, slow as dawn over a graveyard. Birds chirped in the eaves of the freight house, not singing so much as arguing over who had claim to what part of the sky.

Jack guided the locomotive down the short spur and onto the turntable like a man steering a church pew into place. The engine clanked and rumbled, a heavy beast with steam on its breath, and when it stopped—brakes hissing like snakes—it was with a sharp, final chud that echoed across the yard.

Jack leaned out the cab window and tilted his face to the sun. His eyelids fluttered. He breathed in deep through his nose, the way a man does when he's trying to memorize the world. Then he let it out with a satisfied, gravel-throated "Ahhhhhh," like a man who'd just found the bottom of a good bottle.

His hand slid across his chest like it was searching for an old wound, but found something better: a little bulge in his shirt pocket. He pinched out a hand-rolled cigarette, a crooked thing with flecks of tobacco sticking out the end like whiskers. It clung to his lip while he reached into the hip pocket of his overalls.

The Zippo came out like a relic—chrome, cool and smooth to the touch. One side bore his name, *Jack Luken*—the other, a graceful line of script that didn't fit him at all, words too faint and far away to read.

He held it like a magician palming a coin. *Pop*. One-handed flick. The cap snapped open with a sound that could startle crows, and a heartbeat later he struck the flint. The wheel rasped and spat flame like it had been waiting for this exact moment. The acrid tang of lighter fluid filled his nose.

He lit the cigarette, took a long, thoughtful drag—eyes half-shut—and let the smoke pour out slowly. It drifted through the cab, curling around iron levers, pressure gauges, and steel rivets like a ghost deciding whether it should haunt this place or keep moving. It trailed back across the boiler, then spiraled toward the ceiling and vanished.

Jack exhaled again, quieter this time, and tapped the edge of the lighter against his knee. Somewhere behind his eyes, a thought stirred. But it passed. Like the smoke. Like everything else.

The turntable let out a low mechanical groan as it began to spin, its gears grinding beneath the weight of the locomotive. Eddie crouched by the fireman's window, one hand braced on the sill, the other gripping a brass pipe overhead. The world outside turned in a slow, deliberate arc, the yard reorienting itself like a sundial shifting with the sun. As the engine came to a stop, it now faced a single main line that forked outward like fingers on an open hand—dozens of tracks snaking away into the distance, each one leading to somewhere different, somewhere unknowable.

The next hour was spent collecting cars, and Eddie quickly lost track of how many. They picked up everything: coal cars with black grit caked along the sides, slatted livestock cars that bleated and shifted as pigs and cattle kicked nervously at the planks, boxcars of grain, fruit crates packed in straw, steel vats of milk that clanged hollow against their fastenings, pallets of newsprint and bundled lumber strapped down with rusted chain. A little bit of everything America had to give. Jack and Red worked in rhythm, calling out signals, checking brake lines, crouching under couplers with lanterns swaying in the shadows. Every hiss of air and metal ping seemed to speak its own language.

When they finally rolled out, pushing west toward Iowa, the engine gave a long, echoing whistle that scattered a flock of crows from the wires overhead. A few hundred yards out, with the cars bumping and jangling behind them, Jack pulled his head in from the widow and hollered across the engine cab to Eddie, "Why don't you come outta that corner and take a proper seat?" and pointed to a small ledge at the top of the coal bunker.

Eddie stood, dusted his jeans, and stepped past Red, who nodded without looking up from a grease-slicked gauge. He found the narrow ledge on the coal bunker and scrambled on top—it was high enough to see over the engine cab, but low enough to take a break from the wind when needed. He perched there carefully, knees drawn in, arms draped across them.

Eddie sat up, wind rushed over the open cab, tugging at his hair. The scent of wheatfields mixed with pine sap hit him like a lungful of memory, and for a moment he felt like he was flying, not riding. Ahead, the twin rails shimmered in the late afternoon light, vanishing over a hill in the distance. It looked like the whole train might just sail off the edge of the world.

By the time they rolled back into Proviso, the sun had dropped below the rooftops, taking the color with it. The yard was black now, soaked in shadows, lit only by the wandering glow of truck lamps and the far-off blink of engine headlights. The roundhouse glowed ahead like a jack-o'-lantern in the dark, warm orange leaking from its windows and vents.

The engine crept forward like a tugboat threading through fog. Jack eased it through the yard with a feather-light touch, pistons whispering while crickets chirped beneath the steel.

They eased onto the turntable. The engine shuddered as it crept forward, metal grinding in long, miserable groans that bounced around the curved concrete walls. The table rotated and lined them up with the engine bay, and the locomotive rolled in like a tired beast seeking shelter.

Then silence.

Jack, Red, and Eddie gathered their things—oil rags, lunch tins, water jugs—and clomped down the iron steps. Keena sprinted down the metal deck, down off the front to the dirt, and followed behind them.

Wrong Place, Wrong Time

Late one afternoon, after hours of sorting bolts the size of thumbs and lining up tools like soldiers, Eddie made his way to the outhouse—not out of need, but because sometimes the body needed a different kind of relief. A break from the hammering, the steam, the stench of sweat and steel. The world out here smelled like smoke and piss and rusted ambition. Still, it beat sorting bolts.

He reached for the outhouse door, but something prickled at the base of his neck. He froze, then knocked instead.

The door creaked open like it didn't want to, and there was Arthur—Horse, slouched on the bench inside, knees up to his chest, a look on his face like a dog who'd been caught chewing through a Bible.

"Hey, Eddie," Arthur said, his voice cracking on the first syllable like a pre-teen.

Eddie squinted. "You… hiding in here?"

Arthur's eyes danced left, then right, like they were doing a jitterbug across his face. "Nah. What? Me? Hiding? No sir." He chuckled. A bad chuckle—thin and nervous and full of jittery energy, like it might snap in half under its own weight.

"You're lookin' crazier than a outhouse rat—and you've been duckin' folks all day, Horse. Looks like death left you a love note." Eddie stepped closer. "What's going on?"

Arthur didn't answer. Just jerked his chin toward the tracks. "C'mon. Not here."

They walked. Across rails that hummed faintly under their boots. Past rusting switchbacks and crooked telegraph poles that looked like they were about to surrender to gravity. It took ten minutes, maybe more—long enough for Eddie to feel the air get heavier, like the sky was slowly pressing down on them. Finally, they reached Building 5, the freight house. The big bastard loomed like a sleeping giant, its wide trackside door yawning open.

Inside, it was all gloom and dust. Arthur led him to the far corner—one of those forgotten places where sound died and shadows hung like cobwebs. He turned, face taut.

"You remember those Dicks everyone's been whisperin' about?"

Eddie nodded.

"They're lookin' for me," Arthur said. "Been askin' around. I talked to one of the car cleaners—they were askin' about my tattoo."

"What?" Eddie blinked. "What'd you do? You get into

something bad? Did you… damn, did you kill somebody?"

Arthur shrugged. A dead kind of shrug. "Not that I know. But hell, maybe. Sometimes you don't know the outcome of a fight."

Eddie opened his mouth, but then he heard it—footsteps. Heavy, echoing. And then the door behind them opened again.

Three men stepped inside, their silhouettes crisp against the gray light. Long coats. Tall boots. Peaked caps like shark fins. One had a billy club swinging from his belt like a tail. They walked like they owned the place—and maybe they did.

Eddie's throat tightened. "Cops," he whispered.

Arthur didn't respond, just pressed himself into the shadows. Eddie followed. They both squeezed into the corner, their breath shallow and hot. Eddie's nose twitched. A sneeze crept up, cruel and untimely.

Don't. You. Dare.

The officers drew closer. One peeled off, pulled a crumpled pack of cigarettes from his coat and struck a match.

First try—nothing.

Second—still nothing.

Third—*fssk*—and the flame bloomed, casting an orange halo.

The light hit their corner.

"Run!" Eddie shouted.

Arthur exploded forward, barreled into the cop with the

cigarette, sending both man and matchstick flying. The flame died on the cold concrete.

Eddie saw him go—saw Arthur turn into a goddamn freight train himself, ramming past the other two officers like a fullback on fire. Bodies hit the ground. Shouts rose.

"Stop right there!"

Arthur didn't.

"I said STOP or I'll SHOOT!" The officer grabbed his gun.

Arthur froze a half second, then slowly dropped to his knees. His hands hovered a moment in the air—torn between surrender and shame—before he eased himself onto his stomach. Palms out. Face in the dirt.

His breath hitched. That was all.

The officers moved fast after that. No shouting now—just a tangle of arms, knees, boots. They swarmed him like hornets kicked from the nest, efficient and angry.

One of them grabbed Arthur's wrists and yanked them back hard, cuffs snapping tight with a hollow click-clack that echoed off the rafters. Another crouched beside him, jabbing a finger toward the inked shape on Arthur's arm.

"That's him. Right there. The Quarter Horse."

A third officer—thicker than the rest, with a worn leather billy club hanging from his belt—stepped forward. He looked down at Arthur like he was a sack of meat in the road.

"Good," he muttered, voice low and mean. He pressed one heavy boot onto the side of Arthur's head and ground it into the floor. The metal eyelet of his boot tore skin as Arthur's cheek scraped across the concrete. Blood bloomed, just a little, but it was enough.

"Let's wrap this up," the cop said, flexing his shoulder. "I'm starving."

Then they dragged Arthur up by the cuffs and out the way they'd come. He didn't fight. Didn't shout. He was just…gone.

Eddie stayed crouched in the shadows, chest tight, sweat crawling down his back. The air felt hotter now, like the room had closed in. He stared at the spot where his friend had been lying only seconds before, as if his outline might still be there in the dust.

His fingers twitched. His mouth was dry. His brain scrambled to make sense of it all.

The horse tattoo.

The match in the dark.

The paper the cop had pocketed.

The Dicks looking for something they already knew.

He didn't know what Arthur had done—didn't know if he'd done anything at all—but one thing was clear.

Whatever this was…

It wasn't over.

It was just the beginning.

6 Months Later

Sometimes Eddie vanished for days, slipping out under the cover of night with nothing more than a satchel, a lie, and a dream. He told his mother he was staying with friends—enough truth to quiet her questions—then hustled off to the yard to meet Jack and Red for their long-haul runs across the country. It had become their secret ritual, these trips. The smell of grease and coal, the click-clack rhythm of steel on steel, and the constant motion of the landscape rolling by—it felt like freedom, like purpose.

Jack made a point to use those long stretches of open track to pass on what he knew—not just about trains, but about life. The quiet wisdoms you can only learn from a man who's watched more sunsets from a cab window than he has from a front porch.

One evening, as the locomotive hummed under them and the sky turned soft with twilight, Jack leaned back in his seat and looked at Eddie. "So, what gets your furnace burning, kid?" he asked. "What's in your heart?"

Eddie was quiet for a moment, watching the fields blur past. Then he said, "Horses."

Jack raised an eyebrow. "Horses?" Red chuckled.

Eddie nodded. "When I was eight, Uncle Charlie gave me this collection of hand-carved horses for Christmas. Each one was different—mustangs, Clydesdales, quarter horses—small enough to fit in your palm, but carved so perfect they felt alive.

I played with them every day. I'd build whole ranches out of shoeboxes, pretend they were racing or herding cattle."

Jack chuckled, tapping a cigarette from his pack. "You ever ride one?"

"Once," Eddie said. "A pony at the fair. It wasn't much, but… I'll never forget how it felt. Like I was born for it. Like I belonged on a horse more than anywhere else."

Jack lit his cigarette, the tip flaring orange in the dark. "Then that's where your compass points," he said. "You hang on to that. Most men go their whole lives never figuring out what stokes their fire. But you—Eddie—you already know."

Outside, the moon broke through the clouds, casting long silver ribbons over the countryside.

Throughout the night, Jack and Red took turns dozing, slumped against the steel wall or folded into the corner by the heater. Every so often, one would wake, rub the sleep from his eyes, and trade places with the other.

Eddie tried to catch a few minutes here and there, but the engine cab wasn't built for comfort. The metal floor hummed with vibration, the space tighter than a can of sardines, and every shift of the train sent a jolt through his spine. He sat wedged between the boiler's backhead and the sidewall, knees pulled in, coat collar turned up against the draft sneaking through the seams.

But truth be told, it wasn't sleeplessness keeping him up—it was his conscience. His body was tired, sure—but his mind was running on high steam. The night, the rails, the sense of being out there with nothing but motion and moonlight—it all filled him with a kind of restless wonder.

The Next Morning, 7 AM

The locomotive cut through the morning like a warm blade through butter, its whistle crying into the windless summer air. The sun was low but already golden, casting long shadows over the sleeping fields. Eddie stirred awake, wiping the grit from his eyes. The cool breeze teased his hair as he sat up and peered over the top of the cab. Then he saw it—off in the distance—was a sight that made him catch his breath.

A ranch stretched out across the plain, endless and alive. Dozens of quarter horses roamed the fenced-in land—some tan with white snouts, others black as coal, their coats slick and shining in the sun. A few were dappled white with patches like ink spilled from the sky. They trotted in groups, flicked their tails, chased one another in lazy loops through the morning haze.

"That's it," Eddie said softly, more to himself than to Jack. "That's the dream."

Jack, sitting beside him in the cab with a tin cup of coffee resting on his knee, turned and squinted toward the pasture. "The horses?"

"The whole thing," Eddie said. "The land. The quiet. Riding the range at first light, hearing nothing but the wind and the hooves. Taking care of them—feeding, grooming, training 'em. I want that. A place to call mine. Maybe a dog or two. A barn that smells like hay and saddle leather."

Jack sipped his coffee and nodded. "Sounds like peace."

"That's the idea," Eddie said, eyes glinting.

Jack looked ahead, the silver track vanishing into the soft heat of the horizon. "You go after it, Eddie. No matter how far it seems. A life like that… that's not a mistake. That's a calling."

Eddie turned to him. "You really think so?"

Jack didn't answer right away. He took another sip, then rested the cup between his hands, letting the silence stretch just long enough for his next words to land softly but heavy.

"You know," he said, "we all get a moment when the heart says 'Go,' and fear says 'Stay.'"

Eddie stayed quiet, watching Jack now instead of the ranch.

Jack went on, eyes still fixed on the horizon. "Long time ago, I met someone. One of those rare souls that only comes once—maybe twice if you're lucky—in a lifetime. But I didn't go. I stayed. Made excuses. Said I had things to take care of, people counting on me. Truth is—I was scared."

He looked down into his cup.

"She left. Life moved on. Occasionally, I'll get a reminder about what could've been if I'd just… followed my heart."

Eddie nodded slowly. "You regret it?"

Jack's eyes met his. "I regret letting fear write the end of that chapter."

He took a breath, then offered a tired smile. "So don't

make that mistake, Eddie. Whatever calls to you—horses, land, love—you chase it down like your soul depends on it. 'Cause maybe it does."

The engine rumbled beneath them, powerful and patient, pulling them forward as the ranch faded into the distance behind.

The Quiet Before It Came

They were halfway through Kansas when it happened—flat land all around, no trees, just wheat stubble and wire fences disappearing into the horizon. The train had been moving fine, steady as ever, when a shrill metal scream tore through the air, followed by an explosion of sparks seen out the back of the cab, down the line of cars like fireworks gone wrong.

Jack pulled the brake.

The wheels screamed and groaned, the cars screeching in protest until the whole locomotive came to a grinding halt. The silence afterward felt too still—like the wind was holding its breath.

Jack stood. "Something's dragging. Could be a busted brake shoe. I'll check it."

"Want me to come?" Eddie asked, already hoping from the ledge.

“Nah,” Jack said, climbing down the steel ladder, tools jangling from his belt. “You stay with Red. Keep an eye on things.” Keena stood up and sniffed the air, unsettled. Even Red stood stiff, hands planted on his hips, staring off to the west.

Then the wind came.

Not a breeze. A sudden, hollow gust that made the freight car rattle and moan. Eddie turned, squinting into the distance. His heart skipped. “Red,” he said, pointing.

Out on the horizon, a wall of cloud was moving toward them. Not white, not gray—but pink. Pink and tan and chalky white, like some angry ghost marching over the plains. It billowed high, swallowing the sun.

Red’s face paled. “Dust storm.”

Suddenly, they heard shouting. Faint, chopped up by the wind, but definitely Jack’s voice. “He needs help,” Eddie said, already climbing down the ladder.

Red was right behind, but Keena needed to take the longer route—racing down the boiler’s narrow walkway, claws clicking on steel, bounding down the metal steps to the ground.

They sprinted down the length of the train, boots thudding over railroad ties, wind growing stronger with every step. Dust began to lift and whirl around their ankles. They found Jack kneeling beside the wheels of a livestock car, his arm buried up to the shoulder in the undercarriage.

“Brake rigging’s locked!” he shouted. “She’s twisted on the pin. I need leverage!”

Eddie dropped beside him, grabbing hold of the thick

metal bar that Jack had jammed a wrench under. Red braced the opposite end. "On three!"

"One!"

"Two!"

"Three!"

They all heaved. Metal groaned. Dust swirled in their eyes, their teeth, their hair. Then—*crack*—the piece gave way, popping loose with a loud bang. The bar snapped back, and Jack tumbled onto his rear in the gravel.

"She's free!" he shouted, already scrambling up.

The wind screamed louder now. Visibility dropped fast. They couldn't see beyond the length of a single car. The dust storm had arrived. It wasn't just blowing anymore—it was shaving them raw. The grains of sand stung like bee stings.

They ran.

Back down the length of the train. Up the ladders. Into the cab. Jack hit the throttle. The engine started crawling forward, wheels grinding into motion.

But—

"Where's Keena?" Eddie yelled.

They all turned.

She was gone.

Jack leaned out the cab, eyes straining through the swirling sand, but saw nothing. Then—a faint bark, barely audible over the thunder of the engine and the grinding of steel. "Keep 'er runnin'" Jacked yelled to Eddie. Jack jumped from his seat, rounded the door, tore down the side of the boiler, wind lashing sand into his face like needles. He hit the steps at a run, boots clanging on metal, descending fast toward the ground to the bottom step.

Then he saw her—just a blur in the storm, a ghostlike silhouette streaking alongside the train, ears pinned flat, legs churning through the dust like pistons, barely visible in the swirling chaos.

"KEENA!"

Jack reached out from above—hand strong, sure—grabbed her by the scruff, hoisted her up like a sack of grain and dropped her down on the step above him.

They fought through the ripping wind and stinging grit, heads down, eyes slitted against the storm, clawing their way up the side of the boiler. Sand lashed their faces like needles. The cab offered no shelter—just a perch in the open air, exposed to the wrath of the dust-choked sky.

Jack threw himself into the engineer's seat, hands trembling as he gripped the throttle and slammed it full forward. Eddie and Red ducked low, yanking their shirts up over their mouths. Goggles came down. Keena crouched between their boots, her ears flat.

And then the world vanished.

For twenty endless minutes, there was nothing but roar and

rage—wind howling like a freight of banshees, sand swirling so thick the locomotive's headlight bounced right back in their faces. The train charged forward blind, steel on steel, through a wall of fury.

Then—quiet.

The storm broke.

It peeled away like a curtain yanked from the sky. The dust thinned, sunlight seeped through in hazy golden shafts, and the land returned, ghost-like and still. Particles of dust settled gently on the boiler, on their clothes, in their hair—powdering the world in dull gray like the ash after a fire.

Jack looked over at Eddie and Keena—filthy, wide-eyed, breathing.

He spat dust from his mouth, wiped his sleeve across his brow, and said, "Well… reckon that earns us a lunch break."

Eddie let out a disbelieving laugh.

Red shook his head and muttered, "Ain't right, what we just lived through."

Keena sneezed and thumped her tail once against the floor, like a drumbeat of survival.

The countryside rolled past in a slow-motion flicker, fields gone copper in the last light. The locomotive chuffed and hissed, a steady heartbeat under the sky's dying red. Eddie leaned into the wind that knifed through the open cab and raised his voice.

"Hey, Jack," he shouted over the grind of steel. "Where'd you come up with Keena's name? Never heard anything like it."

Keena lifted her head from the slatted floorboards at the sound of her name, one ear cocked, eyes catching the amber of sunset. Then she settled again, muzzle on paws, tail giving a single sleepy thump.

Jack chuckled, a low rasp. "Got her from a farmer years back. Thought hard on a name. Wanted something different. One night it just came in a dream. Woke up, and there it was: Keena. Liked the sound, so it stuck." He tipped his cap back and gave Eddie a sideways grin. "Funny thing, though. Didn't know it then, but it's Irish—means 'brave' and 'courageous.' Pretty fitting, huh? I'm mostly Irish myself." Jack chuckled.

He fished his Zippo from the front of his overalls. Chrome metal flashed like a spotlight, sharp enough to catch his eyes. He flicked it open with a single squeeze and spark—*pop-ching*—and a clean blue flame bloomed.

Eddie blinked, impressed though he'd seen it a dozen times. "How do you do that?"

Jack's grin widened. "Here. Try it."

The lighter was warm and heavy in Eddie's palm. "Two parts," Jack said, demonstrating with scarred fingers. "Pop the lid, strike the flint. Thumb underneath, index and middle on top. Squeeze till the cap slips free."

Eddie set his grip and squeezed. The Zippo shot from his hands and clattered on the floor. He scrambled after it, cheeks burning.

Jack barked a laugh that disappeared into the engine's roar. "Again."

Second try—no luck. Third—closer. On the fourth squeeze the cap snapped open with a clean metallic click.

"There you go, kid," Jack said, eyes bright behind coal-dust lashes. "That's the hard part. Now bring your thumb down, strike the flint."

Eddie dragged his thumb across the wheel. A spark leapt, caught. Flame danced, quick and eager. He grinned like he'd lit the whole world.

"Not bad," Jack said, reclaiming the lighter with those weather-bitten hands. "Never seen anyone pick it up so fast."

The train thundered east toward Chicago, a ribbon of fire in the dark.

The Fall of a Hero

It was the fall of '34 when Eddie first noticed something wasn't right with Jack. The air was cooling, the leaves were curling in like old paper, and the rails glinted sharper under a lower sun. Something about the season seemed to match Jack's change—slow at first, like the early signs of rot.

At the beginning, it was just the fatigue. Jack would toss a few shovels of coal into the firebox, then slump down on the little engineer's bench, elbows on knees, wheezing like he'd run up five flights of stairs. His head would hang low, eyes hidden beneath the brim of his cap, chest heaving in long, rattling pulls. That was the first red flag.

It wasn't normal—not for Jack Luken. Almost a year earlier, the man had been a legend. He'd once shouldered a railroad tie across his back like it was a sack of flour. Picked up an 80-pound grain bag with one hand and slung it into a boxcar like he was tossing laundry. He could out-eat, out-drink, and outwork any man in the yard. Everyone had a Jack story—usually ending in laughter or awe.

But now? The man could barely keep up a conversation without leaning on something.

The appetite was the next thing to go. Jack—who used to order seconds before anyone else had finished their first—started pushing plates away half-full. He'd always been proud of that story from the '31 summer fair, where he devoured 52 hot dogs in twenty minutes flat and walked away without so much as a hiccup. Folks talked about it like it was war hero stuff. But now, Jack would poke at a meatloaf like it might bite back.

Then came the weight loss.

It wasn't gradual—it was like something was eating him from the inside out. His full, ruddy face, the kind that used to jiggle when he laughed, started to hollow. His neck shrank. His belt rode low, loose even with the extra holes he'd poked into the leather. People around the yard began whispering behind their gloves. Some asked directly, "Jack, everything all right?" And Jack would beam that signature grin—those teeth still bright, still perfect—and say, "Just trimming the fat, boys. Nothing wrong with tightening the bolts once in a while."

But Eddie could see the cracks in the armor. The smile was slower. The eyes didn't shine the same. Jack was afraid—but damned if he'd show it. He hated pity more than pain.

Then the coughing started.

Not the casual, smoker's hack he'd always carried with

him like a stray dog. This was deep, sharp, constant—like his lungs were being scrubbed with steel wool. Every ten seconds it would cut through the air like a saw. Sometimes it came with blood.

A bright splash into his handkerchief. Sometimes more than a splash.

He started keeping that rag folded in his coveralls, pulling it out like a magician mid-trick—wiping the corners of his mouth, dabbing his palms. His chest hurt too. He told Eddie once, during a long haul out toward Iowa, that every deep breath felt like a knife slipping between his ribs. Sometimes, when the train jolted, he'd clutch his side and freeze, jaw locked, knuckles white. It was the only time Eddie ever saw the man look older than forty.

Red saw it too. They both did.

As Jack kept spiraling, Eddie and Red started pushing him to see a doctor. Jack refused at first. He was a hard man—coal-dust blood, steam in the lungs, pride stitched into every thread of his denim. "If this is my time," he said one night, staring out over the railyard with a cigarette burning low in his fingers, "then I'm ready for it. I don't need some sawbones feeding me sugar pills and bad news."

But even a rock has its limit.

One morning, after a fit of coughing that left him doubled over and gasping, he looked up at Eddie, eyes wet, skin the color of ash, and nodded once.

"All right," he rasped. "I'll go."

It was a Saturday afternoon in the heart of autumn when Jack finally gave in. The leaves had turned, the breeze carried that smoky tang of dying grass, and the sky above Proviso was a bright, cloudless blue—the kind that made everything feel sharper, more final.

Jack showed up to the little clinic around three o'clock, walking slower than usual, one hand in his coat pocket and the other curled tight around the railing as he climbed the steps.

The building was squat and made of red brick, with ivy clinging to the mortar in patches like old scars. Two dormer windows peeked out from the pitched roof like eyes. A whitewashed wooden sign, hand-painted in black stenciled letters, swung gently in the breeze above the door: Doctor Morris.

Inside, the air was cool and faintly lemon-scented. The waiting room was dim and calm, like a church that had long since given up hope. There were a few chairs, a squat wooden table with a stack of magazines that hadn't been touched in weeks, and the ticking of a clock that seemed just a little too loud.

At the front counter sat a round woman in her mid-forties with a kind of soft dignity to her. Her brown curls bobbed slightly as she looked up. She wore a navy blue dress with a garland of little pink, white, and yellow flowers printed across it—like she was trying to bring summer with her wherever she went. Her name tag said "Brenda," and her wrists were stacked with bangles in every color of metal—silver, bronze, gold—the kind that clinked like wind chimes whenever she moved. Her cheeks were downy with peach fuzz, and her wide face held the kind of smile that could melt ice.

Jack approached the counter and cleared his throat, but all that came out was a low, wet cough that rattled like coins in a tin can. He winced, pulled out his stained handkerchief, and dabbed at his mouth.

Brenda gave him a patient look.

"How may I help you today, sir?" she asked, voice soft and sweet, with just a trace of a southern drawl that rounded off her vowels.

"Afternoon," Jack said, forcing a smile. "I've been coughing something fierce lately. Just can't shake it. My boys at the rail yard been on me to come in, so..." He shrugged, like it was nothing. Like it didn't hurt him to admit he was here. "Figured I oughta get checked out."

Brenda nodded, already reaching for the clipboard.

"Well, you've come to the right place," she said, handing him the form and a nickel-trimmed fountain pen, the metal dulled from years of use. "Fill this out best you can and we'll be with you shortly."

Jack gave a little nod, took the clipboard, and turned to sit down in one of the hard-backed chairs. He read through the questions slowly—Name, Age, Symptoms, Duration. He didn't like writing things down. It felt too permanent, like carving his condition in stone.

He handed the form back to Brenda and took his seat

again, wheezing softly.

Jack glanced around. The place was clean—too clean. No soot in the corners. No grease smears or engine hum. Just four squared walls, a potted plant dying in the corner, and a rack of brochures that warned about small pox, tuberculosis, and the importance of hand washing. It was the silence that unnerved him most. It made the rasp of his breath feel louder. Made him feel exposed. Like the room could hear the fear behind his ribs.

He tapped a rhythm on his knee, trying not to think. But the truth was already slipping in, slow and certain as a train at midnight.

Something was wrong.

And Jack knew it.

The room was small, almost claustrophobic, with walls painted a pale baby blue that looked like it had been chosen by someone trying too hard to make people feel calm. It didn't work. The color had faded in spots, and a thin crack ran like a vein down one corner near the ceiling. Along the perimeter sat maple chairs—stiff, straight-backed things with the kind of smoothness that only comes from decades of anxious hands gripping the armrests. The floor creaked faintly when Jack shifted his weight.

To his left was a squat little table stacked with worn magazines. A copy of Cosmopolitan sat on top, its corners curled like old toast. The cover featured a beautiful blonde with glossy hair, red lips, and a dreamy faraway look in her eyes—like she'd never known a hard day in her life.

Jack's heart gave a twitch.

Veronica.

That face—those eyes—the resemblance triggered an immediate rush of memory.

The year was 1913, and Jack was thirty-two—young, strong, still a little raw around the edges. It was the night of the very first Christmas tree lighting in Chicago's history, held in Grant Park. The kind of event that buzzed in the air for weeks beforehand, its promise inked in the pages of every city paper, printed bold and festive.

The park was jammed shoulder to shoulder—hats and scarves and bundled coats packed tight like sardines, breath rising in clouds under the streetlamps. The air was sharp and clean, the kind of cold that bit the tip of your nose and made the inside of your ears sting. But no one complained. Not that night. Everyone was too caught up in the magic of it—the joy that had settled over the crowd like a warm blanket.

In the center of the square stood the tree. A Douglas fir, thirty-five feet tall, anchored atop a forty-foot pole so it soared above the crowd like something out of a fairy tale. Smaller trees clustered around its base like adoring children, forming a kind of forest shrine. Six hundred electric bulbs nestled in the branches—and at the very top: the Star of Bethlehem, all ready to be lit against the ink-black sky.

Jack had come to the lighting with a girl named Marilyn.

They'd grown up on the same block in Pullman, two kids who shared peanut butter sandwiches and played hopscotch in the alley before the factories blew their whistles. Over the years, their friendship aged like old wood—worn, familiar, creaky in places but still holding strong. They played checkers at the corner store on slow Sundays, caught matinees at the Granada when work allowed, and nursed cups of black coffee at the same greasy spoon on 111th Street, talking about everything and nothing.

But underneath it all, Marilyn wanted more.

Jack knew. He wasn't blind or cruel. He saw it in the way her voice softened when she said his name, or how she lingered a second longer when they hugged goodbye. Sometimes, when he caught her watching him, there was a hope in her eyes that made him want to look away.

He told her he was too busy. That his job as a mechanic needed him. That he was tired, too damn tired for anything else. The truth was simpler and sharper than that.

"Hey!" Marilyn said, tugging at Jack's sleeve, her voice bright with wonder. Her cheeks were pink from the cold, and her breath hung in the air like fog. "Have you ever seen a tree so big?"

Jack followed her gaze. The Douglas fir towered over the crowd.

"Well..." Jack said, cocking his head. "I don't think it's as big as it looks. Pretty sure they've got it up on a pole. Might've tucked some smaller trees around the bottom to fill it out."

Marilyn's mouth made a little "oh" as she considered it. "Huh," she said softly. "Still pretty, though."

She tucked her hands deeper into her coat sleeves and shifted her weight from one foot to the other. "It's so cold out," she said, pressing her shoulder gently into his. "What do you think about getting some hot chocolate?"

"That's a great idea," Jack replied, glad for a reason to duck out of the cold—and the closeness.

"You want me to stay here?" Marilyn asked, already staking her spot again with her boot heels. "So we don't lose our place up front?"

"Sure," Jack said with a smile. "I'll be right back."

Off in the distance, just past a cluster of bundled-up carolers and a vendor hawking roasted chestnuts, was a crooked little shack that looked like it had been hammered together by drunks. A red wooden sign hung above the doorway, tilting slightly to the left with snowflakes painted along the edges—clumsy, white and cheerful—and in the middle, in thick, slopping paint strokes it read: HOT CHOCOLATE.

Jack pushed through the crowd, sidestepping elbows and shoulders, the crunch of boots on frozen slush underfoot. The cold bit at the tips of his ears and turned his breath into smoke. Somewhere behind him, a kid screamed with laughter; somewhere ahead, a harmonica struck up a carol in a sad minor key. He squeezed through a final knot of people and found the end of the line.

It stretched out maybe twenty, thirty folks deep—families holding mittened hands, young couples huddled close, old men with red noses and tired eyes—but it moved with a kind of rhythm, like the people knew this was the only place to be and weren't about to raise a fuss.

Jack slipped his hand into his coat pocket and pulled out his timepiece. Its silver case was dented near the hinge, a scar from a long-forgotten drop. He flipped it open. Twenty minutes to go.

Plenty of time, he thought, and closed it with a quiet click. But even as he stepped forward with the line, he couldn't shake the feeling that something was coming—not just the tree lighting. Something else.

Jack scanned the crowd, catching bits of joy like sparks flying off a bonfire—smiling faces, gloved hands pointing skyward, cheeks pink from cold and wonder. Laughter floated above it all, soft and weightless, mingling with the scent of roasting nuts and snow. The tree towered in the background like some holy relic, and for a moment, Jack let himself get lost in it.

Then—just off to the left—he saw them.

Three girls, mid-twenties by the look of them, moving through the crowd like they owned it. Each had a cup of steaming cocoa in her hands, the warm fog rising around their chattering mouths. The one on the left was tall, dark-haired, graceful in that effortless way some women are. The one on the right was shorter, red curls bouncing with every step. But it was the one in the center who made the world drop out from under Jack's feet.

She was maybe five-seven, wrapped in white from hat to coat, like winter itself had decided to take human form. Her hair was a cascade of platinum curls, falling over her shoulders like silk, glowing beneath the lights. The coat she wore hugged her gently and was fastened down the center with shiny black buttons the size of silver dollars. Her hat curled up at the sides like something out of a fairy tale.

And her face—God help him, her face.

Wide blue eyes framed by lashes like feathered ink, a delicate nose that turned up slightly at the tip, cheeks kissed with a chipmunk's charm, and lips painted red as a crime scene. When she smiled, it was like someone lit a match in Jack's chest. Not the slow burn of something familiar, but the violent flare of something long overdue.

She looked at him—head tilted down slightly, coy as a card shark—but her eyes flicked up at him more than once. Not by accident. No, Jack knew that kind of look. Knew it in the way your gut knows when a storm's rolling in.

They passed by, chatting and giggling among themselves, but the giggles bent slightly in his direction. The redhead whispered something, and the blonde smiled without breaking stride. A bold, knowing smile. The kind that came with its own soundtrack.

Are they talking about me? Jack thought, feeling stupid and sixteen again. His gaze latched to hers like a rusted hook, and for a split second, everything else went quiet—the crowd, the cold, even the damn tree. Just two souls staring through the noise, the kind of stare that says I see you, even if neither one knows what that really means yet.

Jack thought she looked familiar, but he couldn't have told you why. He was certain they'd never met—he'd have remembered that face—but something about her tugged at him all the same. A vague echo from a dream, maybe. Or a face from one of those old silent films they showed in the church basement on Saturday nights.

Wow, Jack thought. And somewhere in his chest, something old and heavy turned over in its sleep.

The line moved faster than Jack expected, the cold keeping conversations short and orders simpler. In less than five minutes, he was at the front.

"I'll take two, please," he said, rubbing his hands together for warmth.

Inside the shack, a man stood hunched in the orange glow of a kerosene lantern. The booth itself looked like it had been thrown together in a hurry—planks of green-painted wood nailed crookedly, with gaps wide enough for the wind to sneak through. The man wore a heavy coat, buttoned all the way to the neck, and a cap pulled low over his ears. His breath fogged the air between them.

"That'll be ten cents," he said, sliding two tin cups onto the windowsill with thick fingers stained by years of tobacco and firewood.

Jack reached into his coat pocket, pulled out a handful of coins, and counted out ten pennies into the man's open palm. They made a soft clink—old metal on older skin.

"Thanks," Jack said, nodding.

The man gave a grunt, already moving on to the next order.

Jack took the hot chocolates carefully, one in each hand, and turned back toward the crowd. Steam curled up from the cups like smoke signals, the sweet scent of cocoa rising into the cold night air. He scanned the masses, looking for Marilyn—and somewhere behind that, maybe, those blue eyes again.

He stepped back into the current of bodies, cups in hand, heart beating faster than before.

The image of the blonde girl clung to Jack's mind like a tattoo on a sailor's arm—permanent, impossible to ignore. He wasn't a man blessed with a photographic memory; he often forgot names, misplaced tools, lost track of paydays. But this was different. Her face had burned itself into him with startling clarity—those ice-blue eyes, the wide smile framed in scarlet lipstick, the soft halo of platinum curls beneath her white wool hat. It didn't feel like remembering. It felt like possession.

He weaved his way through the crowd, both hands carefully cradling the hot chocolates like they were holy relics. "Pardon me… excuse me," Jack said, his voice polite but distracted, his mind still somewhere behind him, replaying the way her gaze had locked into his and didn't let go.

The crowd pressed tighter near the front of the park—children on tiptoes, mothers hoisting toddlers, men craning their necks. The chatter was rising like the steam from his cups, sweet and warm and everywhere.

Then it happened.

A hard jolt—his left side slammed by something heavy and fast.

Hot chocolate burst into the air like a geyser, erupting in a hiss of steam that hung briefly in the cold night air before vanishing into mist. Scalding droplets splattered down the front of Jack's overcoat, leaving dark streaks across the tan wool—each one a fresh insult, soaking through with bitter warmth. He gasped, stunned, instinctively raising the second cup like it was something sacred, fragile—something that had to be spared. The first had already met its end, lying sideways on the frozen ground, bleeding cocoa into the snow-packed slush at his feet.

A flash of anger flared in his chest.

He looked down at the mess—his coat ruined, the warm treat wasted—and then shot his eyes upward, bracing himself to unleash a sharp word or two on whoever had barreled into him. He expected some clumsy buffoon with red cheeks and whiskey breath, someone who'd had too much spiked eggnog or mulled wine and stumbled through the crowd like a wrecking ball in mittens.

But instead, he saw her.

It was the blonde.

She stood no more than a foot away, her gloved hand still hovering in the air from the collision, eyes wide with surprise, lips parted as if caught mid-apology. The glow from the lantern-lit booth behind them caught in her curls, turning them to silver fire. Her cheeks were flushed from the cold, and her breath hung between them in fragile clouds.

"Oh my gosh!" the girl cried, her hands flying to her face. "I am so sorry!"

Jack looked into her eyes—wide, sincere—and then at her lips, still slightly parted in shock. Without thinking, he smiled. "That's alright," he said. "I mean… it's just hot chocolate."

The girl, breath catching in her throat, looked truly distraught. "I feel horrible. I'm going to get you new ones."

Before Jack could object, she latched onto his arm and yanked with surprising force—enough to tilt his top hat askew. He reached up with his free hand and nudged it back into place, chuckling to himself as he let her lead.

Her grip was strong, confident, and her voice cut through the festive hum like a conductor's baton. "Coming through! Excuse me! …Coming through!" she called, carving a path through the crowd as if she owned the place. Jack followed, half-amused and half-in-awe. People stepped aside without question.

When they reached the hot chocolate stand, the line had vanished. Everyone else had drifted back toward the tree in anticipation—the lighting ceremony would begin any minute now.

"We'll take two hot chocolates, please," the girl said, peeling off her mittens and stuffing them deep into her coat pockets.

She glanced down, opened her purse, and pulled out two nickels, her fingers moving quickly in the cold.

Jack stood beside her, still trying to make sense of what had just happened. *Was this intentional?* he wondered. *Did she spill the hot chocolate on purpose, just to meet me?* He gazed forward, weighing the odds. *Or was it really just chance?* Either way, he wasn't complaining—but he remained quietly puzzled by the coincidence.

The girl turned from the window with two steaming cups and handed them over. She paused, smiling, the light from the lantern inside the shack glinting off her eyes. "What's your name?" she asked.

"I'm Jack… Jack Luken," he said, setting one cup down on the windowsill so he could extend his hand.

"I'm Veronica—but my friends call me Ronnie. Nice to meet you." She shook his hand, her fingers soft and warm. "And… I'm really sorry about your jacket." She dropped her chin with a playful grin and swayed her shoulders slightly from side to side. "So, are you from around here?"

"Yup," Jack said. "Born and raised."

"I'm from California," Veronica said. "Here visiting family for Christmas. My dad used to do business in Chicago—just sold a coat factory, actually. This coat I'm wearing? One of his." She did a quick spin to show it off, the hem of her white wool coat flaring gently.

Jack gave a low whistle. "Well, that's impressive… and it looks good on you."

"Awww, thanks," Veronica replied, brushing a strand of hair behind her ear. "So what do you do?"

"I'm a mechanic. I work on buggies—fix wheels, replace parts, grease the axles… the usual." Jack gave a half-shrug and smiled from the corner of his mouth.

"Mmm. I figured as much… you look rugged," Veronica teased, eyes bright as she studied him. Then, with the slightest tilt of her head, she asked, "So… do you have a girlfriend? Or was the other hot chocolate for her?"

"I'm here with my friend Marilyn," Jack said. "We've known each other since we were kids, but it's not like that—we're just friends."

Veronica narrowed her eyes playfully. "Hmm… if you say so." She paused, then added, "You seem nice. Are you doing anything tomorrow?"

"Nope. Off on Sundays," Jack said, tucking his hands into his coat pockets, chest unconsciously puffing just a bit.

"Perfect!" Veronica bounced slightly on her heels. "Let's do something! Maybe you can show me a part of Chicago I haven't seen yet?"

"I'd like that," Jack said. "Where should we meet?"

"Outside the Great Northern Hotel. Noon. That's where I'm staying with my folks."

Jack nodded with a smile, then gave his hat a small tip. "I look forward to it."

Jack had completely lost track of time. The tree lighting had slipped his mind entirely—until a collective gasp rose around him, a sharp intake of breath from hundreds of voices at once. An instant later, cheers erupted as the massive Douglas fir lit up in a dazzling display of multicolored Christmas lights, casting the park in a warm, magical glow. The colors shimmered off the falling snowflakes like confetti in a snow globe.

Veronica turned toward the tree, her eyes lighting up for a moment—then she looked back at Jack with urgency.

"I gotta go," she said quickly.

Before Jack could ask why, Veronica leaned in and kissed him on the cheek. Her lips were warm, soft, and gone in an instant.

She turned and disappeared into the crowd.

Jack stood frozen for a second, heart hammering, coat still damp with cocoa. He blinked. *What just happened?*

He turned back toward the hot chocolate stand to collect the cups, and caught the man in the shack watching him with a smirk. The man gave a knowing wink and said, "She's a real doll!"

Jack chuckled, nodded, and grabbed the two cups from the windowsill. His hand trembled slightly, either from the cold—or something else entirely.

He moved through the crowd, carefully weaving between bodies. Carolers belted out "O Come All Ye Faithful" while others clinked flask caps and sipped whatever spirits they'd tucked into their coat pockets. The park smelled like pine and cinnamon and the faintest trace of smoke.

Finally, Jack reached the front, where Marilyn stood with

her arms folded, gazing up at the tree.

"Hey, what took so long?" she asked, turning toward him. "You missed it."

"I'm real sorry," Jack said, handing her one of the cups. "Some girl ran into me while I was coming back with the hot chocolates. Spilled all over my coat." He looked down and gestured to the dark stains on his chest.

Marilyn giggled. "It's okay. It's still early." She took a sip and smiled. "Maybe we can take a walk around the park?"

Jack smiled. "That sounds great."

An Angel from Heaven

It was 11:50 a.m. the following day when Jack arrived at the Great Northern Hotel—an imposing, 16-story giant with red brick walls, ornate stonework, and brass-trimmed revolving doors. With over 500 rooms, it stood like a fortress of elegance at the intersection of Dearborn and Jackson Boulevard. Jack stood on the corner, adjusting his best top hat and smoothing the front of his coat. His freshly pressed slacks creased sharply at the knees, and his boots were polished to a shine that caught the light like glass.

He stared up at the building, feeling the steady pulse of the city around him—the clatter of horseshoes on cobblestones, the jingle of harnesses, the rumble of trolley wheels, and the occasional sputter of a passing motorcar. Jack pulled his coat tighter. For a brief second, doubt crept in.

What if she changes her mind? he wondered. *She's from*

California... from money... and I'm just a mechanic.

"Hey, stranger!"

A voice like sunshine on a cold day broke through his thoughts.

Jack turned—and there she was.

Veronica stood on the sidewalk behind him, smiling brightly. She wore a deep red dress coat with bold black buttons marching down the front, and white frills peeked from her collar and cuffs like delicate lace snow. Her hat sat tilted at just the right angle, its wide brim decorated with pink satin flowers and a burst of feathers that danced in the breeze.

She was even more stunning than the night before.

"So where are you taking me on our first date?" Veronica asked, the corners of her mouth curled in a playful grin.

Jack grinned back, took her hand in his, and gently pulled her toward the street. With his other hand, he brought his forefinger and pinky to his lips and let out a sharp whistle that cut through the traffic like a blade.

"Wow!" Veronica said with a laugh. "You can really whistle loudly!"

Jack raised his arm and waved. "Taxi!"

A horse-drawn cab rolled up almost immediately, its driver tipping his hat.

Jack helped Veronica climb aboard, offering his hand like a gentleman, then stepped in after her.

Over the next four weeks, Jack and Veronica were inseparable. What began as a magical moment beneath the twinkling lights of Grant Park blossomed into something deep, swift, and consuming. From their first date—where Jack showed Veronica hidden corners of the city only locals knew, ending the night with a candlelit dinner at a modest restaurant he could just barely afford—the two fell into an easy rhythm, as if they'd always known each other.

Their connection was electric, the kind of love that makes time irrelevant and the world around you blur at the edges. For the first time in his life, Jack found himself both falling in love and gaining a best friend. They strolled hand-in-hand through the theatre district, skated beneath gaslit streetlamps in the park, shared stolen kisses at street corners, and lingered for hours in cafés talking the way people do when time doesn't matter and silence isn't awkward. The future. Their dreams. Places they'd like to go. The people they wanted to become.

One night, the city lay quiet under a thick blanket of fresh snow. It had started falling just after sunset—fat, lazy flakes that drifted from the sky like ash from heaven. Jack and Veronica wandered along a dimly lit path in Lincoln Park, their footprints the only ones disturbing the powdery white.

The air smelled clean, like pine and cold metal, and the world had gone still, muffled by the snow.

Veronica pulled Jack's hand. "Come on," she said, her cheeks pink from the cold and her eyes alight with mischief.

Jack laughed as she dragged him off the path into an open

clearing. "What are you—?"

Before he could finish, she dropped backward into the snow, arms stretched out wide, legs kicking side to side.

"Snow angels!" she called, grinning up at him. "You've made one before, haven't you?"

Jack shook his head, still standing. "Not since I was a kid."

"Well," she said, "you're overdue."

He smiled, took a breath, and collapsed beside her, sending a puff of snow into the air. For a few seconds, they lay there in silence, arms sweeping up and down like wings, their laughter mixing with the whisper of wind through bare trees.

Jack turned his head and looked at her. She stared up at the sky, flakes catching on her lashes.

"I like to think angels come closer when it snows," she said softly, voice almost lost in the stillness. "Like they're watching. Or maybe visiting. I don't know… snow just feels like them. Light. Gentle. Quiet."

Jack didn't say anything at first. He just watched her, heart thumping in his chest.

"You believe in angels?" he asked finally.

Veronica nodded, eyes still skyward. "I always have. Even when I stopped believing in other things. There's something about them—like they're the one thing left that still feels… pure."

Jack swallowed. He wanted to say something meaningful. Something that might stick in her mind like her words had just stuck in his. But all he could manage was: "You'd make a good one."

Veronica turned her head to face him, her smile slow and warm. "You really think so?"

"Yeah," Jack said, "I do."

They lay there a moment longer before she sat up and looked down at their snow angels side by side—twin impressions of two people caught in a moment of joy.

She laughed. "Look at that. We're already flying."

Jack stared at the patterns in the snow, then at Veronica.

Maybe, he thought, angels do come closer when it snows.

And maybe—just maybe—one of them had found him.

Jack lay awake in his one-bedroom apartment, thinking. The radiator hissed in the corner like an old man muttering in his sleep, and the ticking of the clock on the wall echoed louder than it should have in the silence. Outside, the city was blanketed in fresh snow, muffling the usual nighttime noise into a kind of still that only made Jack's thoughts louder. He stared at the ceiling, arms behind his head, the faint scent of engine grease still clinging to his fingertips, even after two washes.

He was thinking about her. Veronica. Her laugh. The way she scrunched her nose when she was about to say something clever. The way she fit into his side when they walked, like she'd always belonged there. In four weeks, she'd rearranged his life, swept it clean and left something new in its place—

hope. And fear. Mostly both, tangled up like bedsheets after a restless night.

The ceiling didn't offer answers. Just a yellowed crack that reminded him time didn't wait for anyone. Soon she'd go back to California. Sunshine and orange groves. Places Jack only knew from postcards and rumors.

But now, a decision waited quietly at the edge of everything. In the last few days, things with Veronica had deepened, their conversations shifting from playful flirtation to talk of a real future—something lasting. Jack's heart soared at the thought, but beneath the excitement lay a creeping unease, a quiet pressure that seemed to tighten its grip with each passing hour.

What could a girl like her ever want with a guy like me? Jack wondered, over and over. She came from satin and marble, and he came from grease and grit. He knew how to fix a wagon axle blindfolded, but the idea of holding her world together felt like something entirely different.

Even if he made her happy now, could it last? Could he give her the life she was used to—or worse, would she give up hers for him?

Jack began waking each morning with a quiet ache in his chest, dreading the ticking clock of the holidays. He knew what was coming. Soon, Veronica would have to return to California, back to her family, back to her world.

What then?

Would they say goodbye and promise to write, only to fade

from each other's lives like so many fleeting winter romances? Or would she ask him to come with her—offer him something wild and impossible?

He didn't know.

But the thought of losing her made his stomach twist, and the thought of leaving everything he knew behind left his mind racing with fear. Jack had always considered himself a tough guy, sure-footed and unshakable.

But now, for the first time in as long as he could remember, he felt exposed. Vulnerable.

In love.

And terrified.

Snow drifted sideways in soft gusts as Jack pulled open the narrow wooden door of Edelstein's Trinkets & Curios, a small, crooked shop tucked between a tailor's and a tobacconist on Wabash Avenue. A brass bell jingled overhead, announcing his entrance, and the warm air inside—thick with the scent of old wood and lavender polish—rushed over him like a sigh.

The place was dimly lit and cluttered with glass cases, shelves, and spinning racks crowded with charms, lockets, cameo brooches, and oddities from a hundred corners of the world.

An old man with wispy white hair and round spectacles looked up from behind the counter. "Afternoon," he rasped, his voice weathered and calm. "Looking for something in particular?"

Jack removed his hat and stepped closer, brushing a few stubborn snowflakes from his coat sleeve. "Yeah… I need a necklace. For a girl." He paused. "An angel, if you've got one."

The man tilted his head slightly and gave a knowing nod, like he'd heard this kind of request before. "Come with me," he said, and shuffled toward the back of the shop.

He stopped at a narrow display case tucked into a quiet corner, then unlocked it with a small brass key and lifted the creaky glass lid. Inside, resting on a square of blue velvet, was a silver pendant shaped like an angel. The figure was small, delicate, with outstretched wings and a polished gown that shimmered even in the dim light. At the top, where the halo would be, a tiny diamond was set into the silver, catching the light just enough to sparkle like frost in the morning sun.

Jack leaned in, mesmerized. "That's it," he said under his breath. "That's the one."

The old man smiled faintly, lifting the pendant with a pair of tweezers. "Silver. Handmade. The diamond's small, but clean. He looked it with his jeweler's loupe. It'll last. Same as a good promise."

Jack half-smiled and nodded. "How much?"

The man gave a price that made Jack flinch, but only for a second. He reached into his coat and pulled out a small roll of bills—his savings for the month, folded tightly in his pocket since the moment he'd decided.

As the man wrapped the necklace in soft tissue and slid

it into a velvet pouch, Jack felt a wave of nervous energy and quiet purpose. He didn't know what tomorrow would bring, or what Veronica would want with their relationship when the holiday officially ended, but he did know how he felt. And he knew she loved angels.

"Hope she's something special," the man said, handing over the pouch.

Jack took it carefully, the weight of it light in his hand but heavy in meaning. "She is," he said. "More than I ever expected."

The snow came heavy that afternoon, the kind that blanketed everything in silence and made the streetlamps glow like lanterns in a dream. Jack and Veronica sat across from each other at their usual table by the window of the café on Madison—two cups of coffee steaming between them, untouched. Outside, the world blurred white, the city softening beneath the storm.

Inside, it was warm, but the air between them held a chill. Veronica stirred her coffee without drinking it, her eyes low, fingers nervously tracing the rim of her cup. Jack watched her, his own hands curled around the warmth of the mug, even though he didn't feel much of anything in them.

She finally looked up. "I leave tomorrow," she said.

Jack nodded, slowly. "I know."

Veronica's lips trembled just a bit. "Come with me."

The words hung there, delicate and weightless—until they weren't.

Jack's heart stuttered. He opened his mouth, then closed it again. He looked away, out the window, where a man passed by holding a bundle of newspapers over his head. "Ronnie…" he said quietly. "I can't."

The silence that followed wasn't angry. It was something else—sadder, softer. A breaking that didn't make a sound.

Veronica blinked fast, her lashes catching tears she didn't want to fall. "Why not?" she whispered.

Jack struggled to explain it. The fear. The weight of what it meant to leave everything he'd ever known. "I don't know how to be out there," he finally said. "Out in your world. It's not just distance—it's… everything. I'm not ready."

Veronica looked down at her hands, twisting in her lap. A tear slid down her cheek, and she made no move to wipe it away.

Jack reached into his coat pocket and pulled out a small box, worn at the corners. He opened it gently and placed it on the table between them.

Inside was the silver angel necklace, delicate and simple, with a tiny diamond catching the café's yellow light like a star.

Veronica stared at it. "Jack…"

He reached across the table and took her hand. "It's not goodbye," he said. "Not forever. I'll write you every week—long letters, the kind that take time to read. Maybe one day you'll come back… or maybe I'll find my way out west. Who knows?"

She looked up at him, smiling through her tears. "You really think you'll write?"

Jack smirked softly. "You won't be able to get rid of me."

Outside, the snow kept falling. The coffee cooled. But inside the café, in that quiet corner of the world, a promise was made—not of forever, not yet—but of something real.

And for now, that was enough.

Out on the street, the snow had let up, but the air still bit with a bitter wind. Flakes clung to the edges of lampposts and curled around the rims of shop awnings. Jack and Veronica stepped out of the café into the quiet of late afternoon, the dimming sky casting a violet hue over the city.

Just down the curb, a chestnut mare stood tethered to a buggy, its breath puffing in soft clouds. Veronica smiled and reached out instinctively, her gloved hand brushing gently along the horse's muzzle.

"Hey there, sweetheart," she murmured.

The buggy driver, a squat man in a thick wool coat, turned sharply from his bench. "Careful, miss," he called out. "She frightens easy."

Veronica turned her head, but kept petting the mare. "She's beautiful," she said, half to herself.

Jack stood a few paces back, hands deep in his pockets, still feeling the ghost of her fingers in his. He glanced up and saw a trolley turning the corner, slush grinding under its wheels.

Time was running short.

He stepped into the street and raised two fingers to his lips. With a sharp inhale, he let out a piercing whistle that cut through the wintry air.

The horse's ears twitched. Then, in one swift motion, it reared up with a startled scream, hooves slicing the air like blades.

"Veronica!" Jack shouted.

She turned—but too late.

The mare came down hard.

There was a sickening thud. Veronica crumpled beneath the weight of the animal, her red coat crumpling into the snowy street like a dropped flower. A shriek rang out from someone nearby, and the street exploded into chaos. A woman screamed. A man shouted for help.

The buggy driver jumped down, shouting curses, tugging hard on the reins to pull the horse back.

A uniformed officer came sprinting down the sidewalk, whistle already in his mouth. "Clear back!" he barked. "Everyone move!"

Jack was already on his knees, slipping in the snow as he reached for Veronica. Her eyes were closed. Her hat lay a few feet away, crushed and soaking. The silver angel at her neck glinted faintly in the growing dark.

"Ronnie," Jack whispered. "Please—no, no, no…"

The officer dropped beside them, yelling in panic over his shoulder. "We've got a woman down—Grant and Madison. Get an ambulance here now!"

Snowflakes began falling again—quiet, unbothered—as the city held its breath.

Suddenly, the memory dissolved. The cold from the snow, the weight of the necklace in his hand, Veronica's tear-streaked face—gone in an instant, like a curtain falling.

Jack blinked and looked up. The sterile hum of fluorescent lights buzzed overhead. The waiting room had grown quieter. Across from him, the clock ticked with patient indifference.

Brenda stood in front of him, her clipboard pressed against her chest. She gave a small, apologetic smile.

"Dr. Morris will see you now," she said gently.

Jack's body stirred before his mind did. He stood, dazed, eyes still half in another time. The past clung to him like a coat he hadn't yet taken off.

Jack stepped forward without a word and fell in behind her. The hallway ahead stretched long and dim, lined with closed doors and the faint scent of antiseptic.

Brenda led him to the exam room and it was even quieter than the waiting area. Pale tan walls, a ticking wall clock, and the low hum of a radiator filled the silence. Jack sat stiffly on the edge of the exam table, hands resting on his knees, trying to keep still—trying to keep from coughing. The paper beneath him crackled every time he shifted.

A moment later, the door opened and in stepped Dr.

Morris—a tall man in his early sixties with white hair combed neatly back and deep lines carved into his face like the rings of an old tree. He wore a stethoscope around his neck and carried a clipboard under one arm.

"Mr. Luken," he said with a slight nod. "I'm Dr. Morris. Let's have a listen, shall we?"

Jack nodded silently.

The doctor stepped forward, placed the cold diaphragm of the stethoscope against Jack's back, and said, "Deep breath in… and out."

Jack did as he was told, wheezing through clenched teeth.

"Again."

Jack coughed halfway through the inhale, a dry, hacking sound that rattled in his chest like nails in a tin can.

Morris moved the stethoscope to Jack's chest and repeated the process, listening closely. His brow tightened slightly, but he said nothing right away. He stepped back, scribbled something on his clipboard, and said, "I'd like to get a radiograph of your chest. It won't take long."

The x-ray machine was wheeled in, and with the help of a nurse, Jack stood and faced the cold plate, arms raised as instructed. The image was captured in a flash of light, and the nurse gave him a reassuring pat before stepping away with the film.

Ten minutes passed.

Then twenty.

Jack sat there again, staring at the wall, mind wandering.

The weight in his chest felt heavier than usual.

Finally, Dr. Morris returned. He shut the door behind him, the click sounding louder than it should have.

He didn't speak at first. He slid the film into the backlit panel on the wall, clicked the light on, and studied it with his arms crossed.

Jack watched his face more than the image.

The doctor sighed and turned.

"Mr. Luken," he began, voice low, grounded, but not without kindness, "I won't dance around it. The scan shows a large mass in your right lung. It's in a late stage, and there's some indication it may have spread."

Jack didn't blink. He stared straight ahead, as if the words hadn't quite landed.

Dr. Morris continued. "You're dealing with a form of lung cancer. I suspect it's been developing for some time. The shortness of breath, weight loss, the blood—it's all connected."

Jack looked down at his calloused hands, resting motionless in his lap.

"How long?" he asked.

The doctor didn't hesitate. "Without treatment, one to three months, possibly. With treatment… it might extend that. But we're not talking about a cure, Jack. I'm sorry."

The words hung in the room like smoke.

Jack nodded once. No tears, no words. Just a quiet acceptance, like a man hearing the sound of the whistle one last time.

Dr. Morris placed a hand on Jack's shoulder. "Take some time. If you want to discuss options, I'll be just outside."

Jack didn't answer. He kept his eyes on the x-ray, glowing softly on the wall, as if it were trying to say something he already knew.

The clock on the wall ticked. The radiator hummed. Outside, the wind pushed against the windows like it was trying to get in.

The wind howled outside the narrow windows of Jack's top-floor apartment, rattling the panes and carrying the bitter cold of late autumn. Inside, the place was dim, lit only by the soft amber glow of a single oil lamp on the nightstand. The wallpaper—faded and peeling in the corners—cast long shadows across the walls. A kettle clicked as it cooled on the stove in the kitchen. The floorboards creaked with each gust of wind, like an old ship adrift.

Jack lay in bed, propped up against the headboard, wrapped in a thick wool blanket. His boots sat by the door, dusted with dried mud from earlier that day. Beside the lamp on the nightstand sat his Bible, worn and underlined, with the edges of its pages curled from years of use. Next to it, a hand-rolled cigarette burned slowly in the ashtray, its smoke rising like a spirit toward the ceiling.

He stared at the ceiling.

One to three months.

The words had echoed through his mind all evening, repeating in different tones—first clinical, then final, then almost comforting.

He wasn't afraid. Not really.

A man like Jack had made peace with his own mortality a long time ago. It came with the job. With the life. With watching steel twist and engines break, and good men vanish without warning under wheels and time. He had seen enough to know how it ended for everyone, sooner or later.

He shifted slightly, pressing a hand to his chest. It ached there, deep inside—like a knot tightening more each day. The cough had settled in, hollow and constant. But the fear? That hadn't taken root.

"I'm good with God," he whispered to no one. "I always have been."

He closed his eyes for a moment, then opened them again and looked toward the window. Flurries had started, and began to thicken, frosting the world white. It dusted the tiny deck beyond his door, a thin white icing over wood long past its prime.

No hospitals. No doctors. No sharp smells of medicine or whispered condolences in hallways. No needles. No machines.

He wasn't built for that kind of dying.

He reached for the lamp and turned down the flame. The room fell into soft darkness, the kind that wraps around you like an old coat.

Outside, the snow kept falling.

And inside, Jack Luken closed his eyes, ready to let nature run its course.

Early Morning - Proviso Yard, Roundhouse

The cold was already beginning to lift as the first rays of sunlight broke over the eastern edge of the yard. Gold light poured through the open bay doors of the roundhouse, cutting through the lingering steam like a blade. The smell of coal dust, grease, and morning frost hung thick in the air.

Inside their bays, the engines sat brooding in the shadows, massive and unmoving, lined along the perimeter of the giant turntable. Tools clinked in the distance. A crow cawed from somewhere high on the rafters.

Jack stood near Engine 2745, one foot up on the iron step, a rag slung over his shoulder. He looked smaller than usual, not just from the weight he'd lost, but from something deeper—like the world had shifted beneath him, and he was just now learning to stand on it again.

Eddie came in first, wiping his hands on his overalls. Red followed behind, lighting the stub of a cigarette with a match he struck off his boot.

"Morning," Jack said. He spoke with a calm that felt nailed in place.

"Hey, boss," Red muttered. "You're here early."

Jack nodded. "Didn't sleep much. Figured I'd get a jump on

the boiler checks."

Eddie studied Jack's face. "You alright?"

Jack looked out through the bay doors, the sunlight gleaming off the rails. For a moment, he didn't say anything.

Then, with the same calm he used when guiding a locomotive down a steep grade, he turned and said, "I saw the doctor."

That stopped them both.

Red shifted. "And?"

Jack took a deep breath, then let it out through his nose. "Lung cancer," he said. "Bad kind. Said I've got maybe a few months. Could be less."

Eddie's face fell. Red pulled the cigarette from his lips but didn't say a word.

"I'm not scared," Jack added quickly, like he was trying to get out ahead of their emotions. "Been thinking about it. Thinking about a lot of things."

He looked at them both—really looked—and smiled faintly.

"I believe there's something waiting on the other side," Jack said. "Always have. And if not, well… at least I'll get some peace."

Red rubbed a hand over his mouth. Eddie blinked hard and looked down at the floor, chewing the inside of his cheek.

"You're not… gonna fight it?" Eddie asked quietly.

Jack shook his head. "Nah. No hospitals. No wires. Just… gonna keep doing what I do till I can't anymore. When my time comes, I'll go the way I came—covered in soot and headed toward the light."

No one said anything for a long moment. The roundhouse groaned as the old steel structure warmed in the sun.

Finally, Red spoke, voice soft: "You're a hell of a man, Jack."

Jack gave a tired chuckle. "Don't make a fuss about it. Not yet. Still got tracks to run and engines to fire. Let's get to work."

And with that, he turned and climbed up into the cab of 2745, the metal echo of his boots on the ladder sounding both hollow and strong.

Eddie and Red stood for another moment, still rooted in the sunlit quiet, before slowly following after him.

Outside, the trains waited.

And the day moved forward, as it always had.

Where the Tracks Divide

The sun had dipped low, casting long shadows across the rail yard as Eddie wiped grime off his hands and watched Red demonstrate the oiling of the piston rods for the second time that week. Jack had taught him the basics, but now Red was filling in the gaps—reluctantly, but with a seriousness Eddie had never seen in him before. The unspoken truth hung between them like a low-hanging cloud: Jack wouldn't be around much longer.

"Don't overfill the bearings," Red muttered, wiping his own rag along the valve guides. "And if she hisses too loud when she's building pressure, it means your governor ain't set right. Got it?"

Eddie nodded, committing every word to memory like scripture. "Got it."

The rest of the day went by in steady rhythm—grease, steel, the hiss of steam, and the clang of tools in the roundhouse. By the time most of the yard crew had disappeared into the dusk, Eddie grabbed a broom and started sweeping the floor near the office. His movements were slow, methodical. He wanted to be seen. Sure enough, Fleming passed by, gave him a grunt of approval, and shuffled off into the night with his newspaper tucked under one arm.

Eddie kept sweeping until the last light in the office blinked out. Then he made his way to the locker room.

The metal door creaked as he opened his locker, the scent of coal dust and old leather greeting him. On top of his lunch pail sat a folded piece of paper, yellow and creased like it had been pulled from someone's pocket in a hurry.

He opened it. The handwriting was rushed, the letters sharp and tilted:

"Meet at the railroad ties - 10pm."

No name. But he didn't need one.

Arthur.

Eddie checked the clock on the wall. 9:22.

He stared at the note for another second, then folded it and tucked it into his coat pocket. Something in his gut told him this wasn't just a reunion. Something was coming.

Eddie zipped his coat to the top and crossed the gravel lot behind the roundhouse, careful not to draw any attention. The night was cold and damp, with a thin mist crawling in from the south end of the yard. He passed rows of idle freight cars, their hulking frames black against the yard lights, and made his way through the dead grass toward the stack of railroad ties near the fence line—the same place the kids ate their lunch each day at noon. Out of sight, and away from Mr. Fleming.

He climbed to the top of the ties and sat, elbows on knees, boots resting in a patch of cinders. From here, he could see the yard come to life in its quiet way—steam engines breathing and clanking in the dark, headlights sweeping the gravel, truck doors slamming in the distance. Even now, this place never really slept.

He checked his watch. 10:12.

Did Arthur actually break out? Was he released early? Or was this some kind of prank?

The idea felt impossible, but the note in his locker was written in Arthur's familiar scrawl. Nobody else wrote their "e"s like that.

Eddie waited, scanning the shadows between passing trucks and signal poles.

Then—behind him—gravel shifted.

"Hope I didn't keep you waiting," a voice said casually.

Eddie flinched and stood, heart jumping.

Arthur stepped out from behind a flatbed, arms raised like a magician's assistant. He looked rough—his coat torn at the cuff, face thinner, eyes bloodshot—but alive. Smiling.

"Holy hell," Eddie said. "You really did it."

Arthur grinned. "Good to see you too."

They clapped hands and pulled each other into a quick hug.

"You're crazy," Eddie said. "How?"

Arthur wiped his nose on his sleeve. "Slipped under a prison bus when no one was lookin'. Wedged my boots into the crossbeam, gripped the paneling like a tick. Soon as we cleared the outer gates, I let go. Rolled into a cornfield and ran until my legs gave out."

Eddie shook his head in disbelief. "You could've snapped your neck."

"I didn't," Arthur said. "Freedom is worth the risk. Now I'm here."

Arthur crouched near the edge of the ties, his hands stuffed deep into the pockets of his coat, shoulders hunched like he was bracing for a punch that hadn't landed yet. His eyes were bloodshot, but not from crying—Arthur didn't cry. It was the kind of haunted look that came from sleepless nights and too many memories clawing to the surface.

"They pinned it on me, Ed," he said finally, voice low and hollow. "Said I set the fire. Said it was murder. First-degree, all three."

Eddie stared. "Who?"

Arthur shook his head, eyes flicking toward the shadows. "Some neighbor. Said they saw me outside the house, night of the fire. That it looked planned. Like I just stood there and watched it burn."

Eddie said nothing. He couldn't. The image was too heavy. Arthur, standing in the dark, smoke curling up behind him, flames dancing in his eyes.

"But it wasn't like that." Arthur's voice cracked. "I swear to God, Ed. I went out my window—just out onto the roof over the patio. Wanted a smoke. That's all. Just needed to breathe for a minute, y'know?"

Eddie nodded slowly.

"I sat there, lookin' at the stars, thinkin' about nothin'. And when I was done, I put it out on my boot. Thought I killed it." He looked down. "Really thought I killed it."

The silence between them filled with a train's horn mourning in the distance and the soft creak of timbers shifting in the cold night.

"It's never been clear what started it," Arthur said, softer now. "Coulda been the smoke. Coulda been somethin' else. But it don't matter. Cops didn't care. Three people dead—my mom, my dad, my little brother—and I'm the last one standin'. Easy math for 'em."

Eddie's voice was barely a whisper. "Jesus, Arthur…"

"I can't stay here, Ed." Arthur stood up, pacing now. "They're lookin' for me. Dogs, roadblocks, whole damn city breathing down my neck. Chicago's a cage, and I'm the last rat inside."

"Where will you go?"

Arthur stopped. Shrugged. "Don't know yet. Somewhere west, maybe. Maybe hop a freight, keep low. Just gotta move."

Eddie stood beside him now, hands buried in his coat, staring out over the darkened rail yard. Lights flickered in the distance. A truck's brakes hissed. The wind carried the faint scent of oil and iron.

They see a dim light approaching—a low rumble building with it, steel grinding against steel. Headlamp glow spilled over the tracks in a widening cone, slicing through the foggy air like a knife. Arthur's body tensed as he threw his bag over his shoulder.

"Eddie!" Arthur called over the rising noise. "Maybe our paths meet again one day!"

He backed toward the tracks, boots crunching gravel, eyes never leaving Eddie's. "Follow your heart, Eddie. Follow your dreams!"

Then, without another word, Arthur turned and sprinted toward the train as it thundered past like a runaway beast. His coat flared behind him. He scanned the blur of cars, eyes sharp, searching. Boxcars. Boxcars. A flatbed.

There.

With a running leap, Arthur grabbed the side, swung his legs up, and rolled across the flatbed deck like a soldier escaping under gunfire. He popped to his feet, wind in his face, and turned back.

He raised a hand high and waved—a wide, defiant, lonesome wave—and Eddie lifted his in return, the two of them suspended across the space of everything unsaid.

Arthur's figure shrank, swallowed bit by bit by the night, until there was nothing left but the hum of the steel wheels and the echo of what used to be.

Eddie stood still, wind tugging at his coat, staring into the dark like it might give him something back. His chest was tight. His stomach hollow.

His heart sank—for the second time.

And just like that, Arthur was gone.

Two Days from Forever

The hospital room was quiet except for the low hum of machines and the occasional shuffle of nurses passing in the hallway. Jack lay propped up in the bed, a thin quilt tucked around his frail frame. His face had hollowed further, cheeks sunken, lips pale, but his eyes—though tired—still had their old glint. The kind that held something deeper than pain.

A cold wind rattled the windowpanes. Outside, the gray light of late afternoon filtered weakly into the room through the curtains.

Jack lay motionless. The rise and fall of his chest was shallow, slow, like a tide going out for the last time. His arms rested at his sides, limp and bone-thin, an IV line trailing from the back of his hand.

Eddie sat beside him in a hard vinyl chair, hunched forward, elbows on his knees. His boots were still caked with mud from the rail yard. He hadn't stopped at home. Hadn't wanted to. Jack reached to his side and fumbled at the nightstand drawer. Eddie stood to help, but Jack waved him off with a faint smile.

"I'm dying, kid," Jack muttered, pulling out a small burlap sack tied with twine. "Not helpless."

He held the sack out with a trembling hand.

Eddie hesitated, then took it. It was heavier than it looked.

Jack breathed slow, deliberate. "That's everything I got left. Savings from over the years. I don't trust banks, never did. It's not much, but it's enough to get by for a while."

Eddie looked down at the sack in his lap, then back at Jack. "Jack, I can't—"

"Yes, you can," Jack cut in. "And you will."

He took a long breath, the kind that made his whole chest rattle. "When I go… Keena's gonna need someone. She's a tough girl, but she's been through hell. She loved me better than I ever deserved."

His eyes drifted to the corner of the room, where Keena lay curled on a folded blanket. Her head lifted as if she knew she was being spoken of, but she didn't move.

Jack turned back to Eddie. "I want you to look after her. Feed her. Talk to her. Don't leave her wondering why I didn't come home."

Eddie blinked hard, his throat tightening. "I will," he said. "I promise."

Jack nodded once, slow and heavy. "Good. That's all I need."

He shifted against the pillows, a faint wince crossing his face. "There's...something else," he rasped, fumbling at the nightstand until his fingers closed around a set of keys. The metal jingled softly as he lifted them, catching a slice of lamplight.

"Here," he said, holding them out to Eddie. "The Chevy's yours now."

Eddie stared, wide-eyed.

"You just turned sixteen—old enough to drive," Jack went on, a tired smile tugging at the corners of his mouth. "Couldn't be better timing."

The keys glinted in his trembling hand as he handed them over to Eddie, Jack's face faint with pride.

Outside, the rain kept falling. Inside, the quiet settled again.

And for a moment, neither of them said a word. Just sat there, listening to the sound of time slipping away.

Eddie stood outside Jack's room for a moment, rubbing his hands together absently. The hallway smelled like antiseptic and warm rubber. A nurse passed by, then paused and turned back—short, maybe fifty, with kind eyes and a tired smile. Her name tag read "Karen."

"You here for Mr. Luken?" she asked gently.

Eddie nodded. "Yeah... I'm his friend. Been with him a long time."

Karen gave a slow nod, her smile fading just a little. "I'm

glad. He's been asking for you when he's awake."

She glanced at the clipboard in her hands, then met Eddie's eyes. "I won't sugarcoat it. He's only got a few days left. Maybe less."

Eddie swallowed and looked past her, back through the small window in the door. Jack's outline barely moved beneath the sheets.

"There's something else," Karen said. "When it starts getting close… some folks prefer to die at home. It's quieter. More comfortable. Less… clinical. If that's something you think Jack might want—we can help arrange it."

Eddie stared at her for a long second, then nodded. "Yeah. I think he'd want that. He always said he wanted to be in his own bed when it came."

Karen reached out and touched his arm lightly. "Alright. When the time comes, we'll make sure you have what you need to get him there."

Eddie nodded again, this time slower. "Thanks," he said, voice tight. "I'll take him home tomorrow."

Eddie pedaled hard, his boots grinding the rusted pedals as he cut across the wide stretch of the rail yard. The sun had slipped behind the roundhouse, leaving long slashes of gold spilling over the gravel and rails. Keena loped behind him, paws thudding in steady pace with the wheels, tongue out, breath puffing in short bursts. She stayed tight on his trail, weaving through brush and scattered pallets, her eyes fixed on him like she understood—like she knew he needed her close.

They slipped through the edge of the yard, into the patch of woods, and out the other side into the city. The cracked sidewalks gave way to cobblestone streets and flickering lamp posts, and Eddie's breath puffed in quick bursts as he climbed the last hill to their apartment.

When they got to the door, the place was quiet. Too quiet.

"Catherine?" Eddie called, peering into the front room. No answer. The only sound was the ticking of the clock above the stove and Keena's nails clicking on the hardwood floor. Catherine was gone again.

Eddie's mom sat at the kitchen table, her hair wrapped in a loose bun, fingers pressed to her temples. The overhead bulb swung slightly from its chain, casting slow, ghostly shadows across the room.

"There you are," she said, glancing up. "We were just wondering if we'd have anything to eat tonight."

Eddie yanked a chair out, and Keena immediately claimed the space beside it, plopping down with a sigh.

"I can look around. Maybe find some canned soup," Eddie offered.

His mom let out a tired breath. "The school wrote again," she said, sliding a torn envelope across the table. "You've missed too many days. They're talking expulsion."

Eddie didn't touch the letter. He just stared at the grain of the table, at a scratch he remembered making with a fork when he was ten.

"I don't care," he finally said. "I can't stop working. The railroad is my life now. It's better than any college."

There was a long silence.

His mother's eyes narrowed. "The railroad?"

Eddie looked up—he'd said too much. His mouth mistakenly said what he was secretly thinking.

She nodded, slowly, the truth settling in like dust. "I knew it. You've been at the rail yard this whole time, haven't you?"

Eddie didn't deny it.

He just reached down and scratched behind Keena's ears. Her tail thumped once against the floor.

"I had to," he said. "I'm needed there."

His mother looked at him, at the young man sitting across from her—calloused hands, circles under his eyes, dirt still smudged behind one ear—and saw, maybe for the first time, that the boy she'd raised was gone. In his place sat someone else entirely. Someone older. Harder. Someone who'd already seen too much.

A sudden crash at the front door snapped everyone's attention to the hallway. Raised voices. A sharp slap. Then Catherine stumbled inside, sobbing, her hand clutched to her cheek, the shape of a palm already blooming red across her skin.

Eddie shot up from the table.

"Catherine?" he breathed.

She didn't answer—just sank to the floor in tears.

Eddie bolted, Keena right behind him. They tore down the hallway, hit the stairwell at a run, and burst out onto the stoop, scanning the sidewalk—and there he was. Ray. Backlit by a streetlamp, already turning to walk away, shoulders hunched beneath his coat.

"Ray!" Eddie shouted, fury in his voice.

Ray stopped, slowly turned, and smiled like the devil himself.

Keena's growl started low, deep in her throat, then erupted into a bark as she ran and lunged.

Ray's grin twisted. He pulled his coat aside—and reached for the gun tucked in his waistband.

But Keena was faster.

She hit him like a bullet. Her teeth sank into his forearm with a wet, tearing crunch, shredding cloth and flesh. Ray screamed as blood ran down his hand, fingers slipping on the grip. He staggered, flailing, Keena thrashing and hanging on as he tried to raise the gun with his free hand.

The shot went off—one deafening crack.

Keena yelped and tumbled sideways.

"Keena!" Eddie shouted, dropping to his knees beside her.

Blood ran from a crease in her ear—a clean graze, but still enough to make her whimper and shake.

Ray, blood running down his arm and pale with panic, backed away slowly, then turned and bolted down the street.

Eddie started to rise, rage boiling again—but then headlights cut through the darkness at the end of the block.

A car engine roared to life.

"Get back!" Eddie yelled, scooping Keena into his arms.

The tires squealed, smoke rising from the rubber as the car peeled out—hurtling straight toward them.

Eddie dove, hitting the pavement hard with Keena in his arms. The car missed them by inches, roaring past in a blur of chrome and fury as it tore off into the night.

Then silence.

Only Eddie's ragged breath and the drip of rain from the awning above.

Ray was gone. For good this time.

Eddie never saw him again. Neither did Catherine.

It was a cold, gray afternoon when the hospital transport van pulled up to the old duplex. Two orderlies eased Jack out slowly, bundled in blankets, his face pale against the wool. They carried him upstairs, careful and quiet, and settled him gently into his bed—propping him up with pillows, adjusting the covers, making sure he was warm. The room felt still, heavy with the quiet understanding that Jack had come home to die.

Rain lashed the rooftop of Jack's apartment in steady sheets, the sound filling the room like a thousand quiet drumbeats. From the top floor, the water was relentless—hammering the shingles, overflowing the rusted gutters, cascading to the gravel driveway below in gushing streams that carved tiny rivers through the mud.

Eddie sat beside the bed, still and silent, his fingers gently wrapped around Jack's hand. It was cool to the touch—no longer warming, no longer gripping back.

The rain tapped against the windowpanes like soft knuckles, and somewhere deep in the walls, the old pipes moaned. The whole house felt like it was holding its breath.

Keena lay on the floor near the foot of the bed, her body curled in tight, ears flat against her skull. She didn't whimper or bark. She just lay there, unmoving, her snout resting on her front paws, eyes cast away from the bed. She refused to look. It was as if she already knew—had known for hours—that Jack was slipping away.

A single tear traced down Eddie's cheek and fell, soundless, to the worn wooden floor.

He didn't speak. There was nothing left to say.

As the sun lowered it got colder, near freezing outside—just cold enough for the rain to consider turning to snow. A chill crept through the house like an unwelcome guest, settling in the corners, seeping through the walls. Jack had kept the heat low during his final months—partly to save money, mostly because he no longer cared.

Inside Jack's bedroom, the cold was worst. Drafts slipped in through the loose seals of the windows and slithered across the floorboards. Eddie had tucked him in tight beneath a stack of heavy blankets—quilt over quilt, like the layers might somehow keep death at bay—but still, Jack trembled. His body shivered involuntarily, a failing furnace with no fire left inside.

He barely resembled the man he'd once been. The muscle and mass that had once made Jack Luken a figure of strength at the yard were gone, wasted away. His skin hung loose on a scaffold of bone, and his face—once round and red with laughter—was sharp and hollow now, his eyes sunken into dark hollows. Even his hair, once thick and black as coal, had turned brittle and thin, falling out in patches on the pillow. He looked like a ghost already, one foot still tethered to this world, the other halfway beyond.

Each breath came with effort—drawn slowly, painfully—ending in a wheeze that rattled deep in his chest like wind through an empty tunnel. Eddie sat by the bed, watching, listening, waiting. And somewhere in the silence between those struggling breaths, he felt the quiet presence of goodbye drawing near.

In the stillness of the room, just moments before the end, Jack's eyes shifted toward Eddie. He couldn't turn his head—didn't have the strength—but his gaze locked on, clear and deliberate. He hadn't looked at Eddie all day, and Eddie had known why. It was the kind of pain that cut deeper than any words. But now, as the end loomed, Jack needed him to see.

His lips moved without sound: Eddie.

Eddie leaned in quickly, placing his ear beside Jack's trembling mouth. "Yeah, Jack. I'm here."

"The dresser… on top," Jack rasped, barely audible.

Eddie stood, moved across the creaky floorboards, and found the Zippo resting exactly where Jack had said. The chrome glinted in the gray light filtering through the rain-streaked window. He picked it up and turned back to the bed. Jack's eyes followed every step, sharp with intention.

"Read the back," Jack whispered.

Eddie turned the lighter over. The words were engraved in a delicate, old script. Finally, it was close enough to read:

"Your word is a lamp to my feet and a light for my path."

Jack, with the last flicker of strength left in him, reached out. His fingers curled around Eddie's hand, slowly guiding it shut around the lighter.

"Take it," he murmured. "I want… you… to have it."

A faint smile touched Jack's hollow face, warm and strange—like the last flicker of a candle before the flame vanishes.

"They're here," Jack whispered. His eyes widened, not in fear, but wonder. "I see them…"

A silence followed, soft as breath.

Then, from outside, the sound of tires crunching wet gravel. A car door slammed. Footsteps thundered up the stairs. The bedroom door flew open.

Red stood in the doorway, soaked, panting. "Did I make it? I tried—I tried to hurry."

Eddie turned back to the bed—but Jack was gone. The glow was extinguished. His eyes stared blankly at the ceiling, glassy and still. Whatever had been Jack Luken was no longer in the room.

A guttural cry tore loose from Eddie's chest. "No!"

He kicked the metal wastebasket, sending it clattering against the far wall. His hand clenched around the Zippo until the edges bit into his palm. With a snarl, he slammed his fist onto the nightstand hard enough to rattle the lamp.

Then he turned, shoved past Red with a force that knocked him into the doorframe, and burst down the stairs—out into the pouring rain.

Behind him, Keena let out a single bark, sharp and trembling.

She darted from the bedroom, down the stairs, and through the open door—her paws skidding across the wet, slushing porch before launching into the storm.

She tore after Eddie, through the sleet and trees, soaked to the bone, but undeterred.

She didn't know where he was going.

She just knew he shouldn't go alone.

The Fade-Out

Two years had passed since Jack's death when Red finally found love in an unexpected place.

The brakes screamed as the freight ground to a stop, couplers slamming together in a final metallic jolt. Red swung down from the boxcar ladder, boots hitting the dirt with a jarring thud.

He wiped the sweat from his brow and glanced across the yard—then his gaze caught on movement.

She was there, cutting through the noise and diesel haze like a blade. Clipboard tucked under one arm, she walked with long, purposeful strides, the loose ends of her hair snapping in the breeze. A sharp gesture sent one truck backing toward the grain chute. Another flick of her wrist redirected a second, the driver scrambling to adjust under her command. Her voice—clear, firm—carried over the clang and rattle of the yard.

Red's eyes locked on her and refused to let go.

He tracked her instinctively, pivoting with her turns, following the sway of her stride as if the rest of the rail yard had gone silent.

Then she looked up—just for a moment—and it felt like she'd caught him in the act. For a breathless second, the world narrowed to that look—dark eyes, steady and unblinking, reading him like a page.

And just like that, she turned back to her work.

But Red couldn't.

After that day, he started writing her letters—long ones, filled with charm and honesty. Every time the line brought him back through her father's station, he made a point to ask her out, even if it was just for a walk around the depot while the crew unloaded grain. At first, Cynthia brushed him off politely. But Red was persistent in the way only a good-hearted man could be.

"Afternoon, Miss Dawson," Red called, walking up with the slow, careful confidence of a man approaching a skittish horse.

"You're early," she said, glancing at him from the corner of her eye.

"Figure I'd have more time to talk that way," he said, offering a small box wrapped in brown paper. "Picked this up in Wyoming. Figured a lady who works as hard as you might like something sweet."

She hesitated, looking from the package to him. "You didn't have to do that."

"I know," he said with a shrug. "But I wanted to."

She unwrapped it enough to reveal a tin of butter cookies. The faintest smile escaped her. "You think cookies are going to make me like you?"

"No," Red said, leaning against the dock rail. "I think getting to know me will make you like me. The cookies are just to get my foot in the door."

She laughed—just once, short and light—but it was more than he'd gotten before. "You're trouble, Red Miller."

"Maybe," he said, tilting his hat back. "But I'm the kind of trouble that opens doors and holds chairs."

For the first time, she turned fully toward him. "We'll see about that."

And when the foreman called for the next shipment, she walked off—still smiling to herself.

8 Months Later

The sun lingered low, casting a soft golden glow that rippled across the pond like liquid warmth. Pink and white petals drifted lazily from a nearby cherry blossom, brushing across the blanket where Red unpacked the picnic basket. He set down two plates and napkins, then pulled out a length of salami, a box of crackers, and a block of white cheddar cheese.

"You think of everything," Cynthia said with a smile.

Red shrugged, grinning. "Well, I know you like sharp white

cheddar with your wine."

She laughed softly, brushing a strand of hair from her face.

He reached for the bottle of Cabernet—her favorite—and uncorked it with care. The rich scent spilled into the air as he poured into two long-stem glasses. From the bottom of the basket he took out two flat river stones, placing them beneath the glasses to steady them.

"Coasters?" Cynthia tilted her head, amused.

"Improvised," Red said. "Don't want the whole evening ruined by a spilled drink."

He stood, brushing his palms against his overalls, and extended his hands. Cynthia took them, letting him pull her up from the blanket. He looked into her eyes, the breeze tossing a few petals between them. For a moment he just stood there, silent, the weight of what he carried pressing at him. Then he reached into the front pocket of his overalls, fishing around.

Cynthia narrowed her eyes. "What are you up to?"

"Just… hang on," Red muttered, his fingers finally closing around it. He drew it out but kept it curled in his palm. Then he dropped to one knee.

Cynthia gasped, her hand covering her mouth.

Red opened his hand to reveal the diamond ring, the stone catching a shard of sunlight. "This diamond," he said, voice low and resolute, "started as something simple, ordinary. With time, it became this—brilliant, lasting, one of a kind. That's us, Cynthia. What we've found together is rare, and it only grows brighter. And that's what I want for the rest of my life—

with you."

Her eyes shone wet, her voice breaking. "Oh, Red... yes. Yes!"

He slid the ring onto her finger. She turned her hand in the light, the stone flashing, then looked back at him with tears brimming.

"It's perfect," she whispered. Then her tone softened, almost pleading. "Red, I need you to do one thing for me. You have to leave that rail yard. Proviso's no place for you anymore. Come live with me and my family. We can start planning the wedding right."

Red's chest tightened. He forced a smile, but behind it guilt pricked at him. He thought of Eddie—alone, hardened by loss. He could already picture Eddie's face when he found out. Red hated the thought of it, but the path was set. Cynthia was his future now, and the rail yard belonged to a past that already felt behind him.

"Yeah," Red said quietly, kissing Cynthia's hand. "We'll figure it out."

Back at Proviso, the air was thick with diesel, the clang of couplers echoing across the yard. Red found Eddie by the switch house, grease on his hands, a half-burned cigarette hanging from his lips.

"I'm leavin', Eddie," Red said, assured but quiet. "Cynthia wants me at her family's place. We'll be planning the wedding there."

Eddie's jaw flexed. He didn't answer right away, just stared at the rail stretching into the horizon.

Red shifted his weight, trying to bridge the silence. "I want you to be my best man. Couldn't do it without you."

Eddie finally looked at him. His mouth curved into something that was supposed to be a smile, but his eyes betrayed him—dull, heavy, wounded. "Best man, huh? Yeah… sure, Red. I'll do it. Be an honor." His voice was too light, too forced, like he was acting in a play he hadn't wanted to be cast in.

Red nodded, grateful but guilty. Eddie crushed the cigarette under his boot and turned back to the tracks, pretending to study the steel.

Inside, though, it was another stab in the chest. Another thing taken. Another piece gone.

Hooray for Red!

The tavern's lantern light spilled across the worn pine floor, catching in the swirling haze of cigarette smoke. Outside, the night air was cold enough to bite, but inside, the heat from bodies, beer, and laughter wrapped the room like a thick coat.

Red sat at the head of a scarred oak table, his father to his right, his groomsmen flanking him like a rowdy honor guard. The smell of pinewood mingled with the yeasty tang of draft beer, and every slam of a glass on the table sent a ripple through the mugs and shot glasses.

"Tomorrow, you're a married man," one of the yardmen said, raising his pint. "No more chasing skirts at the depot!"

The men roared. Red grinned, shaking his head, and clinked his glass against his father's. Foam spilled over his knuckles as he drank deep, the bitter bite of beer warming his chest.

Stories flowed like the beer itself—tales of frozen brakes in January, near misses on the main line, and the kind of rail yard pranks that never made it into the company logs. Red laughed until his jaw ached, his voice raw from the noise, the sound of it bouncing off the low-beamed ceiling.

When someone called for a toast, they all stood, boots thudding against the floorboards in unison. Glasses were raised high under the flicker of the tavern's light.

"To Red!" his father bellowed, his deep voice cutting through the din.

"To Red!" the others echoed, the cheer spilling out into the night like steam from a whistle.

For a moment, Red let it all sink in—the warmth, the faces, the knowledge that tomorrow everything would change. But there was only one problem.

Eddie hadn't arrived yet.

And Eddie was Red's best man.

It was nearly 11 o'clock when the saloon doors burst open with a bang that turned every head.

"HEEEEY, everybody!" Eddie shouted, arms flung wide like he owned the place. His mud-covered boots scuffed across the floor as he staggered to the bar, dragging a stool with a scream so sharp it scraped the nerves.

He plopped down beside Red, grinning crookedly. "Made it, didn't I?"

Then, with no warning, Eddie leaned in, let out a sharp, foul belch near Red's face, and threw his head back in laughter that was just a bit too loud, too forced, too empty.

Red tried to smile, but behind his eyes there was worry. Something wasn't right with Eddie.

This was supposed to be a night of celebration—Red's last night as a bachelor. And Eddie, his best man, should've been the one to keep things light, to give a toast, to slap him on the back and help calm the nerves. That's what Jack would've done.

But Jack wasn't there.

And Eddie wasn't himself.

"Well, well, Mr. Red..." Eddie said with a loose grin, his voice syrupy and slow. "Looks like you're about to ride off into the sunset with one classy lady."

He swayed on his stool, blinking slow, eyelids drooping like curtains at the end of a long show. His smile wobbled—half warm, half mean.

Red turned toward him, jaw tight. One look told him everything—Eddie was drunk, deeper than Red had ever seen. And when Eddie drank too much, the words started to spill out sharp.

"So tell me," Eddie slurred, leaning in too close, "what's a woman like that see in a guy like you?"

"Eddie," Red warned, voice firm as stone.

Eddie laughed, but there was no joy in it. "C'mon, you had to notice... the way she was looking at me during the rehearsal dinner? You sure she's marrying the right guy?"

A silence fell over the group. Red's knuckles whitened around his glass. Earl, Red's father, pushed up from his stool and walked over, quiet and calm. He laid a hand on Eddie's shoulder.

"Alright, son. It's been a long day. Maybe it's time to call it a night. Get some rest. Big day tomorrow."

Eddie slapped the hand away, eyes flashing. "Don't touch me, old man!"

The bartender gave a small nod to someone behind Eddie, and a broad man in a leather vest and steel-toe boots rose from his stool like a storm cloud.

"That's enough," the bartender said flatly. "You leave on your own… or we help you."

Eddie looked around—at Red, at Earl, at the stranger now standing behind him—and something behind his eyes flickered. He swayed again, swallowed hard, and stood up without a word.

Eddie didn't make it to the door on his own.

He'd barely taken two stumbling steps when the big guy in the leather vest grabbed him by the collar and belt and hauled him backward like a sack of grain. Chairs scraped. Someone muttered, "About time." Another voice cursed under their breath.

"Hey—hey! Get your damn hands off me!" Eddie shouted, flailing, but his words slurred into nonsense, swallowed by the jukebox and clinking glasses.

The bartender gave a quick nod. "Out."

The door burst open with a bang as Eddie was shoved through it and out into the night. He landed hard on the wooden boardwalk, palms scuffing against the wet slats. The saloon doors clapped shut behind him.

Rain had started, soft at first, just enough to darken the dust. Eddie sat there, blinking, hunched over with his elbows on his knees. His chest heaved. He spat into the street and swore, fists balled at his sides.

Inside, laughter resumed—quiet at first, cautious—then louder, as if the room had exhaled.

Eddie sat in the dark, soaked and shivering, staring at the glowing windows of the bar. He could still see Red in there, talking low with Earl and the others. Laughing maybe. Probably pretending none of this had happened.

A bottle clinked in Eddie's coat pocket. He pulled it out with a shaking hand, unscrewed the cap, and took a long swig.

His best friend was getting married tomorrow.

And Eddie wasn't sure he'd be invited anymore.

Eddie stood alone by the tracks on the edge of town, his collar flipped up against the cold drizzle, the bottle still clutched in one hand. His head pounded, but not as hard as the guilt rattling inside. The screeching of steel in the distance told him a freight was coming—westbound first, then the one he needed, headed back east.

Back to Chicago.

Back to nowhere.

The massive engine growled past, and as the final car of the westbound vanished into the dark, Eddie spotted it: another train, its dim yellow headlamp cutting through the fog like a beam from a lighthouse.

He tossed the bottle into the brush.

It was nearly empty anyway.

The gravel crunched under his boots as he jogged alongside the eastbound train, scanning for an open latch, a low step, something. One of the boxcars had a loose latch. It clanked rhythmically with each turn of the wheel. Eddie grabbed the handle, ran a few more strides, and heaved himself up with a grunt.

Inside, it was cold and pitch black. Smelled like old hay and rust. The door slammed behind him.

He slid to the floor, breathing heavy, soaked and filthy.

He would miss Red's wedding.

He knew it the moment the train began to pick up speed.

He closed his eyes and leaned his head against the wood-planked wall, the whistle echoing through the hollow car. The weight of what he'd done settled on him like wet cement.

No toast.

No speech.

No goodbyes.

The Breaking Point

It had been thirty years since Jack died. The world had changed a dozen times over, but Eddie hadn't—not really. It was 1962, and he was still on the railroad. The boy who once chased engines down the yard was now an engineer, forty years old, with a permanent squint from sun and diesel smoke.

He didn't talk much anymore. Didn't need to. The men in the yard knew him as the kind who kept his head down and his eyes on the track. Somewhere along the way, the dreams had drained out of him. So had the friends.

Years ago, Eddie lost his mother to sudden cardiac arrest—a quiet morning turned sideways by a phone call that still echoed in his memory. Catherine and Margaret—his older sisters—had long since drifted into lives of comfort, each married to men with tidy bank accounts and big houses. Their connections to Eddie existed mostly on cream-colored Christmas cards, the kind with embossed wreaths and signatures that felt like afterthoughts. Calls were rare, visits rarer. Whatever closeness they'd shared as kids had thinned to something formal and brittle, like old paper left too long in the sun.

He'd been married twice. Both times, he'd torched it—maybe not with matches, but with the same careless flame that ate through everything he touched. The whiskey. The nights gone missing. The fights that started hot and ended cold. What he didn't drink away, he gambled or let slip through his fingers.

He carried that same slow burn onto the rails. Signals blurred, rules bent. Some mornings he climbed into the cab with a hangover sour enough to make his eyes water, shrugging off the stares of the crew. Brake tests got skipped, paperwork went half-finished. It wasn't that he wanted to crash anything—he just stopped caring if he did. The hiss of steam and the clank of couplers no longer stirred anything in him; it was all noise, a job to survive rather than a craft to take pride in.

And then there was Keena. The only thing that ever stayed. She'd been with him through the wreckage—riding shotgun in the truck, sleeping at the foot of his bed, watching over him with those eyes that saw too much. But time caught up quick, the way it always does. Degenerative myelopathy, the vet called it, like putting a name to sorrow made it any easier. Her back legs went first, then her strength, then everything else. It was fast—too fast—and one day he found himself sitting on the cold tile of the vet's floor, Keena's body trembling against his legs, her breath coming hard and shallow. The vet crouched beside them, whispering words of comfort that didn't help. Eddie kept his hand on her side and stared her deep into her eyes, feeling her fade, until the only sound left was the hum of the overhead lights—then nothing at all.

The yard was settling into evening, that soft hush after the day's racket when only a few diesels grumbled in the distance. Eddie trudged down the row of lockers, boots scuffing at the grit, the smell of oil and hot iron still clinging to his clothes from three days on the rails.

Something white caught his eye. A single sheet of paper, folded sharp and taped dead center on his locker door. Chicago North Western letterhead, the black logo stark against the yellow light.

He peeled it free and unfolded it, the tape snapping like a small gunshot.

Mr. Edward Ross, it read in crisp type. Report to Yardmaster Pullman's office, 8:00 a.m. tomorrow.

That was it. No signature beyond the blocky stamp of the yard.

A crease carved its way between Eddie's brows. He was scheduled to roll out again at the same hour, a shipment headed westbound. A quiet twist of unease tightened in his gut. You didn't get a summons from the yardmaster for nothing.

He stood there a moment, the letter trembling slightly between his fingers, the hallway around him echoing with the distant clang of a coupling. Trouble, he thought. Could be nothing—but probably wasn't.

Dawn still clung to the yard when Eddie coaxed Jack's old truck into the employee lot. The '34 Chevy coughed like a two-pack-a-day smoker, engine knocking in protest until he cut the ignition. The roundhouse loomed ahead, a massive brick horseshoe haloed by the first hard light of morning. Sunbeams knifed through its high windows, catching motes of coal dust so they hung like gold flecks in the cool air.

He shoved his hands into his jacket pockets and headed inside. The place smelled of iron and old grease, the floor echoing each step with a hollow clang. A steel staircase curled up along the wall, black paint chipped to raw metal. He climbed, boots ringing against the treads, past the smell of hot oil and the low murmur of crews starting their shift, until the noise thinned and the top floor opened into a quieter corridor—the executives' perch.

Eddie rapped twice on the heavy oak door, the sound swallowed by the hum of morning activity outside. A brass plate gleamed at eye level: Yardmaster, the word engraved in black enamel that caught the light like a wink. Beneath it, smaller letters spelled out Robert Pullman.

"Come in," a voice called—smooth, measured.

Eddie eased the door open and stepped into a room that smelled faintly of polish and warm leather. Sunlight poured through two tall bay windows with arched tops, slicing the yellow haze into sharp angles across the carpet.

Pullman sat behind a broad executive desk of dark oak, everything on its surface squared to perfection. He was younger than Eddie expected—thirties, maybe—clean-cut hair, crisp white shirt, and the kind of confidence that suggested family connections or city hall favors had helped him into the chair.

"Morning, Mr. Ross," Pullman said, gesturing to a maroon leather chair across from him. "Have a seat."

The chair gave a soft creak as Eddie settled in, brass upholstery buttons catching the light. It smelled rich, like the leather had been recently conditioned, the scent almost sweet. Every slight shift sent another quiet groan through the cushions.

Pullman folded his hands on the desk and studied Eddie with a polite, unreadable smile. "I appreciate you coming in on short notice," he said, voice carrying a hint of something Eddie couldn't quite place—businesslike, but with an edge that made the room feel smaller.

Pullman let the silence hang for a beat, fingers drumming once on the oak. Then he drew in a slow breath and leaned forward, elbows on the desk.

"Eddie, I didn't call you in here for pleasantries," he said, voice calm but edged with steel. "I've had multiple complaints about your conduct on the job. Serious ones."

Eddie sat a little straighter, heart ticking faster. The leather chair creaked beneath him.

"First," Pullman continued, flipping open a manila folder. "Substance abuse on duty. Operating a locomotive while under the influence of drugs or alcohol is an immediate termination offense. I've got reports from your fellow railmen saying they've smelled alcohol on your breath more than once."

Eddie opened his mouth, but Pullman raised a hand. "Don't. Just listen for now."

He turned a page, eyes scanning the next sheet. "Second—operating past a stop signal. You know as well as I do what that can mean. Catastrophic consequences. I got this complaint just last week."

The room seemed to shrink. Eddie could hear the faint hiss of the steam heat behind the walls.

"And third," Pullman said, his gaze sharpening, "failure to perform the required brake tests. During a city inspection, you were seen leaving the yard without checking the brakes on a shipment. You know the rules. Proper brake testing isn't optional."

Pullman closed the folder with a quiet snap and set it aside. "Any one of these could end a career. Together? They paint a pretty grim picture."

Eddie swallowed, the leather chair groaning again as he shifted, searching for words that wouldn't come.

Pullman rubbed the bridge of his nose, the folder still at his elbow. "Look," he said, softer now. "Corporate records show you've been with the Chicago North Western since you were thirteen." He let out a short breath, half a chuckle. "Huh… guess we took some chances back then. Probably wasn't even legal."

He leaned back, chair groaning. "Up until recently, Eddie, your record's been spotless. Impeccable. I'd rather not lose a man like you. So here's what I'm offering—a warning. A second chance to shape up, so we don't have to ship you out."

Eddie stared at the grain of the oak desk, jaw tight. The words settled like grit in his teeth. A warning. After all the years. After the long nights, the storms, the endless clatter of wheels on steel. This was the thanks.

His face went flat, cold. "Don't worry about it," he muttered.

Pullman blinked. "What's that?"

"I quit." Eddie pushed the chair back, the leather groaning one last time. His expression didn't flicker. No anger showing, just the hollow calm of a slammed door.

Before Pullman could form a reply, Eddie stood and walked out, boots thudding against the polished floor, leaving the smell of oiled leather and sunlight behind him.

By the time the echo of his boots faded down the hall, Eddie was already a man without a plan. Whatever cash he'd stashed over the years disappeared in a blur—bar tabs, six-packs, the kind of late-night card games where you win just enough to lose again. When the money ran dry, he didn't bother looking for work.

Jack's old truck became his address. He parked it in a weed-choked lot where rusted-out hulks sagged on flat tires, a graveyard of forgotten steel where his own heap fit right in. Nights were a mix of engine creaks and cold drafts through the floorboards; days, a slow shuffle from street corner to street corner, palm out for enough change to buy the next case of beer and square of cigarettes.

Months slid past like empty bottles until summer's heat began to fade. The first sharp nights of September gnawed at him, a chill that crawled under the collar and stayed there. Chicago's winters were a different animal—wind that could skin you alive, snow that turned streets into ice-bound trenches. Lying in the truck's cab one brittle evening, Eddie stared at the sagging headliner and finally let the thought surface: *What happens when the real cold comes?*

That night, sleep dragged him under like a riptide, and the dream came in fits and starts—hazy flickers, like an old film strip fed through a rusty projector.

A flare of light: Jack's weathered hands, the creases etched deep as rail ties.

Click. The Zippo's cap popped open, the sound sharp as a snapped twig.

A flash of Jack's grin, tobacco-stained and proud as ever.

Scritch. Thumb to flint, a blossom of flame that burned gold against the dark.

The scenes refused to stay still. Jack's voice slipped in and out, words chopped by static:

"Steady, kid…always steady." The lighter floated in the dream, metal gleaming like a captured star.

Another quick cut—Eddie fumbling with the trick, Jack's laugh rolling like a distant train.

Click-snap. Light, dark. Light, dark. A staccato heartbeat.

Eddie reached for the lighter, but the frame wobbled, warped. Jack's face blurred to shadow. Only the flame stayed clear—bright, patient, unyielding—before the reel burned white and the dream ended.

A brittle crack echoed in the cab as Eddie's eyes snapped open. Frost feathered the inside of the windshield, pale as smoke. He sat up stiffly, joints popping, and for a moment just watched his breath bloom white in the half-light. The truck's cab smelled of cold metal and stale beer.

He shoved the door open. The hinge shrieked, and the predawn air knifed in, raw enough to sting his lungs. Eddie climbed out, boots crunching on frozen gravel, and pulled his coat tighter. The lot lay silent except for the distant rattle of an L train and the whisper of wind through weeds.

From the bed of the truck he dragged a burlap sack filled with scavenged fuel—broken branches, splintered pallets, wads of old newspaper gone soft with damp. He crossed to the rusted oil barrel set in a ring of stones and began feeding it, first the paper, then the wood, the sound of each drop echoing hollow against the steel.

The wind knifed through the weeded lot, carrying grit and the sour smell of the city. Eddie hunched deeper into his coat and stood beside the oil drum. The sky had that bruised Chicago color—steel and purple—and the first flecks of snow needled his cheeks.

He flipped open Jack's Zippo, the engraved chrome catching the dim light. *Click*. Flame bloomed, bright and sudden. He crouched, feeding the fire until it hissed and popped, smoke curling like black rope into the dark.

"Mind if I borrow that light?"

Eddie jerked upright. A figure stood just outside the circle of fire, a hood pulled low enough to swallow his face. The long, cowl-like folds reminded Eddie of pictures he'd seen of Gregorian monks.

The man stepped closer, a cigar between his fingers. "Your lighter," he said again, voice soft but clear. No breath clouded the air.

Something cold slid down Eddie's spine. "Yeah… sure." He held out the Zippo. "How'd you—"

"Eddie." The man said his name like he'd known it forever.

Eddie froze. "How do you know—"

The hooded man sparked his cigar, the flame blooming bright—but even in that sudden glow, his face stayed buried in shadow. The man thumbed the lighter's engraving, then spoke as if reading from memory. "Your word is a lamp for my feet and a light for my path. Psalm one-nineteen, verse one-oh-five." His voice carried an odd calm, almost musical. "It means the wisdom of God lights the way that's meant for you."

Eddie blinked. "What?"

The stranger snapped the Zippo shut with a soft metallic click and, without a word, flicked it back through the air. Eddie caught it by reflex, the chrome warm from the flame.

When Eddie looked up, the man was already a darker shape melting into the night. One heartbeat, two—gone. The lot was empty except for the soft crackle of the fire.

Eddie spun, scanning shadows. Nothing. No footprints in the thin snow that just started blanketing the ground. Only the flame and the quiet rush of wind. His pulse thudded in his ears.

He stared at the Zippo in his hand, its chrome warm against his palm. Fear pricked him, sharp as the cold, but beneath it something steadier took hold—a low, surprising warmth, like a coal hidden under ash.

He didn't understand who the stranger was, how he knew his name, or how he'd just vanished into thin air, but the words lingered, bright as the flame: a lamp for my feet, a light for my path.

The next morning he sat on a rotted stump next to Jack's old truck, a stack of yesterday's newspapers spread across his knees. His stomach growled, but he ignored it and ran a finger down the smudged classifieds. Welders. Car sales. Night security. Nothing he could—or wanted to do. Then a small ad snagged his eye:

Janitor Needed - Lincoln Elementary - Walking distance from downtown.

A janitor. He almost snorted. But he'd started his life with a broom in the roundhouse, sweeping up coal dust and shoveling ash. He knew the smell of ammonia, the slap of a mop against concrete. It wasn't glory, but it was something. Better than freezing to death in Jack's old truck, better than being another stiff the city would haul off when winter finally showed its teeth.

Eddie used the cracked mirror on the truck's visor to shave, a dull razor dragging through days of stubble. He scrubbed his face with a rag dipped in cold water from a gas-station sink, then buttoned the cleanest shirt he owned—a pale blue thing that still smelled faintly of smoke. The old truck coughed but started, and he eased it out of the lot, the rising sun flashing across the windshield.

Wildcat Elementary sat on a quiet side street, its brick walls glowing in early light. Kids' chalk drawings—rockets, flowers, crooked hopscotch squares—brightened the walk. Eddie parked a block away, combed his damp hair with his fingers, and walked up the steps, each creak of his boots echoing against the school's broad front doors.

Inside, the halls smelled of waxed linoleum and pencil shavings. A man in a tweed jacket—clearly a teacher—was pinning student art to a bulletin board. He turned at the sound of Eddie's boots.

"Can I help you?" the teacher asked, brow raised.

"I'm here about the janitor job in the paper," Eddie said, shifting his weight.

The teacher's face softened into a friendly half-smile. "Oh, great." I'm John Keller—fifth grade." He wiped his hands on his slacks and extended one to shake. Eddie gave it a firm squeeze, surprised at how steady his own hand felt.

"Come on," Keller said. "I'll take you to his office." In that moment, Eddie felt a strange flicker in his chest, a mix of nerves and anticipation. It reminded him, faintly, of the day he first met Arthur at the roundhouse—back when the world seemed vast and full of possibilities, before the years had carved their weight into his shoulders. Only this was different; there was no roar of engines, no grease under his nails, no whistling wind through the rails. Just the polished floors, the smell of chalk dust, and the echo of their footsteps down the quiet hall.

He led Eddie down the polished corridor, the faint smell of chalk following them, and stopped at a door marked Principal. "Here we are," Keller said with an encouraging nod before knocking lightly and opening the door.

"Mr. Harris? We've got an applicant for the janitorial job, his name's Eddie."

Mr. Harris, the principal, stood—a lean man with a warm but cautious smile. "Morning. Sit wherever you like."

"It was nice meeting you, Eddie." Keller said before turning from the door to head down the hallway. Eddie gave a nod.

Eddie lowered himself into the chair, aware of the way his knees trembled from the uncertainty. No doubt a lack of alcohol wasn't helping. Normally, Eddie would have had a drink or two by now—but today, Eddie knew he couldn't blow it; he needed to be on his best behavior.

"Normally we have folks fill out an application and we get back to them." Harris said. "But seeing how you're here already and I have a few minutes, we can do an impromptu interview."

"You've done maintenance work before?" Harris asked.

"Yeah," Eddie said, voice rough but steady. "Started out cleaning the rail yard when I was a kid. Kept at it for years. I know how to keep a place running."

"What about your most recent employment?" Harris asked, cocking his head.

Eddie shifted in his chair, hands resting on his knees, trying to appear calm. "I… I was a railroad engineer for about thirty years," he said, letting the words fall carefully, measured. "Loved the work, loved the rails… but the multi-day trips, being gone for so long, I just—well, I wanted to be closer to my family. Thought it was time to stay put, keep a routine, be around people I care about."

He let the pause hang just long enough for it to sound sincere. Harris raised an eyebrow, nodding slowly, clearly weighing the story. Eddie kept his expression flat, hiding the truth behind a thin veil of weary pride and practicality.

Harris leaned back in his chair, fingers steepled, studying Eddie like he was weighing a complicated equation. "Thirty years, you say? That's quite a tenure," he said slowly. "So you're looking for something… quieter now? More predictable?"

Eddie nodded, careful not to blink too fast or fidget.

"Exactly, sir. Something steady. A place where I can contribute… and still be home at night."

Harris tapped his pen against the desk. "I see. And why janitorial work, if you don't mind me asking? Seems like quite a change from operating locomotives."

Eddie's mind raced, but he held his composure. "I… I've always taken pride in keeping things in order. Clean, organized. I like seeing a space cared for. Figured I could apply the same discipline I had on the railroad here."

Harris's gaze softened, and Eddie caught a glimpse of approval in the man's eyes. Inside, Eddie felt a small surge of hope—but also a twinge of guilt. He was spinning a tale that wasn't quite true, and yet… it might just get him through that door.

Harris studied him for a long beat, then nodded. "It's honest work. We need someone who shows up, keeps the halls clean, looks out for the kids. Think you can do that?"

Eddie met his eyes. "Yeah. I can do that."

The principal's smile widened just a little. "Good. We'll be in touch soon. Can I get your number?"

Eddie was stuck. *I'm so close* he thinks—one last stretch of the truth can't hurt. "Mind if I stop by in a few days to check-in on the decision? I'm between living situations now, and don't have utilities hooked up."

Harris looked at Eddie with slightly suspicious eyes, but trusted his gut anyway. "Ok Eddie, that's fine."

As Eddie stepped back into the crisp air, a faint hum of

children's laughter drifted from the playground. For the first time in years, he felt a flicker of possibility—small, but alive.

Eddie shuffled through the halls of Lincoln Elementary School, mop bucket squeaking against the linoleum, a faint tang of bleach and floor wax in the air. The Lincoln Wildcats' banners hung from the walls, blue and gold, stiff and dusty. He knew these halls—knew how to get them spotless without wasting a second. Vacuuming, scrubbing, wiping, emptying trash cans until even the cafeteria smelled like nothing at all, which, in Eddie's mind, was a kind of victory.

Weeks turned into months. Sweat and small paychecks accumulated. The janitor's job was steady, and Eddie saved every spare cent. Eventually, he had enough for a security deposit.

One Sunday morning, as he sipped lukewarm coffee from a thermos, Eddie flipped through the newspaper. A small ad caught his eye: "Modest attic apartment available. Contact Florence: 555-1212. Quiet neighborhood, private entrance. Reasonable rent."

That afternoon Eddie fed a handful of coins into the payphone outside the corner grocery, the handset cold against his ear. The number from the ad rang twice before a warm, lilting voice answered.

"Hello, this is Florence."

Eddie cleared his throat. "Uh—hi. I'm calling about the

apartment in the paper."

They talked longer than he expected. Florence asked about steady income—he told her about the janitor job at Wildcat Elementary. She asked if he smoked, and he said only outside. Her laugh, light and easy, carried through the crackling line. By the time they hung up, she'd offered to show him the place that evening.

The apartment was exactly what the ad promised: a snug attic perched above her detached garage. Humble, a little cramped—but affordable. And for Eddie, affordability meant possibility.

Eddie handed over the modest deposit he'd scraped together from weeks of careful saving. Florence passed him a small brass key with a friendly smile. That night he carried his few belongings up the steep wooden stairs and set them by the bed, the space warm and still around him. For the first time in a long time, he had a door he could lock behind him—and a place that was his alone.

Florence

Eddie woke with a groan, cheek stuck to the couch's threadbare armrest. His foot swept the floor until it connected with an empty beer can, sending it skidding into the wall with a metallic clink. He pushed himself upright, shoulders hunched, and stumbled toward the kitchenette. The coffee tin sat on the counter, light as a feather when he shook it—empty.

The attic room pressed in around him. The five-foot knee walls made the sloped ceiling dip so low he had to duck unless he stood dead-center. Rough, splintered beams crossed overhead, their exposed nails pushing through the plywood like rusted teeth. The air carried a faint smell of dust and old timber.

A sagging couch, a flickering TV, a narrow bed shoved into a corner, a bathroom hardly bigger than a closet, and a miniature oven with four small burners—that was the sum of it. Barely enough space for a man to live, but it kept him dry, and the rent wouldn't bleed him beyond what he could scrape together.

Eddie threw on yesterday's shirt, ran a hand through his hair, and pushed out the side door. The outside stairs groaned under his weight, the aged wood bending slightly with each step. An angled overhang rattled in the morning breeze, shedding a few cold drops from last night's rain.

At the bottom, he caught sight of Florence. Late-seventies, give or take, with a halo of blue-and-silver curls set tight to hide the thinning. Thick-rimmed glasses perched on her nose, magnifying sharp, birdlike eyes. She was kneeling in the soil, hands deep among the perennials, coaxing them into tidy rows.

The sight of her made his gut tighten—he was late on rent, and it had only been three months since he moved in. Any second now, he expected her to straighten up, brush dirt from her knees, and bring it up. But she didn't. She just kept working the soil, humming to herself, not looking up as he passed.

Florence straightened from her flowerbed, brushing dirt from her gloves.

"Good morning, Eddie. How's the apartment treating you?"

Eddie slowed but didn't stop, hitching a thumb toward the garage. "It's working out great. And don't worry about the noise when you pull in and out—barely notice it." He kept his tone light, hoping to skate past the part where she might remember the rent.

She smiled, the corners of her eyes creasing behind the

thick rims. "I just made a fresh pitcher of iced tea. Lemon slices and everything. You should come sit on the porch with me, take a break from whatever you're up to. I've got two new rockers—thought we could break them in. Talk about the news, politics, life..." She gestured toward the house. "Whatever you like. I enjoy making new friends."

Eddie forced a polite grin, guilt chewing at him. She was too nice. "Can't today," he said, already edging toward the driveway.

Florence's smile didn't fade, but her hands went back to the soil. Eddie trotted down the short drive, past the weathered garage doors, and crossed to Jack's rusted pickup with mismatched green fenders, parked crooked against the curb.

The truck rumbled through the sleepy Chicago suburbs, past rows of brick bungalows and tidy lawns still damp from the morning sprinklers. The streets were quiet—Sunday quiet—until he turned onto the corner where the little store sat wedged between a laundromat and a barber shop.

He pulled in and spotted it immediately: a gleaming white Cadillac convertible with two identical white Labs sitting alert in the backseat, tongues lolling. Eddie's gut tightened. Mr. Boyd.

He killed the engine with a grunt and slid out, keeping his eyes low. Inside, the reindeer bells above the door gave a bright jangle. He gave the clerk a curt nod and made his way down the aisles, pace quick but casual, scanning for any sign of the man. Past the canned goods. Past the freezer section. Finally, the coffee shelf. He grabbed the cheapest dark roast they had—store brand, big red tin—and turned toward the register.

He paid in crumpled bills, receipt already half-stuffed in his pocket when a shadow caught the corner of his eye.

"Eddie! Great to see you."

There he was—Mr. Boyd, short and broad with a clean white beard, his cowboy hat perched like a crown. The man's smile was wide, practiced, the kind that dared you not to return it.

Eddie gave a stiff nod.

"Did you see my boys out there?" Boyd's voice brimmed with pride. "White Labradors—'polar bear labs,' some folks call them. Rare color variation. They've got that iridescent coat, black points on the face. Recognized by the AKC, you know. Smartest dogs you'll ever meet. Trainable, loyal, gentle—everything a dog should be."

Eddie gave Boyd half a smirk, enough to pass for polite. He even tossed out a token, "Yeah, they look like they'd win ribbons or somethin'."

Boyd chuckled, launching into a story about their last show—some out-of-state competition, shiny medals, judges who "knew real quality when they saw it." Eddie let him talk, nodding once or twice, his eyes already drifting toward the door.

After a minute, he cut in. "Well, I gotta get this coffee home before I fall asleep standin' here."

It was blunt, maybe a little too sharp, but Eddie didn't

wait for Boyd's reply. He slipped past, boots scuffing the tile, and shoved the door open hard enough for the bells to give a startled clatter. Outside, the sunlight hit him like a spotlight, and he made a beeline for his truck without looking back.

Eddie rolled past Florence's place slow enough to take in the scene. She'd traded her garden gloves for conversation, standing with a smiling couple beside a shiny red sedan. Brochures flashed in their hands like warning flags.

Eddie eased his truck up the block and parked out of sight. No way he was walking into that. He waited, watching the three of them chat, Florence's smile wide, her head tipping back in laughter. Finally, she gestured toward the house. The screen door squealed open, then clapped shut behind them.

Clear.

Eddie swung the truck to the curb, killed the engine, and hustled out. The rusty door gave a hollow thunk as he slammed it, then he took the wooden stairs two at a time, hunched, hoping no one glanced out a window.

Inside, he tore open a frozen TV dinner, the tray hissing in the oven. A few minutes later, he was on the creaking couch, chewing limp Salisbury steak and watching the fuzzy glow of his battered television.

Then—footsteps. Heavy, more than one set. The wooden stairs outside groaned under the weight of two… maybe three people.

A sharp knock rattled the door.

Eddie's fork slipped from his hand, clattering into a beer

can that spun across the floor like a propeller.

Dammit, he thought, blood rising in his ears. "This is the last thing I need."

The knock came again, sharp and polite. Eddie froze mid-step toward the door. No eyehole. No way to see who it was without showing his face.

He thought about staying quiet—just letting them think he wasn't home. Then Florence's voice floated through the wood, gentle but persistent.

"Eddie, are you home?"

He clenched his jaw. Another knock.

"We have some visitors. They're from the church. They want to know if you have a minute?"

Eddie felt the tug of guilt gnawing at him. His hand hovered over the knob. Then came a lighter *tap-tap*—different knuckles, probably one of the visitors.

He cursed under his breath. Couldn't ignore Florence.

His fingers closed on the handle. The old brass felt cold under his grip. He turned it slow, easing the door open on its stiff hinges.

At the top of the steps stood Florence, beaming wide, her dentures too perfect to be real. A step below her—a young man, trim haircut, crisp shirt, posture straight as a fence post. Another step down, the young woman—striking, with a kind of shy, watchful look in her eyes.

The man reached up past Florence, hand out like he was ready to own the handshake.

Eddie forced his own hand forward, his face neutral while his gut twisted. Their palms met.

Just smile. Just get through it.

It'll be over soon, he told himself. He'd just moved into Florence's attic apartment, and he wasn't ready to be kicked out—not yet.

The young man's grip was firm, his smile effortless. "Tom Jensen," he said. "From First Cavalry Church, off Grove Road."

Eddie said nothing.

Tom tilted his head, still holding that practiced warmth. "Got a few minutes to talk about… you know—" he gestured vaguely toward the sky—"the meaning of it all?"

Eddie's jaw tightened. "I was just on my way out."

"Of course." Tom's tone stayed gracious, unbothered. He pulled a glossy brochure from under his arm. "Here—take this. First Cavalry Church." The front showed a pair of praying hands against a sunburst sky.

Eddie forced a smile, lips tight, and took it.

"Hope to see you at service one day," Tom said.

Eddie gave a nod that was more reflex than agreement, already grunting inside.

The steps creaked as the three of them made their way down. Florence's voice floated lighter now, cheerful as she chatted. The further their footsteps went, the easier Eddie breathed.

He shut the door, flipped the latch, and glanced at the brochure. Then it went into the trash, crumpled with a hollow thunk.

For a moment, a shadow crossed his mind—unwelcome, unfinished. Then he let it die, slid back onto the couch, fork in hand. The Salisbury steak waited. So did *The Price is Right*.

Eddie stayed in the attic apartment eight years. Somewhere along the line the calendar lost its weight. The seasons looped past like scenery outside a train window—fall's crackling leaves, winter's knife-edge cold, spring drizzle, the brief burn of summer—and each turn came faster than the last. He'd blink and it was November again. Nearly sixty now, the speed of it made him dizzy.

The habits piled up with the years: too many cigarettes, too much cheap whiskey, too many TV dinners eaten off the wobbly card table by the flicker of an aging television. Money was always just enough to scrape by, never enough to feel safe. Whatever dreams he'd carried as a boy—back when anything seemed possible—had long since dried to dust. Distraction became his best defense. He kept his mind busy so it wouldn't wander into dark alleys of memory: the losses, the old failures, the nights when the world had felt wide open.

Florence became the bright spot in that narrowing world. She reminded him of his late mother, a steady warmth that softened the edges. His sisters—nearly gone now—their lives bound to wealthy husbands. He rarely laid eyes on them anymore, years slipping past without so much as a visit. But

Florence was there in the small daily ways: waving from her garden, sharing leftovers, calling up the stairs when a storm blew through. Eddie, in turn, maintained her house, tuned her sputtering car, replaced the porch boards one summer.

One bright Sunday morning, Eddie balanced on the third rung of Florence's old aluminum ladder, a screwdriver tucked behind his ear as he worked at a stubborn clog in the gutter. The air smelled of cut grass and the faint sweetness of late-blooming lilacs.

Around the corner came Florence, her house shoes whispering across the walk. She carried a plate piled high with freshly fried chicken, steam curling in the sun. "You hungry, Eddie?" she called, her voice warm as the July morning.

He turned to answer, the ladder giving a small metallic groan. The sudden shift made the world tilt. Eddie grabbed the gutter with one hand to steady himself, heart kicking once in his chest.

Florence gasped, clutching the plate closer. "Careful up there!"

"I'll be down in just a bit," Eddie hollered, forcing a grin while his knuckles whitened on the metal. "Need to clear the gunk from this downspout first."

He tipped his chin toward the darkening sky. "Storm's rolling in—if I don't clear it, the water'll spill from the elbow again and keep chewing up the siding."

Florence shook her head but didn't argue, the smell of crisp chicken drifting up as Eddie turned back to the task, the warm sunlight catching the fine dust of leaves that floated from the eaves.

The small kitchen smelled of butter and warm breading. Eddie sat across from Florence, a paper napkin tucked into his collar while she moved with gentle grace between counter and table. She lifted a scoop of mashed potatoes and plopped it beside the golden drumsticks already on his plate.

"Eat up before it cools," she said.

Eddie set his hat on the table, brim up. "Smells like Sunday at my ma's," he said, picking up a piece of chicken.

Florence settled into her chair, folding her hands for a moment before reaching for her own plate. "Eddie," she began, her voice gentle but certain, "why don't you come with me to First Cavalry sometime? Might be good for you. I know it's helped me."

Eddie looked over, his face blank as cooling ash after a fire.

"It'd get you out of that apartment, away from the TV. You can't meet a nice lady sitting inside all day. And who knows—you might like it. Good people go there."

Eddie paused mid-bite, the words catching him off guard. "Don't know if I believe in God," he said finally, trying to sound casual. "Not sure I'd fit in. Don't hardly got the time either, with work—and I need my leisure on the weekend. Only way I can reset, unwind."

He set the chicken down and wiped his fingers on a napkin. "Plus," he added, voice lowering, "if there were a God, I'd have a good place to unload plenty of blame for the things I've been through. The losses, the failures, the burned-up dreams. Probably best I don't go."

Florence looked down, pressing her napkin softly to her lips. "Won't bring it up again, Eddie. Sorry for that."

A heaviness settled between them, the clock ticking in the quiet. Eddie's chest tightened. He hated that look on her face—like he'd kicked something fragile. His heart sank as he reached for another piece of chicken, wishing he could pull the words back into his mouth.

One warm evening they rocked side by side on the porch as the sun bled out behind the maples. Florence's hands rested like pale birds on the armrests. She talked, gently, about feeling the nearness of her own ending—about where she might go next, about the comfort her faith gave her. She chose her words with care, knowing Eddie's stance, but to her it felt too important to leave unsaid. Eddie listened, the old floorboards creaking beneath them, the twilight stretching long, and for once he didn't interrupt.

Dusk settled like a blue veil over the neighborhood. The last scraps of daylight bled into the trees while moths wheeled and tapped at the porch light, soft wings whispering against the glass. Eddie rocked in rhythm with the old boards, the chair creaking in time with Florence's beside him.

"I figure I've only got a handful of years left," she said, her voice almost cheerful. "No one in my family's ever made it past eighty-nine. I'll be eighty-seven come Tuesday."

Eddie shifted, uneasy. "Ah, don't start talking like that," he said, eyes fixed on the street where the shadows pooled.

"I'm just being honest." Her chair kept rocking, back and forth like a metronome marking the silence. "Not much time left for me, Eddie."

He grunted, tried to change the subject—something about the tomatoes in her garden—but the words felt tinny in his mouth. He didn't like thinking about the future anymore. Too many busted dreams behind him, too many people buried. Better to coast until the lantern burned out, let the dark have its way and maybe find peace at the end of it.

The evening deepened until the blue of twilight drained to black. A cool dampness crept across the porch, carrying the smell of cut grass and the faint sweetness of Florence's flowers. Eddie rose, brushing the chill from his sleeves. "Guess I'll head upstairs," he said, nodding toward the attic steps. Florence gave a small, knowing smile and kept rocking, the porch light haloing her silver hair. Eddie climbed the narrow staircase, each board groaning under his boots, the night closing in around him.

Inside, the apartment smelled of old wood and rain-soaked earth drifting through the screened window. Forty-five years to the day since Jack died. That was excuse enough. Eddie uncapped the bottle and poured shots by candlelight until the lines between the flicker of flame and the shadows blurred. He stopped counting somewhere after the fifth.

The box of Jack's things sat on the coffee table, dusty but close. Eddie dug through it with slow hands, pulling up a black-and-white photo: Jack in his thirties, smiling wide beside a blonde with bright platinum curls. Veronica, Eddie guessed—the one who'd slipped through Jack's fingers, the story Jack had only told once and never again.

Outside the wind stiffened, a storm rushing in fast. Rain hammered the roof, the same hard rhythm that had played the night Jack passed. Eddie thumbed the Zippo Jack had left him, the chrome winking in the candlelight. He read the engraving under his breath, the words soft and strange in the dark.

His mind drifted to younger days—dreams of a ranch out west, of wide plains and cattle drives. Jack telling him to chase those dreams like they were meant for him. None of it had come true.

A flash of red and blue pulsed across the wall. Eddie lurched to the window, heart stumbling. An ambulance idled at the curb, its lights strobing through the rain. Two EMTs carried a gurney up Florence's walk. Minutes later they rolled her back out, a pale outline under a sheet.

The next day the newspaper made it plain: natural causes, old age.

Something inside Eddie cracked lower than ever before. He sat in the silence of the attic, staring at the empty rocker on the porch, the moths still circling the bulb like lost souls. Restless. Hollow. Searching for something he couldn't name.

That night, the thought of First Cavalry needled at him

like a loose stitch. He drifted into a shallow sleep and dreamed of the church—its white clapboard walls lit by morning sun, doors open wide as if they'd been waiting. He heard Florence's laugh somewhere inside, steady as sunlight through lace curtains, and smelled the faint sweetness of her fried chicken carried on a breeze. When he jolted awake, the picture lingered, sharp as the scent of her old rose lotion.

For days the notion trailed him like a shadow. He argued with it while shaving, while folding his threadbare shirts, while staring at the television's dull glow. He didn't believe in God—never had, he told himself—but the image of that wide-open door wouldn't quit.

Finally, one cold dawn, Eddie sighed and muttered into the empty room, "Alright, Florence. I'll go." At the very least, he figured, he owed her that much.

The Visit

Morning light leaked through the crooked blinds, pale and cold. Eddie sat at the window with his coffee-stained mug of tap water, watching the quiet street come alive. Couples strolled past in pressed slacks and shining shoes, women in bright skirts and tidy hats, kids tugging at sleeves—each of them wrapped in that Sunday shine.

He rubbed a hand over his unshaven jaw. *That's what you're supposed to wear to church*, he thought, eyeing his own heap of clothes on the chair. Most were stained or frayed, a record of years lived rough.

Eddie pulled open the dresser drawers, stirring through old flannels and dusty jeans. At last he found a pair of black pants that still held a crease if you squinted, and a white button-down that smelled faintly of lavender from Florence's laundry soap. He shook the shirt out, ran a damp cloth across the collar, and slipped it on.

In the cracked mirror by the door he studied the man staring back—gray creeping through his hair, eyes rimmed with sleepless years. He tugged the collar straighter, gave a single nod. Good enough.

Eddie eased Jack's old truck into the far corner of the First Cavalry lot, gravel crunching under the bald tires. Chrome and waxed paint gleamed everywhere—late-model sedans, a few polished SUVs, a candy-red convertible that caught the sun like a flare. His truck, a relic with flaking green fenders and a door that creaked like an old knee, looked like it had wandered in from a junkyard.

He killed the engine and sat for a beat, palms on the wheel. The white clapboard church stood ahead, its steeple cutting into a pale-blue sky. Voices drifted on the breeze—laughter, a burst of organ music through an open door. Eddie smoothed the front of his shirt and felt the rough stubble on his chin. Too late to shave now.

When he finally stepped out, the cold air wrapped around him, sharper than he expected. Gravel crunched loud under his boots, each step like a gunshot in his ears. He kept his eyes on the ground, but he could feel it: the weight of glances sliding across him. Or maybe it was just his nerves. Hard to tell.

As Eddie made his way along the row, the white Cadillac convertible caught his eye. His gut tightened; the last thing he wanted was a run-in with Boyd. The two white Labs lounged across the back seat, their heads lifting as he approached. One gave a soft whine, tails flicking against the white leather. Eddie shoved his hands deeper into his coat pockets and moved past without a glance, muttering a low grunt.

A couple passed by, perfume and aftershave trailing behind them. The man gave a polite nod. Eddie answered with a stiff twitch of his head, heart thumping faster. The door ahead swung open, spilling warm light and the hum of hymnals onto the steps. He adjusted his collar, wondering if it was crooked, wondering if everyone could tell he didn't belong.

Just walk, he told himself. *It's only a building. Only people.* But the back of his neck prickled as if a hundred eyes tracked him all the same.

At the top of the stone steps a woman in a navy cardigan held the door, her smile soft and inviting. "Good morning," she said, voice bright as the bell overhead. "Welcome to First Cavalry."

Eddie tipped his chin in something like a nod. "Morning," he muttered, his throat dry.

"Service just started, but you'll find a seat easy enough," she added, pressing a folded bulletin into his hand. The paper felt warm from her fingers.

Inside, the change hit him all at once. The entryway breathed heat, a gentle floral scent riding the air—roses maybe, and a faint sweetness like baby powder. After the chill of the parking lot it felt almost too warm, a comfort settling over him like a quilt.

He stepped farther in, boots silent on thick carpet, and

caught the murmur of the congregation beyond the double doors. Through a narrow gap he saw rows of bowed heads, a sea of silver hair gleaming in the soft light. Elderly couples shifted in pews, shoulders touching, hymnals open in lined hands. A low organ note trembled through the rafters.

Eddie paused, letting the door close softly behind him. For a moment he just stood there, the scent of flowers and powder filling his nose, the warmth seeping through his shirt, unsure whether to keep moving or turn right back around.

"Eddie!" shouted someone in a whisper.

The voice was familiar. Eddie looked. It was Tom Jensen.

"Glad to see you here!" Tom said, sliding to the side of the church pew. "We've got room right here." He patted the oak twice.

Eddie was stuck—no way out.

Eddie eased into the pew beside Tom, the wood worn to a dull shine from decades of bodies shifting, coats sliding, fingers drumming. The sanctuary glowed with a honeyed light that made the brass organ pipes wink like quiet sentinels.

The pastor strode to the edge of the pulpit, silver hair catching the glare of the overhead lights. His dark suit flashed like storm clouds when he moved.

"Brothers and sisters," he thundered, voice filling every corner of the sanctuary, "God set a course for your life long before you drew breath. A purpose. A calling. But don't fool yourself—there is an enemy who burns to wreck it."

He jabbed a finger toward the back pews, eyes blazing. "The

devil doesn't knock polite. He breaks in. He lies, he tempts, he whispers that your plan is better. And every whisper is meant to drag you off the road God laid for you."

His palm came down hard on the pulpit, a sharp crack like a gunshot. The pastor leaned in slightly, eyes bright behind thick rimmed glasses. "Even when the night howls. Even when you can't see more than a single step. God's plan is fire—don't let the devil douse it."

The choir stirred behind him, a low hum rising like wind through pines. Heads bowed and murmured amens drifted like soft echoes. Eddie shifted, the pew creaking under his weight. The pastor's voice droned on, smooth as a lullaby to everyone else, but each word scraped across Eddie like sandpaper. God's plan. God's path. What bull. If there was a plan for him, it sure looked like a blueprint for misery—loss after loss, a lifetime of busted dreams and unwanted memories.

He felt a slow burn rise in his chest, creeping into his face until his cheeks prickled hot. His pulse hammered in his ears, so loud he swore it might give him away. Sweat beaded at his hairline as he yanked a handkerchief from his pocket and blotted his forehead, hoping no one saw. But the itch for a drink scratched at him, sharp and insistent. *Just get through this*, he told himself. One more hymn. One more prayer. Then a stiff pour waiting at home.

Time stretched, each second thick as molasses. He clenched his teeth until his jaw ached, molars grinding in a slow, angry rhythm.

Tom leaned closer, eyebrows raised. "So, what do you think? Enjoying the service?"

Eddie blinked, caught off guard. "Oh—yes," he said quickly, forcing a smile that felt stiff and foreign. "Very interesting."

Tom gave a small nod and turned back to the pulpit. Eddie exhaled, long and shaky, his jaw still twitching like a live wire.

The final hymn faded into a warm murmur of voices and shuffling feet. Sunlight streamed through the stained-glass windows, splashing the aisle with fractured color as the congregation filed out. Eddie moved fast, angling for the door, hoping to beat the crush in the lot, but was stopped at the bottleneck. A moment later, Tom's hand landed on his shoulder.

"Eddie, good to see you here," Tom said, his smile loose and friendly. "We're having a little brunch over at our place—my wife's gonna get the griddle going. Come by, meet a few folks."

Eddie offered a polite half-smile. "That's kind of you, Tom, but I should probably head back. Got a few things I need to tend to." He kept his tone friendly, but his mind was already on the familiar burn of whiskey waiting at home.

Tom looked as though he might press the invitation, then simply nodded. "Another time, then. Glad you came."

"Appreciate it," Eddie said, giving a quick handshake before slipping through the crowd and out into the crisp midday air.

The parking lot was alive with motion—Cadillacs and late-model Mercedes humming to life, SUVs easing out with quiet efficiency. Gravel crunched under Eddie's boots as a gust of wind whipped through, stirring up a dry swirl of dust and brittle leaves.

He kept his eyes low, heading for the far corner where Jack's old truck waited like an unwashed secret.

He climbed in and turned the key. The engine coughed once, then fired with a deafening bang—a sharp backfire that cracked the Sunday calm. Several people ducked and looked around, startled. Eddie hunched instinctively, heat rising to his face. He eased the truck into gear, the muffler grumbling as he rolled toward the exit. Dust kicked up behind him in a pale brown cloud as he pulled onto the street, leaving the polished cars and polite goodbyes behind.

For the next two weeks, Eddie moved through his days like a man half-awake. The attic felt too still without the soft shuffle of Florence's feet on the porch beside the garage, or the warm drift of her humming through the screened window as supper sizzled in her house.

But underneath the quiet grief was a gnawing worry he couldn't shake. Florence had been the reason he had a roof at all. Her kindness had kept the attic warm in winter, kept the hot plates and sandwiches coming when his own cupboard was bare. Without her, the arrangement felt flimsy as cardboard. How long until her kin showed up with keys and told him to clear out? He had no savings, no real plan, not even a clean place to land. He imagined himself on a cot at the mission, or worse, curled up in the cab of Jack's old truck again with a blanket over his shoulders and frost blooming on the glass. The thought made his chest seize. Every creak of the stairwell set him on edge, every car that slowed in front of the house made him think of Florence's children coming to sort her things, to sweep him away with the rest of the clutter.

Eddie never set foot in First Cavalry again. Once was plenty. The memory of that first service clung to him like smoke, hard to wash out, and the guilt that had crawled up his back that morning still made him itch if he thought about it too long. He told himself it was the pastor's fault—too much fire and brimstone, too much talk about "plans" and "paths" and "holding fast." What did any of that have to do with a man like him? He already knew what his life amounted to: broken promises, busted knuckles, and a liver that throbbed most mornings like it was begging for mercy. If that was God's plan, it was a cruel one, and Eddie wasn't about to sit through another hour of being reminded.

So he put the church out of his mind the same way he dealt with most things that threatened to dig too deep: he pushed it down and poured liquor over the top. If Tom ever mentioned the service, Eddie changed the subject quick or acted like he hadn't heard. And when Sunday rolled around, instead of pews and hymnals, Eddie stuck to the things that dulled the edges—smokes, daytime programming, and the bottom of a good bottle.

One Sunday afternoon, when Eddie eased the truck into

the drive, a flash of white in the yard caught his eye.

A wooden post, fresh in the soil. A sign:

ESTATE SALE – Next Weekend.

Eddie cut the engine and just stared. The words wavered in the heat shimmer. He climbed the stairs to the attic, shoulders heavy, and changed into an old flannel and worn jeans. He poured a cheap bourbon over two melting cubes and let it burn down his throat.

That's when he heard it—grit crunching under tires. A car pulling in.

He set the glass on the sill and looked out. A silver sedan idled behind his truck. A man in a pressed shirt stepped out, a leather folio tucked under one arm. Papers in his hand. He started for the stairs.

Eddie's gut tightened. He didn't move until the knock rattled the door.

"Mr. Ross?" the man called, voice clipped.

Eddie opened the door a cautious inch. "Yeah?"

The man gave a polite smile. "I'm sorry to bother you. I'm Mark Taylor, with Harlan Realty." He held out a sheaf of papers like a peace offering. "I'm afraid I've got some tough news. With Ms. Florence's passing, the property's going to market. We'll need the apartment vacated before the estate sale next weekend."

Eddie's jaw worked, silent.

"I know it's sudden," Taylor went on. "Truly sorry for the inconvenience." Then he tried a weak grin. "Rough run of luck, huh? First the owner passes and now this notice. Guess when it rains it pours."

Something in Eddie snapped hot and quick. Florence wasn't an owner. She was Florence—warmth in a cold world. His fingers itched to slam the door. Instead he said, "Yeah. Real funny."

Taylor's grin died. He cleared his throat and retreated down the steps, shoes crunching fast on the pavement.

Eddie shut the door hard enough to rattle the frame. The papers trembled in his hand. He looked around the attic—one chair, a narrow bed, the TV humming low—and felt the walls close in.

By nightfall he'd packed everything he owned into a single duffel: spare shirts, a razor, a dented thermos. He swung it over a shoulder, descended the stairs, and heaved it into the bed of Jack's old truck. The slam of metal echoed through the quiet yard.

The weeded lot greeted him like a bad memory, the city's sour smell rising with the night mist. He parked near the oil drum, sat in the cab with the engine ticking cool, and lit a cigarette.

A janitor's wages barely covered Florence's attic. No fixed address, no chance—an ordinary lease might as well have been a penthouse on the moon. The math was merciless.

And so the thought returned, steady as a rail line stretching to the horizon: the yard.

The locomotives.

The work that had once been his whole life.

He flicked ash out the window, eyes narrowing at the dark. Maybe it was time to climb back into a cab, feel the diesel rumble beneath him, and reclaim what he'd lost.

Redemption—that was the word that kept gnawing at him.

He pictured the old locomotive cab: the smell of diesel, the tremor underfoot as the throttle opened. Years back he'd walked away in a blaze of anger, left behind a spotless record turned sour in a single meeting. They'd called him reckless, careless. Maybe they weren't wrong.

But the rails were in his blood. He knew every signal light, every yard curve, every sound a healthy engine made. Going back wouldn't just mean a paycheck—it would mean proving that the man who quit in a storm of pride could still steady his hands, climb back in, and run a train clean and true.

He didn't want forgiveness from the bosses or even from God. He wanted to prove it to himself: that the railroad hadn't beaten him, and that he hadn't beaten himself.

Two nights later, Eddie turned the truck toward the old rail yard.

The city thinned to cracked asphalt and warehouses. Sodium

lights buzzed overhead like tired wasps. He rolled down the window, letting the damp air slap his face, and for the first time in weeks he felt something like a pulse quicken. The smell came first—diesel and hot metal—a scent that clung to his bones even after years away.

He eased through the chain-link gate, the one still hanging crooked on its hinges. No guard tonight, just a floodlight throwing hard shadows across the gravel. The yard opened before him, a maze of rust-striped tracks and hulking silhouettes of engines asleep under the moon.

He parked at the edge and stepped out. Gravel shifted under his boots with the same crunch he remembered from a lifetime ago. His breath fogged in the cool air. Somewhere down the line a coupling clanged, a hollow ring that echoed through the yard.

He walked slowly, fingertips brushing the flaked paint of a boxcar as he passed. Each step pulled a memory loose: the hiss of air brakes, the deep bellied horn at dawn, Jack leaning from a cab window with that half grin. Nights when the yard roared alive—steel screaming, lights blazing—while the rest of the city slept.

At Track 7 a big GE locomotive loomed, paint dulled to a bruised red. Eddie climbed the ladder to the catwalk, hands steady on the cold rungs. Inside, the cab smelled of oil and dust. He slid into the engineer's seat, the leather cracked but familiar, and laid his palms on the console.

A slow exhale. For a heartbeat it felt like time rolled back:

him at thirty, eyes clear, the future wide and loud with promise.

"Damn," he whispered to no one.

A yard light flickered across the windshield, painting the rails silver. He could almost feel the machine stir under him, waiting for a throttle he no longer had the right to pull.

But maybe he could again.

The thought landed heavy. He wasn't sure if it was hope or a challenge, but it set something moving inside, something he hadn't felt since Jack was alive.

He sat there a long while, listening to the quiet tick of cooling metal, the distant groan of a freight settling into place, heavy and tired as the day itself, until the night deepened around him and the idea of starting over no longer felt impossible.

The next morning, Eddie woke while the sky was still the color of cold steel, the sun nowhere in sight. His eyes opened sharp, not from rest but from a restlessness that hadn't let him go all night. The thought of Proviso filled his head like a drumbeat—steady, loud, insistent. Go back. Try again. See if there's a place for you.

Even in his sleep, the idea had circled him like a moth to flame. Half-formed dreams tugged at him: flashes of steel wheels, smoke curling up against the sky, the turntable at the roundhouse spinning like the center of the universe. It was the same kind of dream he'd had when he was thirteen, night after night, when trains weren't just machines—they were destiny.

He rolled over, grabbed a cigarette from the crumpled pack on the bench seat and lit it. The flame trembled in the dark. Eddie sat up and put an elbow on the window, exhaled a long stream of smoke, and tapped the ash. Three perfect rings floated into the night, wobbling, stretching, then unraveling into nothing.

The black outside softened. A knife-edge of sun broke over the treetops, spilling weak light through the windshield of Jack's old truck. Eddie stubbed the cigarette, shoved on his jacket, and turned the key. The truck coughed once, then fired, rattling awake like it had something to prove. He dropped it into gear and rolled out.

By the time he pulled into the employee lot at Proviso, the sky had gone pale. Eddie parked crooked between a Chevy and a rust-red Pontiac and just sat there for a moment. He scanned the rows, searching for anything familiar—an old Buick he remembered, a Ford with a dented fender—but nearly ten years had passed. If any of those cars still lived, they weren't here today.

He got out and started across the gravel. That's when he saw it—the stake. The one Jack used to tie Keena to on long days, before Eddie and Keena got to tag along on the runs. The wood was splintered and gray now, leaning at an angle, but it hit him hard, like stepping into a photograph.

The memory rolled forward uninvited. Arthur, rounding the corner with a burlap sack of sawdust slung over his shoulder, asking if Eddie wanted to help mop up an oil spill. That was the first time they'd really talked, the beginning of something like brotherhood. And like everything else, it had faded away.

Eddie stopped mid-step. Where's Arthur now? Dead? Alive? Behind bars? Married with kids somewhere, never thinking twice about him? The thought pressed down, heavy and useless. He shook it off, spat on the gravel, and kept walking.

The roundhouse loomed ahead, wide and black against the morning sky. Eddie grabbed the cold iron handle and heaved the door open. The hinges shrieked in protest.

Inside, a low echo swallowed his steps. In the distance, locomotives sat in a ring, hulking shadows, patient and waiting. He felt his throat tighten. Across in the far corner, the black iron spiral staircase climbed upward, twisting toward the executives' perch.

Eddie marched to it, boots clanging on each step as he wound up and up. At the top, a narrow corridor stretched ahead. His chest swelled tight. Pressure pushed in behind his eyes. His vision pulsed, dark at the edges.

Slow motion took over. The lights buzzed and flickered like they had before. The corridor smelled the same—oil and paper and dust. The same time of day. The same chill in the air. The same ache in his gut. Frame by frame, the past folded over the present until Eddie wasn't sure which one he was in. Then, like smoke slipping through fingers, it was gone.

He blinked, steadied himself, and looked up. The sign on the wall came into focus:

Yardmaster.

And underneath, the same as it had been almost ten years ago:

Robert Pullman.

Eddie's knuckles rapped once, sharp against the heavy oak. He held his breath, ear pressed to the door. Silence. He tapped again, softer this time.

Then came a voice from down the hall—low, clipped. Eddie spun his head. A tall figure moved toward him, shoulders squared, stride steady. For a moment Eddie thought maybe he'd dreamed it, but as the silhouette stepped into the spill of light from a high window, his stomach tightened.

Pullman.

Older now, with hair grayer at the temples, deeper lines cut into his face. *Rustic*, Eddie thought. The rail yard aged a man the way wind and salt aged a dock piling—fast and merciless.

"Hello, sir." Eddie managed, straightening. His voice cracked faintly. "I'm sure you don't remember me. Name's Edward Ross. Used to be a railroad engineer here at Proviso—until I messed up badly."

Pullman squinted, eyebrows knitting. Then his mouth

twitched into something close to a smile. "Ah. I do remember you." He let out a dry chuckle. "I guess we've both aged some over the years."

He gestured to the office door. "Come on in."

The leather chair behind the desk gleamed, its brass studs winking in the slanted light. The scent of conditioned hide hung in the air, rich and heavy. Sun poured through the tall windows, spilling across Pullman's oak desk, across the framed timetables and the railroad clock ticking loud in the corner.

"Have a seat."

Eddie lowered himself into the chair opposite, palms slick, and began spinning his story. His words came halting at first, then faster, like water down a slope. He talked about regret—about quitting when he should've swallowed his pride, about the mistakes of a younger man who thought too much of himself.

"I had a drinking problem," Eddie admitted, lowering his eyes for effect. "But that's behind me now. I've changed." He added quickly: "Found God. I'm not the same fella I was."

Pullman's face gave little away. He leaned back, fingers steepled, watching Eddie as if waiting for the mask to slip. Still, when Eddie asked—pleaded, almost—for another chance, Pullman exhaled through his nose and gave a small nod.

"Luck's on your side," he said finally. "One of our engineers just retired. We've got an opening."

The words hung in the air like a bell struck clean. Eddie felt the ground return under his feet.

"I'll take it," he said and nodded his head, "Gladly."

They shook hands across the desk, Pullman's grip strong and dry.

In the parking lot, Eddie strode back to Jack's old truck, heart racing. He slid in behind the wheel, slammed the door, and yanked open the glovebox. The flask winked in the sun. He unscrewed the cap, tilted it back, and let the whiskey burn its way down, a celebration and a betrayal in the same breath.

Wiping his mouth with the back of his hand, Eddie slammed the flask shut and tucked it away. Time to tie up loose ends. He turned the key, the engine coughing awake, and pointed the truck toward Wildcat Elementary.

Principal Harris would need to hear he was quitting.

When the Steel Met (1978)

It was a morning like a thousand others—cold, bleak, the kind of December dawn that made men curse when their boots hit the ground. Twenty-eight degrees, snow still crusted from the day before, and the whole yard breathing steam like some iron beast. From the bays of the roundhouse poured thick clouds of vapor, smoke and shadow curling together under the glare of the floodlights bolted to the power poles. The light turned the fog into ghost-faces that shifted and vanished, leaving behind only the reek of fuel and soot. Diesel engines muttered to themselves in the dark, a low metallic grumble that bounced off the sides of the boxcars like voices arguing in another room.

Eddie pulled his red dented Dodge Ram into the lot—the two-tone beater he'd gotten after trading off Jack's old truck for next to nothing, a deal that still burned a little when he thought about it. His head throbbed with hangover, that sour-bellied ache that begged for coffee before it tipped over into full-blown nausea. He cut the engine, sat for a moment, then fished out a cigarette.

The lighter flared, the smoke caught, and Eddie tilted his head back toward the sky. It was 4:50 a.m., black as tar, stars faint and pinched behind the clouds. He pulled deep, and the cold air knifed into his lungs, sharp enough to make his eyes water. Jack came to him then, as sudden as the sting—Jack with his ruined lungs, the rasp in his chest at the end.

Eddie thought, *If I'm lucky, maybe these things will kill me too*. The idea wasn't sad, wasn't even frightening. Just flat. Like a fact written on a scrap of paper.

He exhaled—steam and smoke twisting together in the bitter dark. At 5:12 the clock on the dash glowed green, a silent shove. Time to move.

Eddie hauled the thermos from the seat, then the backpack, the thing stuffed with the usual survival kit: a crumpled bag of chips, peanut-butter-and-jelly in wax paper, a fistful of candy bars, a couple greasy magazines, spare gloves, a little lumbar pillow for the bad back that never stopped nagging him, and the bottle of rum tucked down deep like a secret.

At the tailgate he dragged out the satchel of tools, the leather cracked and worn from years of grease and weather, then circled back around to the front. He kicked at the frozen slush clogging the wheel well, a hollow whack against the metal, and started across the yard with his head down, boots crunching on hard-packed snow. Each puff of smoke from his cigarette came out like a ghost trailing him in the dark.

He passed a line of boxcars that loomed up, their sides scarred with rust and graffiti, when his foot found ice. Just like that, his legs shot out from under him. The sky reeled and then *wham*—his back hit the ground with a flat, sick sound. "Damn it!" Eddie barked, the word steaming up in the air.

He lay there for half a second, snow biting the back of his neck, before scrambling up and brushing himself off. His palms were raw, his ass was wet, and he already felt the bruise blooming. He struck the Zippo, lit a fresh cigarette with shaking hands, and kept moving, smoke curling around his head like a halo gone bad.

Inside the roundhouse, the first thing that hit him was the cold, sharp and biting, crawling under his coat and through his sleeves. The smell came next: oil, iron, and the faint tang of diesel, mingling with the ghost of burnt coffee from a pot long since emptied. Max was there waiting, hunched over his desk like some old bird perched too long. Max had always looked like he'd been carved from dried leather—cheeks lined deep, skin tanned into hide, grin full of gums with a single crooked tooth hanging on for dear life.

He smiled at Eddie, and the smile made the crows-feet etch even deeper down his cheeks. "Eh, Eddie," Max rasped, his voice half gravel, half smoke, "you're lookin' a little tired this morning."

"Oh, why don't you keep your comments to yourself," Eddie muttered, not meeting his eye.

Max only chuckled. He had a knack for getting under Eddie's skin, and the old bastard knew it. That was half the fun. Watching Eddie twitch was easy sport, and Max never minded a little fun before the trains started rolling.

The day's manifest read like a death wish: concrete pipes, steel drainage, tanks of propane and gasoline, piles of timber and coal. South Dakota was the destination—six hours of iron and snow between here and there. A hundred cars long, heavy as sin. For a load like that, they'd run with three locomotives stacked in a multiple-unit lash-up, Eddie in the front seat with the power of all three under his hand. The thought gave him a flicker of pride and a tremor of dread, both at once.

Max slid him the radio with a grunt. Eddie stuffed it in his coat pocket and trudged across the roundhouse floor. The air hung thick with steam and smoke, the sound of a dozen machines coughing and belching like mechanical beasts chained in the dark. His engine sat waiting: a dark blue Alco RSD-7, grime-caked and tired, yellow trim long since dulled to mustard. The numbers painted on the side read 457.

She was a brute—sixteen cylinders, twenty-four hundred horsepower. A diesel-electric powerhouse that could drag a mountain if you chained it right. Eddie planted a boot on the iron rung, grabbed the cold rail, and hauled himself up. His fingers stuck for a second on the frozen steel.

Inside, the cab was a box of metal and stale air, cold enough that his breath fogged when he exhaled. He dropped the thermos and backpack in the corner, settled into the seat, and felt the ache in his spine remind him just how long it had been since his body was young. He pulled in a lungful of air, let it out with a shudder, and pushed the ignition.

The Alco coughed, sputtered, then came to life with a savage roar. *Chug-chug-chug—VROOM*. The floor quaked under him, the whole machine rattling and shaking as if it might leap free of the rails. Pistons hammered, camshafts spun, and thick black smoke geysered out of the stack, curling into the sky like the breath of some buried demon.

Eddie checked the gauges, half from habit and half from duty, then leaned back. He let his eyelids droop. The hum of the machine, the deep belly-rumble of the engine, almost rocked him. Just for a second. Just a quick nap.

The radio jolted him like a slap. Static crackled, then a voice barking sharp: "Eddie, are you there?"

He snapped upright, heart lurching. He yanked the radio up. "Yes, I'm here!"

"Is Bobby there? He's not answering his radio. You guys are starting to run behind."

Bobby was a conductor by title, but Eddie knew the kid treated the job like a birthright. His old man had worn the cap before him, his grandfather before that, and even further back, some yardmaster kin who'd kept trains humming before radios and electricity were common. Railroading ran in Bobby's blood like iron in water. Barely out of his teens, thick through the shoulders, quick on his feet, Bobby worked with the cocky assurance of someone who believed nothing bad ever really happened to him. Still, for all the swagger, the boy knew his business. He kept his eye on the rules, the regulations, and—whether Eddie liked it or not—made damn sure Eddie stayed inside the lines.

A few minutes later, the door to the cab cracked open and Bobby's wind-reddened face appeared. "Sorry for the holdup, Eddie. We can go." His breath came out in white gusts, and he gave an apologetic half-smile.

Eddie grunted, slid the throttle forward, and felt the Alco lurch like a waking beast. The locomotive rumbled down the short spur, the cab rattling as the wheels clanged over joints in the track. Ahead loomed the turntable, black steel slick with ice. Eddie eased the throttle back and brought the engine to a jarring stop at the dead center of the platform.

With a groan of gears, the turntable began to rotate, grinding slowly into alignment with the main track. Eddie sat back, watching through the frost-streaked glass. The floodlights overhead bled pale yellow through the storm, throwing jagged beams into the dark. The air was alive with a vicious mix of rain, sleet, and snow, slanting sideways in hard diagonal sheets. Each gust rattled the glass and made the engine shiver on its springs. The sound of sleet striking the cab was like a handful of gravel thrown against tin siding, a steady hiss broken by sudden flurries. Beyond that, the wind howled, low and mournful, carrying through the rail yard like something alive.

It made Eddie's skin crawl. He had seen too many wrecks, too many twisted rails and splintered ties not to take weather like this seriously. "Bobby, you been paying attention to the forecast?" he asked. "With conditions like this, the tracks'll freeze slicker than glass."

Bobby leaned against the console, casual as ever. "Nah, I wouldn't worry about it," he said, rubbing his palms together for warmth. "Storm's moving fast. I figure it'll be over in an hour."

Eddie shot him a look, but the kid just grinned. Confidence like that could get a man killed—or worse, get the whole damn train killed.

The turntable ground to a halt, aligning them with the outbound track. Eddie pushed the throttle again, inching forward, the headlight spearing into the dark. Ahead waited the other two locomotives and a string of loaded cars, crouched in the sleet like some giant iron centipede ready to crawl out across the frozen prairie.

Eddie leaned out the side window, breath fogging the air, and watched the rear end draw closer to the waiting engines—two Alco brutes crouched low in the storm, black-blue hulks under the ghostlight of the yard lamps. Beyond them stretched the string of loaded cars, their outlines glistening in the sleet like the armored plates of some sleeping prehistoric creature.

Bobby darted down toward the rear, rain jacket plastered to his body, hood pulled tight around his face. Ice clung to him, thin sheets forming along his shoulders and sleeves, catching the dim light. The sleet pelted his face like needles.

The radio crackled with Bobby's voice, faint and tinny

through the static: "A little more… a little more… okay, STOP!" Eddie's gloved hand pulled back on the throttle, and the locomotive shuddered to stillness. The couplers kissed with a hollow metallic clank that echoed down the frozen line. For a moment, the sound hung in the air, swallowed quickly by the wind.

The three locomotives rumbled as one, a monstrous, synchronized heartbeat pounding through the steel rails. Forty-eight pistons thrummed with unrelenting fury, and Eddie felt it in his hands, in his chest, in the low vibration crawling up his spine. The night—or what passed for it in the pre-dawn darkness—was alive with the metallic symphony of wheels rolling over rails, couplers clanging, chains rattling. Each car's slack pulled taut in succession like the tug of some enormous mechanical beast settling into motion. The yard slipped behind them, lights dwindling, engines huffing like dragons, until the black horizon swallowed it all. It was 6:08 a.m., and the three-headed train was finally on its way.

Thirty minutes into the journey, with the windshield frosting over in delicate, jagged patterns and the snow thickening into a gray-white veil, Eddie needed a moment, a small indulgence of habit. He stepped out onto the front deck, feeling the sting of cold wind cutting through his coat, biting at his cheeks. The train shivered beneath him, a living thing beneath his feet, and he fished a cigarette from his pocket. The flick of the Zippo's flame illuminated his weathered hands for an instant, the familiar engraving glinting in the weak morning light. He inhaled, letting the smoke curl up into the freezing air, a small rebellion against the relentless cold and the endless, looming track ahead.

It was 6:38 in the morning, the kind of hour when the world still feels half asleep and dangerous because of it. The snow had thickened into a steady white curtain that swallowed everything past the length of the engine's headlights. The thermometer on the dash read thirteen degrees, but it felt colder than that—colder in a way that got into your bones and made you wonder if maybe you were turning to ice from the inside out.

Somewhere behind the storm, the sun was trying to crawl up over the horizon, but it might as well have stayed in bed. The light that came through the snow was ghost-light—thin, pale, and cruel. The forest that hugged the tracks was nothing but a smear of black shapes, and the rails ahead stretched into a tunnel of blue shadow, as if the world had been drained of every other color.

The locomotive's twin beams cut through the storm, bright but useless, throwing the snow into mad, swirling patterns like a million tiny ghosts trying to claw their way out of the dark.

Then, through the hum of the engine and the dull throb of steel on steel, the radio crackled to life—a burst of static, and Bobby's voice, sharp with something that didn't sound like his usual easy confidence.

"Eddie," he said, his voice thin and distant through the static. "You see that? Take a look down the tracks. I thought I saw a light down there."

Eddie squinted into the storm. A light? Out here? He leaned forward, eyes narrowing against the snow. And for just a heartbeat—no more—he thought maybe he saw it too.

"Hold on," Eddie said, his voice low but sharp enough to cut through the static on the radio. "There is something down there. Shut off the headlights—I can't see a damn thing with the glare bouncing off the snow."

Bobby didn't argue. A second later, the lights blinked out, and the train was swallowed in darkness. The only illumination came from the faint blue glow—the sickly pre-dawn light of a world half-buried in ice. For a moment, it felt like the train had vanished, like they were suspended in nothing but cold air and the soft hiss of falling snow.

"There," Eddie murmured. "You see it now? Few miles off, maybe more, but it's there. A light." He leaned over the rail, squinting his eyes against the snow and ice. "We're stopping the train."

He said it with a kind of grim certainty, but his mind was already running ahead, faster than the wheels beneath them. What the hell could it be? A car on the crossing, maybe—someone stupid enough to think they could beat the train? Or worse—a headlight. Another train. God, that would be bad.

Eddie's jaw clenched. He took a final drag from his cigarette, the ember flaring bright orange against the blue-black dark, then flicked it off the side of the train. It arced down into the snow and disappeared in a blur.

The wind slapped at him as he pulled himself into the cabin. His boots scraped the metal steps, the smell of oil and steel hit his nose again—comforting, familiar, but not enough to settle the unease crawling up his spine. He shut the door behind him, sealing himself inside the cab's dim glow, and for the first time that morning, he realized how quiet everything had gotten.

Too quiet.

Eddie's face had gone the color of chalk. The blood seemed to drain right out of him as he fell into his seat, the cracked leather groaning beneath his weight. His hands moved automatically—training taking over where thought had stalled. He snatched up the radiotelephone, the coiled cord trembling like it knew what was coming.

"This is engine 457," he said, his voice tight, words pressed through clenched teeth. "We're heading west for South Dakota and—uh—we've got a light down the tracks. Possibly another train. Over."

There was a hiss, then a burst of static. A moment later, the dispatcher's voice came through—flat, professional, too calm. "Copy 457. We are not aware of anything on the tracks obstructing your route. Over."

That was it. No alarm, no scramble, no confirmation—just those cold, useless words.

Eddie slammed the phone back into its cradle, the sound echoing off the steel. For a second, he leaned forward, elbows on his knees, face buried in his hands. His breath came out ragged, loud enough to hear over the engine's low hum. Then he looked up, eyes wild, skin slick with sweat despite the cold.

"Start flashing the lights and lay on the horn!" he barked, voice cracking. "I'm hitting the brakes."

Bobby didn't hesitate. He reached for the light switch, flicking it on and off in quick succession, strobing the snow outside into a disorienting blur. Then he leaned on the horn—one long, bellowing blast that rolled out over the frozen landscape like a wounded animal.

Eddie's knuckles went white on the throttle, the tendons in his hands standing out like wires. The numbers in his head ran like a metronome he couldn't shut off—weight, distance, speed, time—all clicking by in a drumbeat of panic. Nearly a mile to stop, maybe less on dry rails. But these rails weren't dry. They were slick as glass, a thin skin of freezing rain polished over the steel like a promise of death. Two miles between him and that light, maybe. Two minutes at best. One if it was coming straight for them.

"Hold on, Bobby!" Eddie shouted, his voice swallowed by the scream of the horn and the grinding steel. "We could be having a collision in the next minute!"

His hand shot for the sanding lever and yanked it forward, a movement he'd done a thousand times in a calm, controlled way but now it felt like jerking a switch that might mean life or death. Somewhere below them, unseen, valves hissed open and sand rained onto the frozen track. The brakes bit hard, the air compressed with a deafening hiss, and the entire locomotive lurched.

The cabin pitched forward so violently that Eddie's coffee mug skittered off the console and smashed on the floor, hot dregs splattering across his boots. The steel walls trembled like a living thing trying to shake off its own skin. Sparks spat off the rails, a sick orange glow whipping past the windows, tiny comets flaring and dying as they ricocheted into the snow-choked woods. The sound of sand grinding under the wheels was like teeth being crushed to powder.

Bobby grabbed the side of the console to steady himself, his eyes huge, face slick with cold sweat. "I'm not sticking around for this!" he shouted, his voice cracking like a boy's. "I'm going out on the front—and if we're gonna hit, I'm jumping off at the last minute."

Before Eddie could bark anything back, Bobby bolted. He was out of his seat and out the cabin door, the slam echoing in Eddie's skull. Eddie caught one last glimpse of him—hood up, shoulders hunched—disappearing into the storm, into the ghostlight of the engine's lamps, onto the front deck.

Eddie stayed rooted where he was, staring through the windshield. His breath fogged the glass but he didn't even blink. That light up ahead was growing, swelling, burning a hole through the snowstorm. Not a car. Not a truck. Not anything he could name from the highways or the crossings. Just one single light, high in the air, and coming fast—too fast—like the eye of some great thing bearing down on them.

Eddie bolted from the engineer's seat, his boots skidding

on the steel floor as the locomotive bucked beneath him. The hallway between compartments seemed to stretch like a nightmare corridor, the kind where the door you're running toward never gets closer. His breath came in ragged clouds, a ghost following him through the frigid air of the cab. He rounded the corner at the back of the engine, dropped to his knees, and folded himself down against the wall like a man trying to make himself disappear. Arms locked over his shins, head buried between his knees. A kid hiding from thunder. A man hiding from death.

He thought briefly of staying in the chair, of white-knuckling the throttle and staring fate down through the windshield. But he knew what that would mean—his body a ragdoll hurled into steel and glass, bones cracked like ice twigs. If he stayed up there, he wouldn't just die; he'd die awake. That thought broke something in him. Jumping wasn't an option either. His knees were shot from years of climbing ladders, jumping down decks, and winter shifts on frozen rails. He'd never make the jump clean, and he knew it.

Time twisted, slowed, thickened. The seconds went syrupy, dragging by. Eddie squeezed his eyes shut, and all he could see in the darkness of his eyelids was Jack's face—*Is this the day I'm going to die?* the thought whispered, not like his voice but like someone else's, calm and final.

Outside his cocoon of terror, the train screamed. The brakes howled like tortured animals, the metallic shriek of steel on steel cutting into Eddie's skull. The sound of the sand grinding under the wheels was like someone sharpening a blade right beside his ear. And through all of it, he began to hear—not just the noise but the details inside it. The rivets and screws vibrating in their holes, twisting loose. The panels around him rattling like teeth.

The cabin trembled, and so did Eddie. The vibrations came up through the soles of his boots, through his knees, into his chest until it was impossible to tell where the train ended and he began. He was part of the machine now—part of the screaming, the shaking, the waiting. And still, impossibly, there was no impact yet. Only the sound of a giant, unseen fist drawing back before the blow.

Eddie's heartbeat was the only sound left, a heavy drum in his ears. Then, like a flicker of static, a thought slid through the noise: It's been too long. The impact should have come by now—should have been metal on metal, steel shrieking, the end of everything. But there was nothing. Just the endless grinding of the brakes, the hammering of his pulse, and that dead stretch of seconds where nothing happened.

Relief crept in like a weak light under a door. Maybe whatever it was had cleared the tracks. Maybe it was gone. He let out a shaky laugh—half a cough, half a sob—and pushed himself up, feeling the stiffness in his knees. His lungs ached with the cold air as he drew in a long breath, held it for a second, then let it go. He wiped his palms on his pants, trying to shake off the tremor in them.

He moved a few steps ahead, his boots ringing sharp

against the steel floor, the thought of how close he'd come to dying still buzzing in his bones. He lifted his head.

Then—time stopped. Not slowed. Not stretched. Stopped. The shuddering train, the screaming brakes, the rattling screws—all of it went silent, like a reel of film cut clean in the projector. His breath fogged against the glass and hung there, unmoving.

Directly ahead, filling the world beyond the window, was the other train. Black and hulking, its light a white-hot sun burning in the dark. It was so close Eddie could see the frost blooming on its steel skin, could make out the faint crosshatching of numbers on its nose. The sight hit him like a spike through the brain, so vivid and permanent it burned itself into his mind before he even had time to react.

It was the last thing he ever saw.

BOOM!

The sound split the morning wide open—an explosion so violent it seemed to tear the air in half. The two locomotives met head-on with the force of gods at war, steel shrieking and twisting, the world going white with fire and snow and light. The lead engines vaulted off the tracks like thrown dice, rising into the air—thirty feet, maybe more—before veering apart in opposite directions, each dragging a trail of screaming metal behind it. They hit the frozen earth deep in the tree line, bursting into geysers of flame that painted the woods in orange and black.

Behind them, the line of cars began to buckle and fold like a dying snake. One after another, they derailed and jackknifed, piling up into a grotesque sculpture of mangled steel. The sound was endless—iron wrenching, glass shattering, pressure tanks splitting open with ear-splitting cracks.

Concrete pipes snapped free of their flatbeds, hurled through the forest like cannon shells. They tumbled end over end, some spinning like helicopter blades before slamming into the trees with bone-jarring force—*whump!*—bursting into fountains of debris. Shards of concrete and rebar whistled through the woods, slicing branches, embedding themselves deep into trunks, or skipping down the rails in a deadly spray.

Then came the tanks.

BOOM! BOOM! BOOM!

Each explosion was bigger than the last. Propane ignited first—white-hot and fast, a wall of flame roaring skyward. Gasoline followed, rolling up into thick, oily fireballs that mushroomed against the gray sky. The heat was unbearable, melting the snow in seconds, turning the ground into a slush of mud and burning fuel. The shockwaves rippled outward, cracking trees, tearing bark, rattling windows in the nearest town miles away.

Timber from the cargo cars turned into airborne missiles—planks and logs spinning end over end, slamming into the forest with thunderous cracks. Coal poured out of the ruptured cars, scattering down the tracks in a black storm, the chunks pelting through the woods like a volley of bullets.

The sky was a boiling chaos of fire and snow—flakes turning to steam midair as they hit the heat. The ground trembled like it was alive, shuddering beneath the roaring inferno. And then—nothing.

The Other Side

Eddie woke to darkness. His first thought was that he must've gone blind. His second was that he should be dead.

He lay on his side in the cold, his cheek pressed into wet earth. The air was thick with the scent of burned oil and scorched wood. Somewhere nearby, something hissed softly—steam escaping from twisted pipes. He blinked, once, twice, and slowly pushed himself up on trembling hands.

For a long moment he just stayed there, waiting for the pain to come. His breath puffed in short white clouds. He flexed his fingers, then his arms, his legs. Nothing. No broken bones, no gashes, not even a bruise he could feel. His head spun, sure—but when he ran his hands over his scalp and face, all he felt was grime and the grit of ash that clung to his skin. No injuries.

Eddie swallowed hard. It didn't make sense. The collision

should've torn him apart, or crushed him, or at the very least left him bleeding out in the snow. But he felt… fine. Alive. Too alive.

It was night. Pitch black, except for the pale shimmer of moonlight sifting through the trees. The crash had happened just after dawn—he remembered that much. The sun had been coming up through the snow, a dull white disk behind the storm. And now here he was, hours later—maybe more—in a forest that looked carved from shadow and frost.

The snow had stopped. The storm, the wind, the sleet—all of it gone, like it had never been. The moon was out, swollen and white, brighter than he'd ever seen. It washed the landscape in silver light, turning the wreckage into a ghostly sprawl of gleaming steel and blackened ruin.

Eddie staggered to his feet. His knees ached, his ears were ringing, but beneath that, there was… nothing. No cries, no sirens, no echo of the destruction that had torn the world apart only moments before. Just silence. Heavy, unnatural silence.

Here and there, small fires burned in clusters—orange tongues licking at the night air, feeding on what was left of the train. Sections of twisted metal jutted up from the snow like broken bones. Wheels still spun idly in the wreckage, clicking as they slowed. The flames crackled and popped, sending up bursts of ember that floated skyward before vanishing into the black void above.

Eddie started walking through the scorched wreckage and smoking trees. His boots crunched over broken glass and cinders, the snow all melted to a greasy black slush. The air smelled like burnt oil and death. Every breath stung. Every sound—his footsteps, the settling groan of twisted steel—seemed too loud in the awful quiet.

Then he saw it.

A shape lying just ahead, half-buried under a sheet of bent metal. A body.

His stomach dropped clean out of him.

"Oh, Bobby…" he whispered. The words came out like steam in the cold air.

He crept closer, though part of him didn't want to. The head was turned away, the body twisted at a wrong angle—shoulder up high, legs bent under like a rag doll that had been stomped on. The firelight danced over it, showing flashes of pale skin and blood and scorched cloth. Eddie crouched, his knees cracking. He reached out a shaking hand and pushed the metal aside.

What was left of the man's face was… well, it wasn't much of a face anymore. The features were melted, blurred. Eddie felt something sour crawl up the back of his throat and swallowed hard.

He sat back on his heels, heart pounding. *Don't be him*, he thought. *Please, don't let it be Bobby.*

He hesitated, then patted down the man's coat, fingers trembling as he searched the pockets. A lump. A wallet.

He didn't want to look. Didn't want to see the truth staring back at him from some burned, half-melted ID card. But he had to. He had to know.

"Maybe it's one of theirs," he muttered to himself. His voice sounded strange in his own ears—thin, hopeful, cracked. "Maybe he was from the other train. Maybe Bobby jumped far enough."

The wind moved through the trees, soft as breath, and Eddie thought he heard something else beneath it—something shifting in the dark, just beyond the ring of firelight.

He froze, the wallet still clutched in his hand.

The sound came first—soft, fast, and deliberate. A scurrying shuffle that crunched the frozen ground just beyond the reach of the firelight. Eddie froze where he crouched.

The sound came again, this time from behind him. Then from the left. Then the right. Footsteps—light, quick, padding. Animal.

"Wolves," Eddie whispered. His voice cracked like brittle glass. He'd heard stories of wolves out here—lean, hungry things that trailed trains in winter, scavenging the wrecks. He tried to tell himself that's all it was. Nature, coming to clean up the mess.

But then he saw them.

Two eyes blinked from the dark. Too high off the ground, too wide apart. A second pair flickered to life a few yards to the left. Then a third. A fourth. They glowed pale white, like the reflection of the moon.

The fire popped behind Eddie, casting long, jerking shadows that made the trees seem to move. The shapes began to circle—slow, calculated, like they knew they had him.

They stepped closer, just into the edge of the light. Eddie's heart jammed itself into his throat.

They weren't wolves.

They looked like dogs, maybe once, but their skin was all wrong—slick and hairless, the color of skimmed milk with veins pulsing faintly underneath. Their eyes had no pupils, just that blank, milky white. Their lips peeled back in perfect unison, revealing rows of needle-thin teeth, black and wet like oil.

Eddie couldn't move. His breath came in short, whistling bursts through his nose. One of the things tilted its head at him, almost curious. Its nostrils flared, and it made a low, wet growl that vibrated through the frozen air.

Then, from deep in the woods, a sound rose up that made every hair on Eddie's body stand on end—a howl. Long, drawn-out, almost human.

The dogs froze. Every single one turned its head toward the sound, ears twitching. Then, without a sound—not a snarl, not a footstep—they slipped back into the dark. Gone.

Eddie was alone again, the fire crackling weakly behind him, his heart hammering like it was trying to dig its way out of his chest. His hands were shaking as he bent back down to the body. The wallet had slipped from his hand when the dogs appeared. He found it half-buried in the snow, slick with something dark. He didn't want to look—Christ, he didn't—but his fingers moved on their own, flipping it open.

He could barely see. He just needed a name, any name that wasn't Bobby's.

That was when he heard it.

Voices.

Low, murmuring, like a conversation carried on the wind. A man's voice and something else—something softer, like whispers underneath speech. He froze, his breath clouding in the moonlight, and turned toward the sound.

There—beyond the shattered wreckage, past the line of skeletal trees—was a glow. Firelight.

Eddie rose to his feet, every nerve in him screaming not to. But he couldn't help it. Curiosity—fear's cruel twin—pulled him forward. He took a step, then another, boots crunching in the snow. The glow pulsed and shifted, throwing orange tongues of light across the tree trunks.

And then he saw him.

The man stood behind the trees at first, half-hidden, the fire dancing at his back. When Eddie stepped closer, the shape came into focus—and what he saw made the air hitch in his lungs.

He wasn't just a man.

He was beautiful in a way that made Eddie's stomach twist. Tall—absurdly tall, like he'd have to duck to fit through a barn door. His skin looked smooth, pale as bone, and the firelight rolled across it like liquid. His hair was black, thick and gleaming, and his eyes—they were black too. Not brown, not dark gray, but black, like twin pits that reflected the fire instead of catching it.

He sat there atop a pile of something that glittered in the firelight. Eddie squinted. Coins. Gold coins. They shimmered and winked like tiny mirrors in the dark.

The man lifted an apple—red, perfect—and took a slow bite. The sound of it crunching echoed through the trees.

Then he smiled.

That smile was warm and cruel all at once, the kind of smile you'd expect from a card shark who already knows how the game ends. The firelight flickered in his black eyes, and when he spoke, his voice was deep and easy, like warm oil over barbed wire.

"Eddie, I'm glad you're here."

Eddie froze. The man had spoken his name, but not with his mouth. The sound hadn't touched his ears—it had bloomed inside his skull, cold and certain as a thought that wasn't his own.

The man's grin widened as he pointed a finger toward the forest.

Eddie turned, and what he saw made his knees nearly give out. The trees began to move—not swaying in the wind, but peeling back, splitting down the middle like theater curtains drawn by unseen hands. The screech of roots tearing from the earth echoed through the clearing.

Beyond the trees was not more forest, but a wall—flat, black, and impossibly tall. Then came the whirring sound: the old, ghostly chatter of a film projector spinning up from nowhere.

The "screen" shimmered to life, pale and trembling. It began in black and white.

A boy—Eddie, no more than six—sat cross-legged on a kitchen floor made of old linoleum tiles. It was Christmas morning. A thin tree slouched in the corner, its tinsel dull, a few pale bulbs glinting faintly, paper snowflakes hanging like tired ghosts.

The boy tore open a small box and lifted out hand-carved horses, each one shaped and painted with careful, loving detail. He smiled and clopped them across the tiles, making soft little "clip-clop" noises with his tongue.

Then the door opened. The smile died.

Eddie's father stumbled in, red-eyed and swaying, the bottle still in his hand. His mother's voice rose in that high, breaking tone that made Eddie's stomach twist. Then came the sound—the crack of flesh on flesh—and the mother's cry.

On the screen, the little boy froze, then looked away. In the firelight beside him, the man let out a low chuckle, soft and almost pitying.

"Poor kid," he said. "Couldn't even look. Didn't want to see what was already inside him."

The film flickered—colors bleeding in, like watercolor on wet paper.

Now it was years later. The roundhouse. Steam and iron. Eddie laughing with Jack. They were eating sandwiches, sitting on a crate, talking about life, about horses, about the land that went on forever. Eddie remembered this—remembered how good it had felt, how whole.

Then Jack coughed into a rag. The film zoomed in—too close, cruelly close—showing the smear of red there.

The man didn't laugh this time. He just leaned forward slightly, elbows on his knees, eyes black and glinting.

"See that?" he murmured. "You had something like a father. Almost got a second chance. But I was there too."

On the screen, the hospital bed came next. Eddie, older, hollow-eyed, with a bottle waiting at home. The moment Jack died, the light in Eddie's life went dim.

Then the movie began to speed up—jump cuts, flashes of years, empty rooms, unpaid bills, empty bottles clinking together like bones.

"You had help waiting for you," the man said softly. "All the times He reached out. A thousand little moments. You just had to look up."

And then the screen began to show them—those moments: the hand-carved horses, sitting on a shelf in his mother's old house; the ranches that rolled by on long train rides, sunlight spilling like gold over the fields. The things that meant something.

But each image twisted, distorted—drowned in television static, blotted out by flashing neon signs, poker chips, and the dull glow of bar lights.

"You could have had your horses," the man said. "Your land. Your peace. But the world is mine, Eddie. And I'm very good at keeping men busy."

Eddie stood there trembling, his face washed in pale firelight, and for the first time, he understood what distraction really meant.

The film jumped and rattled, its reel spinning faster, the light flickering so hard it stung Eddie's eyes. The black and white bled back into color—cold, silvery tones of dawn—and there it was. Just hours ago.

The roundhouse.

Bobby moving through the sleet, his hood drawn tight, steam coiling around his boots. He was checking the brakes, tapping at the hydraulic lines, his breath showing in quick bursts. Eddie watched himself back the engine up, slow and careful, his face lit by the weak orange glow of the yard lights. He could almost smell the diesel again, feel the vibration under his boots.

The reel clattered on.

Now the storm was raging. Eddie saw himself standing on the front deck, cigarette in hand, snow whipping sideways. He looked older than he ever realized—gray in the stubble, shoulders hunched against the cold, the kind of man time had slowly eroded. Bobby's voice crackled over the radio, thin and distant—"Eddie, you see that? Down the tracks?"

Eddie flinched as the movie jumped again.

The light appeared—small at first, then blinding. The scene expanded to a third-person view, high above the world. The trains collided, metal screaming, the night erupting into an orange bloom of hellfire. Eddie's heart slammed in his chest as he watched himself vanish in the blast. The shockwave tore through the forest, trees bending and snapping like matchsticks.

He wanted to look away. But he couldn't. The film held him. Forced him.

Then came the aftermath.

The reel slowed to a crawl, the sound of the projector deepening into a heavy pulse. Snow, quiet and thick. The wreckage, still burning. Eddie appeared again, stumbling through the woods, steam rising from his jacket. The moon hung too big, too bright. He looked lost, small beneath the trees.

The screen widened.

There was the body—twisted, dark, unrecognizable. Eddie knelt beside it. Watched himself reach for the pockets.

On the massive screen, the image zoomed closer, the film crackling and flickering. Eddie saw himself digging through the coat with shaking hands, the camera focusing tight on every twitch, every grimace. He knew what was coming but couldn't look away.

He saw his own fingers—those same grease-stained, trembling fingers—pull a wallet from the corpse's jacket. His breath caught in his throat.

On the screen, his hands opened the wallet in slow motion, like the film itself was dragging its feet toward revelation. The ID slid halfway out. The light from the fire caught the laminate, just enough for the name to come into focus.

Edward Ross.

The world stopped. No sound, no movement, no air. Eddie's heart didn't so much skip a beat as forget how to beat at all.

He stared, unblinking, his eyes wide and glassy. His own reflection stared back from the ID—his face, his photo, that stiff, familiar smile.

On the screen, the Eddie in the movie dropped the wallet. It hit the ground with a flat, final sound that echoed through the woods like a coffin closing.

Eddie took a step back, shaking his head. "No…" he whispered. "No, that's not—"

But it was.

The realization hit him like a second collision. The dead man wasn't Bobby. It wasn't anyone from the other train. It was him.

He was the body in the snow. The corpse with the twisted limbs and broken face. He was dead.

And yet—he could still see, still breathe, still feel.

A wind cut through the clearing, cold as a morgue drawer, and for the first time Eddie noticed that when it passed through him, he didn't shiver. Didn't feel a thing.

Eddie felt it first through his boots—a dull warmth, faint at first, then growing. He looked down. The frost that had covered the earth only moments ago was gone, replaced by a dull red glow that pulsed beneath his feet like dying coals being coaxed back to life.

Smoke began to rise in lazy tendrils, curling between his legs and drifting into the cold air. The scent hit him next—sharp and sour, like rotten eggs cracked open in the sun. It burned his eyes, made him cough.

The ground gave off a low hum now, deep enough to be felt in his bones. Eddie turned back toward the massive screen—and what he saw wasn't his life anymore. It was a view from high above jagged mountains, white peaks cutting into the sky like knives. The perspective drifted forward, smooth and silent, gliding through icy clouds.

He didn't know how, but he could feel the cold of that place. Could feel the thinness of the air, the emptiness of it. It wasn't like watching a movie anymore—it was like being pulled into it.

The harder he stared, the more the edges of the clearing faded. The trees dimmed, the man on the gold and his fire softened to a distant glow, and all that remained was that view—those mountains, endless and cruel and ancient.

And then—just before the last of the forest vanished entirely—Eddie realized the heat under his boots wasn't just rising. It was spreading.

Eddie's stomach lurched. The ground gave way beneath him—and suddenly there was no ground. He flailed, reaching for anything, but there was nothing to hold onto. The world tilted, the air tore past his ears, and for a terrible, dizzying second, he thought he was falling—until he realized he wasn't.

He was flying.

He twisted in the air and saw his arms stretched out beside him, wind streaming past like invisible current. The world below spun lazily, mountains shrinking beneath him like toys in a snow globe. But then, as he rose higher, the light began to change. The bright silver sky of the mountaintops dimmed, darkened, blackened.

The snow melted. Not slowly, but all at once—like a film reel burning through. Rivers of white turned to ash-gray sludge, then to bare, scorched rock. The air shimmered red and hot, the peaks cracked open like old bones. Down below, a crater yawned in the middle of the ruined landscape, vast and smoking, pulsing with a deep red glow.

He didn't steer toward it, but something—some pull, like gravity—drew him in. The crater widened as he approached, the edges glowing molten.

He tried to fight it. Tried to pull away. But the sky itself seemed to lean in, pressing him downward. The rim of the crater passed over him, and he began to descend.

Slowly. Smoothly.

The walls on either side breathed—moved—as though the rock were alive. Shapes began to crawl out of the stone, peeling themselves from the black surface like shadows learning how to walk.

They had eyes—hundreds of them, blinking open in the dark. The deeper Eddie went, the more of them appeared. Crawling with slick hides and clicking teeth, their limbs too long, their mouths too wide.

And then there were more. Hundreds. Thousands.

The walls churned with them, creatures scaling over one another, their bodies glowing red from the reflected magma below. They swarmed like ants—but ants the size of pit bulls, their mandibles gnashing, their hissing rising into a single, awful chorus that filled the pit.

He flailed, twisting, his arms pinwheeling as he sank deeper. The creatures pressed closer; their pale eyes fixed on him. He tried to breathe, but his lungs refused, seizing up, full of sulfur and smoke.

He thought about church. Just once—years ago. He hadn't wanted to go, but he did it for Florence. He'd sat in the back pew, smelling old wood polish and dust, the air heavy with the hush of people who believed. He remembered that day, the pastor's voice carried through the church like thunder in a far-off valley. "God set a course for your life long before you drew breath," he'd said. "A purpose. A calling. But don't fool yourself—there is an enemy who burns to wreck it." Those words clung to him like smoke, and for a moment, Eddie couldn't tell if the enemy had been out there in the world—or living quietly inside him all along.

At the time the thought of God felt silly, but now—now he was falling, his life burned into ash behind him, and that one small memory felt like the last scrap of warmth he had left. His lips moved, barely forming the words:

"God… please…"

And then—he stopped falling.

Something *grabbed him*.

A Long-Lost Friend

A hand—massive and strong—closed around the back of his neck, not cruelly but with a strange, effortless power. The way a mother cat might lift a kitten out of danger. Eddie dangled, paralyzed with terror and disbelief.

He tried to turn his head, to see who—*or what*—had him.

Eddie blinked, and the blackness gave way to a soft, endless blue. No horizon, no sun—just light, pure and weightless. He was floating, though he couldn't feel his body move. Then, slowly, his boots touched down onto something that looked like snow but wasn't cold.

Clouds wound around his legs, soft and slow, like morning fog lifting off a quiet river. He looked down—there was no ground, just depthless air below him. The light shimmered in a dozen directions, and for the first time in what felt like centuries, Eddie felt… peace.

Then came a sound, faint at first but unmistakable: *Chuff…*

Chuff... Chuff. The rhythmic heartbeat of a steam engine.

Eddie turned just as a plume of white cut through the clouds. The nose of an old locomotive, polished like silver, pushed through the mist. The whistle blew, long and low, echoing through the open sky like a church bell for the dead.

The engine hissed to a stop beside him, the heat of it warming his face. A door swung open, and a figure stepped down from the cab.

Arthur.

He wore the same oil-stained overalls, the same railman's cap tilted back on his head, and the same blond bangs flopped over his eyes, just as Eddie remembered. But his face—his face was clean, shining, and young. The lines of hardship were gone, replaced by a peace that seemed to glow from within.

"Hey kid." Arthur said, his voice carrying through the blue like a ripple across still water. "Glad you made it."

Eddie turned, blinking against the light. "Arthur?" His voice cracked with disbelief. "I can't believe it—it's you, but how...?" He looked around, eyes wide. The world stretched in all directions, an endless wash of blue and white, like he was standing inside the sky itself. "Where am I?" He paused. "Am I dead? Is this... heaven?"

Arthur chuckled softly. "Affirmative on the second one. You didn't stand a chance in that collision. Crushed clean on impact." His eyes, composed and distant, drifted toward the horizon where the old shining engine loomed, silver against the light, hissing softly as it exhaled clouds of white vapor. "As for heaven," he went on, "you could say this is part of it. One of the lower parts. But not the best part—you'll need to go through the Gate for that. But your trip might not be over yet. That's not for us to decide."

"Trip?" Eddie echoed.

Arthur's grin was faint but knowing. "Your time on Earth, kid. What—did you think once you die, that's it? Lanterns out?" He gave a short laugh. "Down there was just the beginning."

Eddie looked down at his hands. They were young again—smooth as milk, unscarred—but something about them was different. Through his hands, he could just make out the mist and clouds drifting past, pale and weightless. His breath caught.

And then he noticed it—how sharp everything felt. The air on his skin. The hiss of the ghost-train through the mist. Every sound, every color, was clear as crystal. Ultra-vivid, razor sharp. Like he'd been living his former life in black and white and now it was full color. The dull ache in his knees was gone, the tired heaviness in his chest too. Time had bled into nothingness. There was no before, no after—just this blue infinity and Arthur smiling at him, like an old friend waiting at the end of a long, strange road.

Arthur watched Eddie study his hands, then said quietly, "You know, Earth—and everything you've ever known down there—it's temporary. Think of it like a season… but not one that's on a cycle. It's a one-time journey.

Arthur smiled, the faint hiss of steam filling the silence between them. "You come to Earth to learn about good and evil, Eddie," he said. "That's the deal. The whole place is a mix of both—light and dark, hope and hurt—and after you've had your fill of each, you've got to make a choice. That choice decides where you spend eternity."

Eddie's jaw went slack. He couldn't tell if he was more scared or amazed.

Arthur went on, voice softening. "You come into the world knowing nothing of it, and that's on purpose. You're not meant to start with the answers—you're meant to dig for them. Those are the rules."

He gave a small grin, eyes catching the strange light. "Seek and you shall find, Eddie. That's the key."

He took off his cap and ran a hand through his hair, sighing. "Earth's a tough joint. Everyone hits a wall sooner or later—when that happens, that's when God expects you to start looking. For something. Answers. Purpose. Truth. That's how you find Him. That's the whole damn point."

Arthur's expression turned grave. "Now the Devil will push you to the edge, Eddie. That's what he does. He crawls into your thoughts, whispers things. Plants doubt. Fear."

He shook his head slowly. "He'll steer your life into places God never meant you to go—dark corners, choices that eat you from the inside out. Arthur looked off into the mist. "To keep you numb, he offers distraction—cheap relief that never lasts. Drink, drugs, mindless noise, cards on the table, a hundred empty thrills. Anything to make you forget who you are and why you're there."

He turned back, eyes sharp now. "That's what he wants—a life with no direction. No Divine purpose. A life without God."

Arthur's mouth tightened into a line. "And once he's got you there, he wants you gone. Dead. Because once you're dead without God, your soul's his." He paused, voice low and final. "That's the Devil's agenda, Eddie. Always has been."

Arthur's expression softened, the light around him dimming just a little. "Before I go," he said, his voice almost a whisper now, "I wanna tell you when the Devil came for me." He paused, drawing a long breath that seemed to tremble through him.

Arthur looked off toward the engine again, where steam curled like ghosts into the blue. "That night," he began, "the night of the fire… when my family was killed—I never told you the whole story." His eyes went distant, and when he spoke again, his voice was small. "I was out on the patio roof, having a smoke. I remember the sky was clear, full of stars. I'd finished my cigarette and didn't want to climb down just to stub it out. So I twisted the cherry off—watched it tumble down the shingles, glowing like a little red comet until it slipped over the edge."

He swallowed hard. "I figured it'd go out before it hit the ground. It was small, harmless… that's what I told myself. But deep down, something whispered otherwise. That little voice in the back of my head—it never shut up after that."

Arthur rubbed his temples, eyes wet. "When the Devil came, he didn't bring fire or brimstone. He brought guilt. Endless guilt. Shame so thick it clung to my bones. He made me believe I deserved every bad dream, every empty day that came after."

Arthur's eyes softened as he went on. "I carried that guilt my whole life, Eddie. Every sunrise, every night I closed my eyes—I saw that little spark rolling off the roof. I saw the smoke, I saw the embers smoking the morning after." His voice trembled, then steadied. "It wasn't until I got here, until I met Him, that I finally understood. That I could finally let it go."

He gave a small, disbelieving smile, like a man remembering a long-forgotten kindness. "And seeing them again—my family—didn't hurt either. Earth, for all its noise and pain, turned out to be more of a crude dream and testing ground than anything."

The blue light around them began to shift, growing brighter at the edges. The engine behind Arthur gave a soft hiss, a slow exhale that seemed to pull at the air.

"I gotta go, Eddie," Arthur said, stepping back toward the train.

"Wait!" Eddie called, his voice cracking. "Arthur—how did it happen? How'd you go?"

Arthur turned, one foot on the iron step, a shadow of that old grin crossing his face. "Caught a freight up north," he said. "Night was wet, latch was slick. My hand slipped." He gestured loosely toward his middle. "Train cut me clean in two. Guess you could say I took my final ride a little too literally."

For a moment, they just looked at each other—old friends across the thin divide between life and whatever comes next.

Arthur gripped the handrail and gave a short nod. "I'm certain I'll see you again, Eddie. If not sooner, then later."

Steam billowed around him, wrapping his outline in white. And just like that cool September night many years ago—when he'd escaped the cops hopping a train out of Chicago—Arthur was gone.

The whistle sounded once, long and low, and the light swallowed him whole.

As the train vanished into the blue, its whistle trailing off like a memory, Eddie stood alone in the quiet. The ground beneath him felt like a cloud—soft, uncertain.

That was when the weight came. Not from above, but from inside. He thought about the guilt he'd been carrying his whole damn life, the kind that seeps into your bones so deep you forget what it's like to feel light.

He'd always blamed himself for what his father did to his mother—the shouting, the hitting, the long nights filled with dread. He was just a boy, but he still thought he should've done something. Stood up to him. Protected her. But he hadn't, and then one day, the chance was gone.

He blamed himself again when his old man left and the money dried up. Thought he should've worked harder, helped more, even though the job at Proviso kept the family afloat. And then there was Red—dear, loyal Red. Missing that wedding had been the last nail in the coffin, the thing that sealed his own little box of shame. He ended that friendship like a fool, with words that cut deeper than he meant.

And it didn't stop there. He thought about Catherine and Margaret—his sisters, his blood. Somewhere along the line, their voices on the phone had turned distant, until finally they just stopped calling altogether. He'd told himself it was life, that people drift. But the truth was uglier. He hadn't tried. Not really.

Then came his mother. Her heart had given out on a quiet morning, and Eddie wasn't there. He should've been. She'd always been there for him—when he was sick, when he came home bleeding from the rail yard, when he sat up nights thinking about Jack. And when it mattered most, he wasn't.

Now, in this strange nowhere between life and death, Eddie realized he'd been dragging that guilt behind him all along—like a chain he'd forged himself.

Eddie just stood there, unsure if minutes or years were passing. Then, something caught his eye.

High above, in the endless sky, a point of light appeared. Faint at first—just a pinprick against the wash of blue—but it began to swell, growing brighter, closer. It wasn't the cold kind of light stars give off. This was warm, alive, and pulsing. Eddie squinted up at it.

The light kept growing and began to move. Slowly at first,

it sank, drifting down through the pale air. Eddie watched it descend, unsure what it was—an angel, a soul, some heavenly machine—but what surprised him most was the absence of fear.

He was a stranger in a strange land, yet peace came over him, clean and quiet, like warm water over cold skin. The kind of calm that silences everything—the doubts, the questions, even the pain of remembering who you used to be.

The light drew closer until it floated before him. Then it stopped.

It was bright—too bright to look at for long—casting shafts of light in a thousand directions. The air shimmered and bent around it, rippling like water, waves of color gliding through the mist.

Slowly, the light began to change. It stretched downward, thinning and elongating, like it was being stretched by invisible hands. Eddie took a half step back, watching as the glow reshaped itself—top to bottom—into something tall and slender.

Then the brilliance started to fade, softening from blinding white to a warm, golden haze. Within it, outlines appeared—shoulders, the curve of a face, features still swimming in the light.

The shape sharpened, gained weight and texture, until it wasn't a light anymore, but a man.

He looked to be young, clean-shaven, sharp-eyed, dressed like he'd stepped out of a sepia photograph from another age. A long overcoat hung to his knees, and a black top hat sat square on his head, slightly tilted like he'd worn it that way all his life.

Eddie stared, breath caught somewhere between his chest and throat. The man stood silent in the soft windless air, hands at his sides, eyes fixed on Eddie with a calm that seemed older than time itself.

The figure stood fully formed now, every line and shadow settling into place. The glow around him thinned to a soft halo, and that's when it hit Eddie—hard, like a punch right to the chest.

Jack.

Younger, early-thirties, with the same easy grin Eddie remembered from the rail yard, the same spark in his eyes that could cut through any dark day. Eddie's mouth went dry. He couldn't speak, couldn't move.

Jack noticed the look on his face and chuckled, tipping his hat. "What," he said, grinning wider, "expecting someone older?"

The sound of his voice—warm, teasing, achingly familiar—carried through the still air like a song Eddie hadn't heard in years.

"I knew you'd make it." He threw Eddie a wink. "Recognize me?" he asked, lips curling to a half-smile.

Eddie blinked, hardly trusting what he was seeing. "Jack—?"

"That's right." Jack nodded. "But a younger version than you knew. Me at thirty-two—back in 1913." He spread his arms a little, letting Eddie take him in. The long coat, the polished boots, the glint of youth still sharp in his face.

"Up here," Jack said, "you're any age you want to be. Most folks pick young—we all like to remember ourselves at our best, I guess." His grin widened, teeth flashing white against the soft gold of the air. "Besides, you and I, Ed—we've got some unfinished business. A story I told you many years ago, but never finished." He tilted his head, eyes glimmering. "I thought my appearance would be fitting." He smiled and tapped the rim of his hat.

Then, suddenly, the blue sky started to bleed out slow, like resin seeping from a wounded pine, the color leaching out until only a dim, smoky gray remained. Shapes pressed through the haze: tall brick buildings shouldering into view, gas lamps flickering weakly in the gloom, and a row of makeshift sheds slapped together from scrap wood. Hand-painted signs dangled crookedly from the fronts, the words barely legible in the half-light: Hot Chocolate, Popcorn, Chestnuts. The air smelled faintly of smoke and winter.

Off to the side, a giant Douglas fir loomed against the fading sky—forty feet of black silhouette, its branches reaching upward like frozen fingers. No lights yet, no sparkle. Just the tree and a crowd that wasn't there.

The scene was exactly as it was that night in 1913—but empty. The park stretched out before them, silent and still, not a soul in sight. The gas lamps burned with a low, steady hiss, their glow pooling on the snow-dusted walkways like patches of amber glass.

Flurries drifted down from a black, depthless sky, the flakes tumbling slow and lazy. Every so often, a sound broke the quiet—a dry, brittle crack as the ice-coated branches of the elms shifted in the breeze. The sound echoed faintly through the emptiness.

Eddie turned a slow circle, taking it in. The vendor huts, the tall fir, the city skyline crouched in the distance—it was a glorious holiday scene… only the people were missing.

From the edge of the park, a figure appeared—Jack—as he was on that night. Young, sure, his stride easy and full of purpose. He was carrying two tin cups brimming with cocoa, their warm sides tarnished and streaked. The steam curled upward into the cold air like twisting spirits.

He didn't see them onlooking—didn't even glance their way. It was like this other Jack existed on a different wavelength, in a different time, a memory caught in motion. Jack and Eddie just stood there watching, silent witnesses, invisible as shadows.

From the opposite side, she appeared—a young woman with a tumble of golden curls bouncing around her scarf. Her head was bowed as she fiddled with a mitten twisting at the strap of her coat, lost somewhere in her own thoughts. The wind lifted a few curls across her cheek, and she brushed them away absently, eyes down, watching her boots break fresh little prints into the new snow.

"That's her," Jack said, tapping Eddie's arm with a smile.

And that's when it happened.

Whump.

The collision was soft but sudden—Jack's breath punched out in a small cloud as a cup of cocoa shot from his hand. He twisted instinctively, arm snapping up to rescue the other before it spilled. Steam and chocolate arced through the air, a brief brown comet under the dim gaslight. And then—everything stopped.

The world froze mid-motion. The cocoa hung there in the air, each droplet caught in its fall. The young woman's curls floated weightless, her face turned upward in surprise. Even the snowflakes had stopped, suspended like tiny crystals in the dark.

"That's the night we met," Jack said, his tone soft. "The night I met Veronica." He glanced toward the frozen scene—himself and Veronica suspended mid-collision.

"Something I learned since I got here, Ed—there's no such thing as coincidence. When things line up too perfectly, like pieces cut to fit, that's not luck. That's God, tapping you on the shoulder, telling you to listen close."

Jack chuckled softly, shaking his head. "For years I figured it had to be a setup—that she'd done it on purpose, maybe to get my attention. I never asked, though. Didn't want to embarrass her if it was true."

Suddenly, the frozen scene released—the world snapping back into motion, splattering hot cocoa down the front of Jack's tan overcoat. The shock hit him a second later, hot liquid seeping through the fabric, steam rising in lazy curls. He looked down, blinking, as if the world had just played a trick on him.

They watched from the edge of the park as the two figures talked, their voices carrying only as faint murmurs. Every so often, Veronica's laugh rose above it, light and distant, like something half-remembered.

Then it happened.

From somewhere unseen came a single thud, deep and resonant, followed by an eruption of light. The towering Douglas fir blazed to life, every branch drenched in brilliance, each bulb a star in its own small heaven. White fire streamed in all directions, turning snow into diamonds.

Veronica gasped—then laughed and jumped up, sudden as a thought, and kissed Jack on the cheek before darting off into the night, her curls catching the light as she ran.

The Jack in the scene stood frozen, one hand rising slowly to his cheek, eyes wide with bewilderment, wonder, and something that would last a lifetime.

"It was a whirlwind romance," Jack said, looking over at Eddie with a faint, wistful smile. "I never knew what hit me. I never felt so alive—so in love—so in fear." He paused, eyes dimming a little. "Followed soon after by the worst pain a man can imagine."

As he spoke, the frozen world around them began to come apart. The grounds—the gas lamps, the Douglas fir, the vendor huts, the drifting snow—all of it started to crack, splitting like dried clay in the sun. Thin fractures spread through the air itself, and pieces began to lift, breaking free in slow motion, until drifting upward and flaking away like ash in the wind.

What was left behind was another scene. It was night again—Chicago—but quieter, softer, wrapped in the hush of falling snow. Jack and Veronica lay side by side in the park, laughing, their arms sweeping wide through the powder. Two perfect snow angels forming beneath them, wings spread in the glow of the streetlamps.

It was snowing lightly, the kind of snow that seemed to silence the world. From the shadows, Jack and Eddie watched them lying side by side in the park, arms sweeping wide, laughter rising like breath into the cold. The white flakes caught in Veronica's eyelashes as she turned her face toward the sky, smiling.

"It was that night I learned Veronica loved angels," Jack said softly. His voice carried a warmth that didn't belong to this cold place. "She said she thought angels came closer when it snowed—thought maybe they were watching. Said the snow was just like them… light, gentle, quiet."

He chuckled, the sound low and fond. "I remember being completely tongue-tied. Lovestruck. Didn't know what to say after all those things. Then it hit me." He smiled faintly, eyes on the two figures in the snow. "I told her she'd make a good one. And right there, it melted her heart."

Just as it had before, the scene began to crack—tiny fissures splintering through the air, faint at first, like glass under pressure. Then the breaks spread wider, faster, until the whole park began to come apart. The snow, the benches, even the night sky fractured into drifting pieces.

The fragments lifted, slow and graceful, catching the light as they rose—little shards of memory peeling free and blowing away like tree petals in the wind. Through the empty spaces they left behind, another scene began to show itself.

Warm light flickered in from the cracks first, golden and soft. Then came the outline of a window display, crowded with glittering odds and ends—porcelain butterflies, pocket watches, and snow globes that shimmered with falling snow. The sign above the glass was painted in curling script: Edelstein's Trinkets & Curios.

"There's me," Jack said softly, nodding toward the window, "at the little trinket shop—Edelstein's. I was looking for an angel necklace."

Through the glass, Eddie watched the other Jack step up to the counter, where an old man with wispy white hair and wire-rimmed glasses stood polishing something small in the light. He hands over the object to Jack, waiting patiently.

Inside, Jack lifted the pendant by its chain, holding it up to the lamplight. The silver flashed, scattering soft reflections across the walls of the shop. For a moment, everything—Jack, the shopkeeper, even Eddie watching from the other side of time—seemed to pause in admiration.

"It was a small miracle they had one," Jack went on, eyes fixed. "Perfect, really—a silver angel pendant with a little diamond right at the top for a halo." He smiled faintly. "What were the chances?"

In the shop, Jack handed over a few folded bills, the shopkeeper wrapping the necklace in white paper, careful as if it were something holy.

"The whole plan," Jack said, voice thinning, "was to give it to Veronica on our last night together. I wanted her to know—really know—that she had my heart." He paused, watching himself walk out of the shop into the cold. "But deep down, I already knew I wasn't going. I let fear talk louder than love."

The world around them began to shift again. The walls of Edelstein's cracked and peeled away like paint curling under heat, fragments lifting and dissolving into the air. The warm glow of the trinket shop bled into a different light—cooler, dimmer, carrying the faint smell of roasted coffee and melting snow.

They were indoors, now, a small coffee shop, narrow and dim, its windows fogged from the warmth inside. Outside, the late afternoon had fallen into that deep blue hush that comes before evening—the kind of light that makes the snow look alive.

In the far corner, they saw them—Jack and Veronica.

The two sat across from each other at a small table, a single lamp above them throwing a soft cone of light that caught the steam from their mugs. Veronica's hands were clasped tight around hers, her knuckles white. Jack leaned forward, elbows on the table, saying something Eddie couldn't hear. Whatever words hung between them, they weighed heavy—the air itself seemed thick with them.

Eddie could feel the tension, even from here. It was the kind of silence that follows after too many things left unsaid.

"Our last night together," Jack said. "I had a choice. Go to California, see where our dreams might lead us, or stay in Chicago. I stayed—I let fear hold me back. And what I wanted—what I really wanted—was to just... let go."

"You see," Jack said, his voice low, almost tender, "up here I learned something else—when your heart's screaming yes, and fear's the only thing saying no... that's the Devil. God wants you to follow your heart—the Devil wants to get in the way of that."

The scene shifted again.

The street outside was washed in deep blue, that strange twilight hue that hangs for a few fleeting minutes before night fully takes the world. Snow fell heavy and fast, the kind that muffles everything and makes the air glow. Gas lamps flickered along the walk, halos forming around them in the swirling flakes.

Veronica stood by the curb, brushing the nose of a chestnut mare hitched to a buggy. The animal's breath came in thick clouds, its eyes wide and wet. She smiled, her gloved hand moving gently over its muzzle.

"The buggy driver tried to warn her," Jack said softly beside Eddie. His voice had gone distant again, like it was coming from some faraway room. "But Veronica ignored him. She just loved animals—never thought they'd do her harm."

He paused, eyes fixed on the frozen scene—the girl, the horse, the falling snow—and the sound of his breath caught, just a little, before the next memory took hold.

The sound of Jack's whistle cut through the quiet like a blade. Sharp. Final. Down in the scene, the other Jack had lifted two fingers to his mouth and blew—a long, clear note meant to hail a taxi.

The mare startled. Her ears shot back, and in the blink of an eye she reared up, forelegs thrashing at the air. Snow flurried around her like sparks from a struck match.

The world froze. Even the steam from the horse's nostrils hung motionless, white ribbons suspended midair. The buggy driver's mouth was open in a shout that never came. Veronica's face tilted up, eyes wide.

Jack's voice broke the silence. "That night, Eddie," he said, low and even, "Veronica died."

He kept his eyes on the frozen tableau. "Crushed by nearly two thousand pounds of animal. Shattered her bones like glass—they said at the hospital there was nothing they could do. They gave her morphine to ease the pain… then she was… gone."

He reached into his coat, hand trembling just slightly, and drew something from his pocket. In the flicker of memory-light, the silver caught fire.

"After the ambulance took her away," he said, "I was standing there in the snow. And there it was—half-buried, catching the moonlight."

He held up the lighter.

The Zippo lighter.

The same one Eddie had carried all those years, the engraving still shining through the chrome.

"Jack Luken," he said softly, running his thumb over the lighter's face. "Engraved on one side. And on the other..." He turned it in his palm, letting the dim glow of memory catch the etching. "A verse. *Your word is a lamp to my feet and a light to my path.*"

He looked at Eddie. The sorrow in his eyes wasn't sharp—it was the slow, tired kind that had worn grooves into a soul. "When Veronica died," he said, "it was her love for angels that led me to Him. This lighter—her gift, the one she never got to give me—it became my reminder. My compass. God was the only thing that got me through."

The snow in the scene swirled faintly around them, though the air where they stood was still. Jack's voice dropped, weighted with memory.

"The biggest regret I ever carried," he said, "was not following my heart. I was too afraid—too damned proud. She came from silk and chandeliers. I came from grease and sweat." He paused, eyes fixed on the frozen image of the horse mid-rear, Veronica caught in its shadow.

"Fear held me back. And she paid the price for it."

His voice cracked on the last word, the sound small and human in the great blue void.

Guilt—that was a given. But this went deeper. It was rot. It was the kind of regret that sank into a man's bones and stank from the inside out. Rotting, reeking regret.

"If only I had gone with her—just said yes—none of it would've happened. If I'd followed my heart and gone to California, we would've lingered at the café that night, maybe an extra cup of coffee, another story. Ten minutes—that's all it would've taken... and everything would've turned out different."

Jack stared at the frozen street, his voice turning to gravel.

"God set a path for me," he said. "I felt it right here—" He pressed a fist to his chest. "But I said no. I told myself I was being practical, sensible. But the truth is, I was afraid. I spent a lifetime regretting that one choice."

He looked over at Eddie, the glow of the lighter soft in his hand.

"Fear'll do that, Eddie. It'll talk to you like a friend, tell you it's keeping you safe. But it's a liar. It steals the life right out from under you. Before you even know, it's gone."

The scene began to unravel like paper curling in a flame. Edges of the street peeled away, the snow, the horse, the glow of the lamplight—all of it disintegrating into drifting ribbons that twisted slowly up into the air. Beneath it, a new world took shape—black iron, billowing steam, the thunderous rhythm of machinery breathing.

They were in the cab of a steam engine. The brass gauges gleamed faintly in the amber light, and coal dust hung thick in the air. Outside the window, the landscape blurred into gold and green—the year 1935, when the world still ran on sweat and fire.

Eddie sat on the lip of the coalbunker, the same narrow ledge where he'd perched as a young boy. The wind rushed over the cab, catching his hair, tugging at his shirt. He closed his eyes and breathed in the sharp tang of creosote, the oily perfume of steel and smoke. Under it all, the scent of wheat fields drifted in—sweet, dry, endless.

It filled him with a strange peace, the kind that hurt. A thousand memories crowded in at once—Jack's hand on the throttle, the rhythmic chuff of pistons, the high wail of the whistle tearing across the open fields. It was the smell and sound of everything good he'd ever known.

Eddie looked down toward the little engineer's bench. Jack was there, older now, just as he remembered him. Broad-shouldered beneath a faded denim shirt, his skin had taken on the tough, weathered look of worn leather, lines carved deep around his eyes and mouth.

Jack looked up, his face breaking into that familiar grin, the one Eddie hadn't seen since before everything went wrong.

"Thought we'd go on a country ride through the plains," he said, his voice a mix of warmth and nostalgia. He gave the throttle a small nudge, and the engine groaned to life, the rhythmic *chuff-chuff* filling the cab.

"I recall it was out here that set your heart on fire," Jack added, eyes cutting to the open landscape beyond the window—a blur of golden fields and far-off fence lines melting into the horizon.

The sound of the train was steady, alive, like a heartbeat that had never really stopped. And as the plains opened wide before them, Eddie felt something stir in his chest—an ache that wasn't pain, but close enough to it.

The plains opened wide, gold spilling out to the edge of the world. Eddie leaned forward, his breath catching as the horizon shimmered like a mirage made real.

There it was.

Just ahead, spread across the rolling plains, stood the ranch he'd dreamed about since boyhood. Acres upon acres of green and gold grass rippling in the breeze. Fenced paddocks dotted with horses, their manes tossing like fire in the sunlight. A white farmhouse rested at the heart of it all, its tin roof catching the light in soft flashes, bright as water under the afternoon sun.

Above it stretched an endless blue sky, painted with drifting white clouds that rolled smooth and patient, like a thought taking shape.

For a moment, Eddie couldn't breathe. It was the dream he'd buried years ago under rust and booze and long nights of self-pity—standing right there in front of him, alive and breathing.

His throat tightened. He swallowed hard, eyes stinging.

"Jack," he whispered, "that's it. That's my place."

Jack smiled softly, hand firm on the throttle. "I know," he said. "Been waitin' for you to see it."

The horses danced across the fields in lazy, easy loops—brown ones with glistening coats, black ones that shone like oil, and a few white ones speckled with gray and black, one with a dark spot right on the nose. They tossed their manes and kicked up little clouds of dust that caught in the sun, halos rising around their legs.

Jack leaned on the throttle, watching the ranch grow larger in the cab window. His voice softened, touched with a weight Eddie hadn't heard before. "Ed," he said quietly, "everyone's life has a purpose—a real one. Something meant only for them." He paused, eyes tracking the motion of the horses as the train clattered closer. "But most never get to fulfill it."

He looked back out the window, his jaw tight. "They get distracted," Jack went on. "They drift off course. And if they're lucky, maybe they still get by. Have a decent life." His hand rested lightly on the lever now. "But it's nothing—nothing—compared to what could've been. What God planned."

The engine roared on, steel and fire carrying them toward that golden ranch—the one that was supposed to be Eddie's.

Jack turned to look at him, eyes narrowing beneath the brim of his cap. The low light from the window caught in the creases of his face, throwing half of it into shadow.

"What happened to those dreams, Eddie?" he asked, voice quiet but sharp enough to cut through the steady rhythm of the rails.

Eddie didn't answer. He just stared out the window, jaw tight, watching the ranch slide past—fences, stables, the white farmhouse glowing in the distance—until it all began to blur together. The horses grew smaller, the fields dimmer, the colors fading into gray.

He sat there, hands limp in his lap, as the dream slipped away—becoming what all his dreams seemed to become in the end.

Another memory left out in the cold.

Jack lifted the Zippo between them, the chrome casing gleaming like fresh ice under a floodlight. It caught every flicker of the cab's glow, scattering it in tiny flashes across the walls—bright, alive, untarnished by time.

"On the night of my death, kid," he said, his voice low, "I wanted you to have this. 'Your word is a lamp to my feet and a light to my path.' He thumbed the lid open and shut, the familiar clink echoing through the cab. "Means the wisdom of God guides the way. Always has, always will. All you gotta do is trust… and listen."

He smiled faintly, eyes crinkling at the corners. "And never quit chasing that thing—the one thing that fills your soul to the brim. Life'll throw you into storms, sure as hell it will. But with God, you'll come out the other side. It might not look how you pictured, but it'll work out. Follow your heart, Eddie… and walk with Him to get there."

He flicked the Zippo shut and turned to face him fully, eyes soft with something almost like pride.

"So this," Jack said, "is a message of no regrets."

Eddie swallowed, the words catching in his throat. "But if

I'm already dead," he said, "why does this matter? Why now?"

Jack's grin widened, that old railman spark glinting behind his eyes. He reached for the horn cord above him, gave it a long, slow pull. The sound wailed out over the plains—haunting, beautiful, endless.

"You're not through the Gate yet, kid."

The sun went down quick, bleeding across the horizon, shifting from gold to copper and finally to a soft, pinkish red. The air was warm and thick—crickets were starting their low, steady chorus out in the fields, the sound carrying that strange mix of comfort and loneliness that only summer nights can hold.

The train slowed to a lazy *chuff, chuff, chuff* as it entered a dense forest. Tall firs loomed on either side, their shadows long and cool, and shafts of sunlight broke through the canopy like rust-colored spears. The world outside the cab seemed to breathe—alive, patient, timeless.

Then came the clearing.

The forest fell away, and what opened before them didn't look like any place Eddie had ever seen. To the left, the pines stood shoulder to shoulder, dark as iron. But to the right stretched a river—a wide, slow-moving band that shimmered like molten glass. It wasn't water that ran through it, but light itself, golden and white, curling and weaving into shimmering strands that painted soft halos on the grass along the banks.

Across the river sat a small log cabin tucked close to the tree line, about a hundred feet from shore. Smoke puffed in gray plumes from the stone chimney, curling softy into the air. Behind it, a pine forest stretched up the mountainside, thinning to smooth ledges—they shimmered pink, drenched in thick ice.

Jack's voice came soft over the engine's hum. "We're at the end of the line, kid." he said, giving a small nod and wink. "At least for now."

Eddie leaned forward, eyes wide, mouth gaped in wonder as he took in the scene, and a strange feeling rose up, soft at first, then stronger—the sense that he'd been here before. Not in body, but somewhere behind the eyes, maybe in a dream. Maybe in another life. He wasn't sure, but it didn't feel like the first time. The glow and curve of the river, the cabin chimney puffing its smoke, even the pink ice shimmering on the ledges—it all tugged at him, like a memory half-remembered. He couldn't say when or where, only that this place had waited for him.

"Where are we?" Eddie asked quietly, as though afraid to disturb the stillness.

Jack's grin was soft—the kind that said more than words ever could. "Upper levels of heaven, but not quite at the Gate yet." He said with a smile. He paused, looking off into the distance, something thoughtful in his eyes. "Why we're here, you might ask?" A quiet chuckle. "You'll find out soon enough."

Then, tipping his cap toward the river, he added, "Listen to your gut, Ed. Let it guide you. Let it be your compass."

Eddie studied him, searching for something in Jack's face—

some hint of what waited beyond that glowing current. But all he found was reassurance. Jack gave him a slow, steady nod, the same kind he used to give before every long haul west.

Eddie swallowed hard, his throat dry, and stepped down the iron rungs. The metal was warm beneath his palms, almost alive. When his boots touched the ground, the earth yielded slightly under his weight. Soft green moss blanketed everything, plush as velvet and glowing faintly under the twilight.

The air was warm and heavy, rich with the scent of loam and rain and something else—something clean and ancient. He breathed deep, the air burning sweet in his chest. Fireflies moved slow through the air, their glow winking like dying stars, brief and beautiful in the deepening dusk.

Eddie stood still for a long moment, letting it all wash over him—the quiet, the warmth, the kind of peace that felt too big for words. For the first time in a long time, he felt… safe. Wrapped in something vast and gentle, as if the whole place had drawn a blanket around him and whispered, you're home now.

Eddie looked back toward the cab, and there was Jack behind the window of the engineer's seat—his outline haloed in the glow from the gauges. He lifted one hand in a slow wave, the way old friends do when words aren't needed.

Then something flickered in the corner of Eddie's eye.

He looked toward the coal bunker and froze. Standing on top of it was a lean black-and-tan German Shepherd. Her fur shimmered faintly in the soft light, muscles trembling with excitement. For a heartbeat Eddie couldn't breathe.

"Keena," he whispered.

It all came rushing back—the vet's office that one gray October morning, the smell of antiseptic, the cold stethoscope pressed to her ribs. The way she had looked at him, eyes wide and trusting, even as the needle slid in. Eddie had carried that memory like a stone in his chest ever since.

Now she was here. Whole again. Beautiful. Her tail wagged once, twice, and she barked—two sharp notes that cut through the warm air like chimes.

Eddie's throat tightened. His vision blurred. For the first time in years, maybe decades, he smiled through the tears.

Eddie turned back toward the river. It shimmered quietly under the red and bruised sky, streams of light like molten silver. The little cottage across the way looked peaceful, inviting—smoke rising from its chimney in gentle puffs, the windows glowing a soft amber that made it feel almost like it was waiting for him.

Eddie turned back around, one last time, to say goodbye. To say see you soon, or farewell forever. He wasn't quite sure which it would be.

But when he turned, the engine was gone—just an empty stretch of moss where it had stood a moment ago. The tracks disappeared into nothing, swallowed by the earth. The spot where Jack, Keena, and the train had just been, only open air now, the clearing bathed in golden riverlight. The coal dust, the scent of oil—gone too, as if scrubbed from existence.

Eddie swallowed hard, his chest tightening. The quiet felt heavier now, a sacred kind of stillness that said everything had come full circle. He let out a long breath, nodded once to the empty air, and turned back toward the glowing current—toward whatever waited for him on the other side.

Heaven's Big on Reunions

Eddie waded in, and the river hit him like a charge. Not cold—alive. It throbbed through him, a warm flow made of feeling instead of water. Joy. Love. Hope. Peace. It poured into him so hard he thought his chest might split with it.

He stood frozen midstream for a moment, light blazing past his legs like molten glass, his chest rising and falling with a charged, reverent suspense.

And then the understanding hit. Hard and clean, right in the center of him.

Everything he'd ever believed—about God, about life, about where he'd been and where he was going—was only the tiniest piece of something vast, infinite. The river wasn't just light; it was the pulse of creation itself. The same current that moved in stars and storms and beating hearts. He realized then that every choice, every breath, every loss had been connected all along.

The world he'd known hadn't been the whole story. It had only been the opening chapter.

He looked up toward the ledges. Thick pink ice clung to the rockface, the color shifting faintly under the light. It gripped the stone like it had been born there, grown from it. Eddie wondered if it ever melted—if this place even knew what melting meant.

About halfway across, Eddie slowed. The current lapped gently at his waist, whispering against him. That's when he noticed movement along the shoreline.

A deer stood there, its coat the color of morning light, ears flicking in his direction. Then another stepped out beside it—smaller, graceful, eyes fixed on him. A rabbit appeared next, nose twitching. Then a hedgehog, its tiny body half-buried in the grass. One by one, they gathered at the river's edge, each of them still, silent, staring straight at him.

For a moment, Eddie thought he must be imagining it. But then something strange stirred in his mind—like a radio tuning in after a long stretch of static. Suddenly, he could hear them. Not in words exactly, but in thoughts, feelings, fragments of understanding.

They were thinking about him.

He felt their curiosity, their quiet wonder. They were asking—without mouths or sound—if he knew. If he truly understood where he was, what this place was. The weight of it. The grace of it. Heaven.

Eddie stood there, chest deep in the glowing light, his heart pounding. The animals didn't move closer. They didn't need to. Somehow, he felt what they already knew: he had crossed into something sacred.

As Eddie neared the shoreline, the world around him seemed to wake. Everything moved—not wildly, but in a slow, deliberate rhythm, like the breathing of something alive. The grass shimmered, bending and lifting in a breeze he couldn't feel. The trees swayed with it, their leaves whispering in perfect time. Even the flowers seemed to pulse, their petals turning gently toward the light that wasn't quite the sun.

It wasn't sound exactly, but there was music in it—soft and wordless, a harmony that hummed somewhere inside him. Every blade, every branch, every petal felt alive with joy, part of a vast song that didn't need to be sung to be heard.

He stepped out of the water, his feet sinking into warm, living earth. Ahead, nestled among the trees, stood the small log cabin. Smoke drifted lazily from the chimney, curling into the violet sky.

In front of it, a young girl crouched low in the soil, her fingers buried in the dark earth as she tended to a patch of flowers—bright blues and yellows, glowing faintly in the light. She hummed something under her breath, a tune Eddie almost recognized.

Eddie stepped closer, the grass soft beneath his feet, the air humming faintly with life. The young girl looked up from her flowers, her smile bright and familiar in a way that tugged at something deep inside him.

She wore a white dress patterned with tiny pink blossoms, each petal stitched with care, the green leaves winding delicately through the fabric. Sunlight—or something like it—played along the hem, turning it almost translucent.

"Hi, Eddie," the little girl said. Her voice was clear and light, carrying a warmth that sank straight into him.

The girl stood, brushing her hands against her knees, bits of soil falling away like flecks of light. Each speck shimmered before it touched the ground, fading into the glowing earth as though absorbed by the world itself. The light in her hair shifted with her movement, a halo of gold and rose that made the air hum softly around her.

"I knew you were coming," she said with a quiet certainty, her voice carrying that same strange peace that filled the air around them. "I prepared some tea."

She reached out and took Eddie's hand. Her fingers were small and soft, warm against his. For a moment, Eddie felt the size difference—the delicate touch in his rougher, work-worn palm. Then he noticed something else. His hand looked older now—weathered, scarred and lined, not youthful like before.

The girl smiled, as if she already knew what he'd seen. Without a word, she turned and led him toward the porch. Two rocking chairs waited side by side, their paint faded to the color of old bone. The porch light by the screen door buzzed faintly, drawing a handful of pale moths that flipped and fluttered in slow circles.

The air smelled faintly of chamomile and wood smoke.

Eddie lowered himself into one of the rockers. The wood creaked under his weight, slow and gentle, like it remembered him. From where he sat, he could see the river racing in front of him—a torrent of light, alive and shimmering as it cut through the valley.

Across the way, the fir trees stood black against a sky that looked caught between day and night. The sunset hung there, unmoving, frozen in that soft place between gold and red—an impossible hue, almost pink, as if time itself had decided to rest a while.

He took a slow breath. Everything felt… known. The rockers. The tea. The red-tinged light bathing the porch. He couldn't place it exactly, but it tugged at something deep in his memory—something small and tender, from a lifetime long gone.

Eddie heard the soft creak of hinges, then the sharp clap of a screen door closing. He turned, heart already stirring with something between recognition and disbelief. Out stepped an elderly woman—blue curls permed tight, large-rimmed glasses perched neatly on her nose. She carried a silver tray balanced carefully in both hands, two porcelain cups resting on saucers, teaspoons chiming lightly with each step. The scent of steeped tea drifted on the air, floral and sweet.

She smiled as she drew near, and the years seemed to fold in on themselves. Her teeth—bright, even, just as perfect as he remembered—caught the light. Only this time, they weren't dentures.

Eddie froze, breath caught halfway between disbelief and joy.

"Flo..." he whispered.

Florence's smile deepened, the same soft, knowing curve she'd given him a thousand times before. "Hello, Eddie," she said, her voice warm and whole again, untouched by time or age.

The tray trembled just slightly in her hands—not from weakness, but from the quiet, trembling joy of a reunion long overdue.

Florence set the tray down on the small table between the rockers, her movements graceful and delicate. She straightened, adjusting her glasses, and gave him a look that carried both humor and love.

"Thought you might recognize me better this way," she said with a light chuckle, smoothing a hand over her hair.

Eddie blinked at her, the pieces clicking together. The child in the garden. The familiar tune she was humming. The tea. The rockers. The way she'd taken his hand. It had all been her.

Now she stood before him exactly as he remembered—an old woman with laugh lines carved deep, the kind that come from a lifetime of smiling through the hard parts.

The sight of her melted him. His throat tightened, and for a moment he couldn't breathe. There she was—Florence—whole and real, eyes bright with that same gentle spark that had carried him through his loneliest years.

He swallowed hard, voice breaking around the words. "You… you look just like I remember."

Florence smiled, the corners of her eyes crinkling. "I figured you'd take comfort in the familiar." She poured the tea, the cups clinking softly in the stillness. "Heaven's big on reunions, Eddie."

They sat quietly, watching the sunset that hung motionless above the treeline. The light was soft, eternal, painting the cabin in hues of rose and copper. The air smelled faintly of earth and tea. Wisps of steam rose from their cups, curling and twisting in the still air like tiny spirits.

Florence broke the silence first. "I knew you were struggling, Eddie," she said gently. Her voice was the same as always—calm, certain, full of that quiet compassion that never needed to be asked for. "I could see it in your eyes. Hear it in your tone. I wanted you to know, in the most sensitive way I could, that He was there the whole time."

She smiled, the corners of her eyes creasing. "I gave you gentle nudges," she said with a soft giggle. "I remember the day I invited Tom and his wife up to your apartment—to talk about church."

Eddie chuckled once, though there was no humor in it. He lowered his head, staring into the tea as the steam swirled. "Yeah," he said quietly. "I remember that day. Not too proud of it."

Florence chuckled, a light, familiar sound that rolled through the air like wind chimes. "Oh, Eddie," she said, shaking her head gently. "It's all right—these things aren't the easiest to figure out."

She leaned back in her chair, the wood creaking softly beneath her. "I just saw you needed help. You seemed lost. Like you were looking for something you couldn't name. At the same time, spiraling into self-destruction." She paused, her gaze settling on him over the tops of her glasses. "The course you were on—it felt like it was being driven by something else. Something that wasn't God." She tilted her head, her eyes twinkling with that same gentle authority Eddie remembered. "If you know what I mean." She raised her eyebrows.

Eddie managed a small nod. He did. More than ever now.

Florence straightened, a spark of youthful energy lighting her face. "I'm glad you went to church," she said brightly. "I know I passed before we had the chance to go together, but little did you know, Eddie..." She smiled softly, her voice turning almost musical. "I was there the entire time."

Eddie looked up at her, the cup of tea trembling slightly in his hands. He thought back to that day, that strange comfort he couldn't explain. He'd told himself it was in his head. But it hadn't been. He knew now, it was her.

The river murmured in the distance, steady as a heartbeat, as the two of them sat beneath a sky that would never fade.

Eddie didn't say much. He just sat there, letting it all soak in—the river of light, endless and alive, coursing through the valley in front of them; the black silhouettes of the fir trees standing majestic on the far side; and above it all, that reddish-pink sky, frozen in place, as if time itself had decided to stop and watch with him.

The stillness wasn't empty—it was full. Every breath, every flicker of color, every whisper of light carried meaning, something deep and wordless that hummed through his chest like a memory he'd always known but never named.

Florence rocked once more, the chair creaking softly beneath her, then stilled. "One more reunion," she said, her voice gentle, almost reverent. "Before you meet Him."

Eddie turned, but she was already rising from her seat. She smoothed her dress, straightened her glasses, and gave him a look that was equal parts love and mischief. Then she moved toward the screen door, the boards sighing beneath her steps.

Eddie rose from the rocker, his knees brushing the edge of the porch rail as he stepped up beside her. Florence turned toward him, her expression calm, glowing with that soft, unshakable assurance.

"Go ahead, Eddie," she said, nodding toward the door. "You don't need me for this."

Her smile lingered—gentle, proud, with something almost maternal beneath it. For a moment, Eddie didn't move. The light off the river shimmered behind them, casting shifting patterns of gold and white across the front of the log cabin. Then, with a deep breath, he reached for the screen door.

The handle was cool under his fingers. He pulled, and the spring gave its familiar groan, the sound of old summers and open windows. The door swung wide, resting against his leg as he held it open.

He paused, turning back to Florence. She met his eyes, and for a moment it felt like all the years between them had folded into one. Eddie gave her a small, grateful smile—one that said everything words couldn't.

Then he faced the door again, placed his hand on the brass knob, and turned. The latch clicked, gentle as a promise kept, before the door eased open.

Eddie stepped through the doorway and was swallowed by light—bright and golden—nearly blinding. Then came the scent. Pine sap. Gingerbread. Wax from melting candles. The smell of Christmas. It came on strong, like stepping into a dream you forgot you had. He was home again—the place he grew up as a boy—1925, his mother's apartment in Chicago.

Somewhere in the apartment, a record played faintly, the needle crackling through a slow holiday tune. The sound was warped but comforting, the kind of thing that lived in the background of a thousand memories.

In the corner stood a little tree, scraggly and lopsided, its tinsel sparking brightly. A few ornaments clung to the branches—silver balls, one glittering red ball with a chip in its side, and some paper snowflakes yellowed with age. A string of lights blinked softly, a few bulbs burned out, leaving small pockets of shadow between the glow.

At its base, a toy train circled the tree in slow loops. The black engine puffed tiny clouds of white steam that hung briefly in the air before fading. Its headlamp glowed a weak amber, flickering as it passed over the seams in the track. The cars behind it rattled softly—red, green, and gold—carrying little wooden crates and a caboose with a broken railing.

Eddie could hear the faint clack of the wheels, steady and rhythmic, the sound threading through the room like a long-lost memory. He thought of setting it up as a boy, crawling around the tree in his pajamas while his mother called from the kitchen. The memory hit him full force—how the lights, the scent of pine, and that tiny chugging sound had once meant everything.

Eddie stopped where he was, his breath catching. The whole room seemed to hum with warmth, alive with something more than light. It wasn't just the sight of it—it was the feeling. Wholesome. Loving. The good days, before everything went south. The laughter around the table, the smell of roast in the oven, his mother humming while she worked. All of it here, folded simply into this one small, imperfect room.

He stood still, the memories washing over him like warm water, his heart aching with both joy and loss.

Eddie stepped carefully through the living room, his boots brushing against crumpled scraps of wrapping paper. By the tree, half-buried under a curl of ribbon, sat a small herd of hand-carved wooden horses. The paint was fresh, still shining faintly under the glow of the tree lights—brown ones, tan ones, a proud black stallion at the front.

His breath caught. They were his—his Christmas presents. Uncle Charlie's handiwork, whittled and painted by hand, still smelling faintly of sap and varnish. He could almost hear the man's gravelly laugh and see the crooked bowtie he wore every year no matter how crooked it sat.

Eddie crouched, brushing a thumb over the smallest horse's mane. The wood was smooth, the detail so fine it almost looked alive. The kind of gift you didn't just play with—you *kept*.

A sudden commotion made him glance up.

Princess—the old house cat—came tearing through the room, tail puffed and thrashing, a bright red bow stuck to it. Her one good eye was wide, the other locked forever in that perpetual wink. She bolted under the table, skidding on the rug, sending a few scraps of wrapping paper flying.

Eddie smiled, the kind that came from somewhere deep, warm, and far away. For a moment, the whole scene glowed—perfect and suspended—the kind of memory too pure for time to touch.

Eddie walked into the kitchen, and the smell hit him first—coffee and sugar, a hint of toast, the faintest trace of lilac perfume. Then he saw her.

His momma sat at the breakfast table, young again—maybe thirty, maybe less—her hair swept up the way she always wore it on Sundays. The same soft eyes, that same knowing smile that seemed to rise before the words ever did. She looked up at him, and for a second neither of them moved.

She didn't have to say a thing. Her eyes said it all.

Eddie took a step forward, his throat tightening, the air suddenly thick with everything he'd missed. She stood then, the chair legs scraping lightly against the worn linoleum. Her arms opened wide, thin and trembling—just like when he was a boy running to her after scraping his knees, or coming home late from the yard.

"Momma..." he breathed, his voice breaking on the word.

Her smile deepened, warm and soft around the eyes. "Come here, Eddie," she said.

And when he did, when she folded him into those familiar arms, it was like time itself exhaled—like the years had never passed.

"Eddie," she said softly, her hand coming up to the back of his head, drawing him close. "I know you've been hurting. I know you've carried what happened back then your whole life." She brushed her thumb through his hair, the way she did when he was a boy. "You've got to let it go, honey. You did more than enough. You were enough."

She pulled back to look him in the eyes. "You were the glue, Eddie. You held this family together when it was ready to fall apart." Her voice trembled, not from sadness but from pride.

"You were always tough as nails," she went on, a small, proud smile forming. "Never could back down from a fight. I remember the day you stood up to Dunn at the Carriage House, when we were about to be tossed out on the street. You saved us that day—saved me, saved your sisters. You did that, Eddie. You alone."

She squeezed his shoulders, firm but gentle, like she was grounding him. "And Catherine," she said, her tone softening.

"You saved her too—from Ray, from that life that would've chewed her up and left her scared forever. You gave her a chance, Eddie. You gave *all of us* one."

Eddie's throat tightened. He wanted to speak, to tell her she was wrong—that he'd failed in more ways than she could imagine—but the words stuck. His mother only smiled, eyes shimmering, as if she already knew.

"You also took on one of the toughest jobs in the whole city," she said, a note of pride curling through her voice. "Getting on at Proviso, the railroad—that wasn't easy. It was no place for anyone's boy to be. The noise, the danger, the hours." She shook her head slowly, a faint smile tugging at her lips. "But you were tough enough, Eddie. Tough enough not just to survive it, but to make a life there. A career. That takes grit."

Her eyes softened. "That's all a mother ever really wants, you know—to know she raised her children well enough to stand on their own two feet someday." She reached out, placing her hand over his. "With you, I never had to worry about that."

Her expression turned tender, touched by something sad and beautiful. "And what you did for Keena..." She paused, swallowing, her voice trembling ever so slightly. "When Jack died, you took care of her. You gave her love right up until you couldn't anymore. That took strength too, Eddie—the kind that breaks the heart and heals it all at once."

Eddie's throat tightened, the memory flickering in his mind like an old film reel—the adventures, the companionship, the way she looked at him in those last moments.

His mother smiled then, her gaze lifting upward, soft and full of hope. "And your sisters," she said. "You'll see them again. Here, in heaven. Once their time comes, I'm sure of it." She reached up, brushing a tear from his cheek with her thumb. "We'll all be together again, sweetheart. Just like before."

"Now," she said, her voice soft but steady, "occasionally, if He thinks your work's not done…"

She turned toward the door, pointing with one hand. Blinding light streamed through the cracks around the frame, pure and alive, spilling across the floorboards like liquid gold. "He might just send you back," she said with a faint smile. "And if that's the case, well—then you'll see them again when you're back."

Eddie followed her gaze, his heart thudding slow and deep. The light was beautiful, but it scared him too—something about it felt final. His brow furrowed as thoughts crowded in.

She noticed. "What is it, Eddie?"

He hesitated, his throat tightening. "I never forgave myself," he said quietly. "For not being there. When you…" He stopped, forcing the words out. "When you died. The heart attack. I should've been there, Momma."

Her expression softened—no judgment, no surprise. Just love. She stepped closer, cupping his cheek in one hand.

"Oh, Eddie," she said. "You need to let it go." Her thumb brushed a tear from his face. "You did more than enough. You always did. There's nothing to feel guilty about."

She held his gaze, her eyes shimmering like they caught the

light from the door. "If anything," she went on, smiling now, "you ought to feel proud. You carried our family through its darkest times. You gave everything you had."

Eddie swallowed hard, a tremor running through him. Somehow, her words didn't just sound like comfort—they felt like truth, deep and absolute, as if they were being spoken straight into his soul.

She turned toward the oven, the hem of her dress catching the glow from the tree. When she opened the door, the warm scent of ginger and molasses filled the room, sweet and comforting, wrapping around Eddie like a blanket from childhood.

She slid the tray out with practiced hands and set it on the counter. The cookies were golden and soft, little men with crooked smiles, steam curling off them in lazy ribbons.

"Only one thing left now," she said, wiping her hands on her apron.

Her eyes lifted toward the door. The light behind it had grown stronger—so bright it seemed alive, pressing through the cracks, spilling across the floorboards in trembling beams. The edges of the door glowed white-hot, the handle glinting like a star about to collapse.

It creaked softly, the sound mingling with the faint jingle of the Christmas tree ornaments and the steady hum of the toy train circling its base. The whole room went still, the air thick with sweetness and wonder, as if heaven itself was waiting for Eddie to take that final step.

At the Foot of Eternity

Eddie stepped through the door—and it hit him like a brick. A burst of light swallowed him whole—pure, endless, absolute. In that instant, Eddie couldn't tell if he stood, floated, or existed at all. The world was gone, replaced by a vast white expanse that wasn't cold or warm, but perfect.

He turned, instinctively looking for the door, for the house, for his mother's face. But there was nothing. No cabin, no porch, no river, no sky. The door was gone—like it had never been there at all.

If there had been any trace of time or space left from the other realms of heaven he'd crossed through, it was gone now, sucked out of existence by this place.

Here, there was no up or down, no horizon, no shadow. Just light—stretching outward forever, infinite in every direction. It didn't end. It didn't begin. It simply was.

Eddie took a slow breath, though there was no air, and felt

something within him loosen—like the final tether unspooling from the anchor of everything he'd known.

The infinity wasn't something Eddie could see so much as feel. It pulsed through him—if him even existed anymore—an endless current of warmth that stripped everything away. His name, his thoughts, his memories, all loosened their grip, floating outward into the great white expanse.

He was bare now—stripped of self and ego, reduced to something smaller and purer. For a moment, he couldn't tell where he ended and the light began. It was all one.

Instinctively, he looked down. But there was no body. No shape, no shadow. He tried to lift his hands, but nothing followed the thought. He was consciousness—nothing more, nothing less.

Then, from somewhere ahead—he felt it. A presence. Massive. Powerful. Not seen, but unmistakably there. It filled the infinite with its weight, its authority, its love.

"Eddie."

The voice rolled through him, a deep and resonant thunder that wasn't sound so much as being. It boomed through the endless white with the same bone-shaking power Eddie remembered from his first day at Proviso Yard—the storm that split the sky when lightning hit, the rail vibrating under his boots.

Eddie looked up—with eyes he no longer had—and knew. Instinct, deeper than thought, told him who it was… it was God.

"I took great care designing you," God said, the sound both thunder and whisper. "Creating your soul and bringing you into the world. You're my greatest creation." He chuckled. "Humanity, made in my likeness."

The words moved through him, pure and heavy with love. Eddie felt them vibrate through the infinite, through whatever passed for his being now.

"At the same time," God went on, "I took equal care crafting the perfect plan to go with each life—your destiny. I buried that seed deep in your soul."

"I brought you into existence with certain passions, talents, and spiritual gifts," God continued, His tone both kind and unyielding. "And I've been trying to guide you, Eddie—first toward me, then toward that plan."

The pause that followed wasn't silence but weight, meaning.

"But little of that seed took root."

The words didn't scold. They simply were. Truth, stripped of judgment. And in that moment, Eddie felt the full shape of his life—every missed chance, every small kindness, every doubt, every love—spread open before him like pages in the palm of God.

"I held the lamp." God said. "I lit the path," the words vibrating through eternity itself. "I sent clues."

Images began to flicker across the white expanse—like ripples of memory painted in light.

"The horse figurines from your Uncle Charlie that Christmas morning when you were a boy. The long hauls with Jack and Red, the ranches stretching out along the countryside—each one a signal, Eddie. All I wanted was for you to walk with me, so I could help you get there."

It came together in Eddie's mind with a slow, undeniable click. His ease with animals, the pull he'd always felt toward horses, the quiet dream of a ranch out west—all breadcrumbs dropped along the path. And wasn't it funny? His best friend "Horse," a Quarter Horse inked on his arm like a prophecy. The church he wandered into by chance—*First Cavalry*. Those moments that used to feel harmless, random, now vibrated with something bigger.

"At your lowest point," God went on, His tone sincere, "I sent an angel. The hooded messenger in the weeded lot—the one who spoke of the verse on Jack's lighter. That, too, was meant to guide you toward me and your purpose." He paused, the silence resonant and full. "Just as Florence and First Cavalry were. Every thread woven into your life had my hand on it."

The light around Eddie deepened, glowing warmer now, fuller.

"I have always loved you," God said. "Always will." The words rolled through Eddie, filling every corner of what he was. Then, softer—but heavier somehow:

"But I'm disappointed," God said. "You let the Devil steal too much of the life I had planned for you."

The words struck deep—not with anger, but sorrow. A father's grief, not a judge's sentence.

Eddie felt the ache of it move through him, pure and undeniable.

"But I thought my life was the rail yard," Eddie said, his voice trembling—not from fear now, but the realization that maybe he'd gotten it all wrong.

The light pulsed softly, like a breath drawn through eternity.

"The rail yard," God replied, His voice vast and kind, "was just part of the journey." The words rippled outward, gentle but firm. "There, you met Jack—the father figure you needed. He built your confidence, steadied your hand, helped you find direction."

Eddie thought of Jack's grin, the smell of grease and steam, the weight of a wrench in his hand. Every clang of metal, every long night on the yard now glowed with new meaning.

"The real destination though, Eddie," God continued, the tone warming, "was the ranch."

A flicker of image passed through the light—rolling hills, red barns, horses running free under a sunset sky.

"Your heart was telling you all you needed to know," God said. "You've known it all along. You just didn't trust it."

The words sank deep, reverberating through the infinite white. Eddie felt them stir something old and buried inside him—an ache, a longing, a truth he'd always felt but never dared to follow.

Before Eddie could speak, the light ahead began to shift.

Out of the white brilliance, form began to take shape—a gate of impossible scale, rising higher than sight could follow.

It shimmered like molten gold and living light woven together, the surface breathing with radiance.

Then he saw movement—small white figures darting above the Gate, looping and diving in smooth figure-eights. They left trails of light behind them, trails that shimmered and vanished in the glow. Angels. Eddie knew it before he could think it. Guardians, circling high above, keeping watch against whatever darkness might dare try to breach this place.

And then came God's voice again—calm, resonant, filling every part of him.

"I'll give you a choice," God said. "Enter the Gate…"

The words hung in the vastness, heavy with finality.

"…or return, to finish my plans for you."

A Second Chance

Eddie was thrown—violently—into something heavy, wet, and solid. It felt like landing inside a sack of dead meat. The impact rattled him from the inside out, knocking the wind from lungs he didn't remember having. His spiritual self crashed back into flesh, into gravity, into pain.

He hit the ground hard. The world around him reeled and spun. His limbs were leaden, his bones thrummed with a deep ache that pulsed in rhythm with the earth itself. He felt like he weighed a thousand pounds.

Cold rushed in—sharp and immediate. His skin prickled, breath fogging in the air. Every nerve screamed awake, raw and electric. His head pounded like a hammer on steel, the pain blooming behind his eyes.

For a moment, he couldn't remember what had happened—why everything hurt, why his body felt broken and strange. Then it came to him, slow and awful.

He hadn't just been hit by something.

He'd been hit by a train.

And this—whatever this was—felt even worse.

The first thing that hit him was the smell—warm antiseptic and plastic. It coated the air like something sterile and alive, sharp enough to make him wince. Somewhere close by, medical equipment kept time in patient, steady beeps that seemed to fill the room with a strange kind of rhythm.

He tried to open his eyes. The light was blinding. It stabbed straight through his skull, so he shut them again, waited, then tried once more. His eyelids felt gummy, heavy, like they'd been glued shut. Shapes blurred and swam in front of him—white ceiling tiles, a metal pole, something hanging beside the bed that dripped clear fluid through a tube.

A groan slipped from his throat, raw and rough. He tried to move, but nothing responded. His body felt like it had been poured full of concrete. With a small tilt of his head, he caught a glimpse downward—and froze.

Head to toe, he was covered in tight white plaster. Every inch of him, sealed.

A full-body cast.

And the ache that radiated from inside it told him one thing for certain: he was still on Earth.

Eddie sank back into the pillow, the weight of exhaustion pulling at him. Then it came—faint at first, then stronger—the scent of perfume. Sweet, warm, and delicate, with a note of something floral and familiar. It was wonderful in every way, cutting through the antiseptic air like sunlight breaking cloud.

Through the blur of his half-focused vision, a figure took shape beside him. A woman—young, maybe mid-twenties. Long golden curls spilled down past her shoulders, gleaming where the light touched them. A small white nurse's cap perched perfectly in place atop her head.

She leaned in, close enough for Eddie to feel the warmth of her presence as she adjusted the pillow behind him. The movement stirred the air—and that's when he saw it.

Something glinted against her neck. Metallic, silver.

It caught the sunlight pouring through the window, a brief spark of brilliance that shimmered and swayed gently back and forth. Eddie squinted, his heart thudding, trying to make sense of it.

Then the blur cleared.

It was a pendant—an angel, its wings outstretched, a single gem gleaming as its halo.

Eddie's breath caught.

The same angel.

She leaned in again, the faint rustle of her uniform brushing against the sheets as she adjusted the cluster of wires and hoses along the wall. That's when Eddie saw it—her name, etched in black across a gold-plated tag pinned to her chest.

VERONICA.

For a moment, his heart stuttered.

"Well, good morning," the nurse said warmly, her voice comforting and patient, like she'd been waiting for him to open his eyes for hours.

Eddie swallowed, his throat dry as dust. "Where... where am I?" he managed, his voice rough.

"Northwestern Memorial," she said, still smiling. "You've been here the past three weeks."

"Three weeks?" Eddie exhaled, turning his head toward the window. The city light filtered through the blinds in soft, gold stripes. "I had the most amazing dream," he said. A faint laugh escaped him, half-broken. "So real..." He paused, shaking his head slowly. "I thought I was dead." He let out another chuckle, softer now. "I thought I was in heaven."

Veronica glanced at him, the corners of her eyes glinting.

"Well," she said gently, adjusting the blanket over his chest, "you've been given another chance." Her words lingered in the sterile air, warm and alive against the rhythmic beeping of the monitor. "I'll make sure to let Jack know you made it back in one piece."

Jack? he thought. *His* Jack? The sound of the name tore through his psyche like a door kicked open in the night.

Eddie forced himself to look back over—every muscle screaming in protest.

But the nurse was gone.

No soft steps leaving the room, no cheerful, "I'll be back to check on you in a little bit." Nothing.

Just gone.

The air still carried her perfume, faint but unmistakable—warm and floral, like a ghost of spring in the sterile cold of the hospital room. The sunlight glinted off the IV pole, throwing a flicker across the floor where she'd just been standing.

Eddie blinked hard, trying to focus, but the doorway stood empty.

Then, movement. Two figures passed in the hall—nurses, chatting and laughing, one holding a clipboard. The sound of their voices felt startlingly normal, almost jarring after the silence.

When they glanced through the doorway and saw him watching, both froze mid-stride.

"He's awake!" the male nurse shouted, his eyes wide.

The clipboard clattered against the doorframe as they scrambled inside, the rush of footsteps and urgent voices flooding the quiet room.

Eddie's gaze drifted past them, back toward the corner where she'd been standing only moments before. Nothing there now. Just sunlight, and the faintest shimmer of dust hanging in the air like the afterglow of a miracle.

"You're awake, Mr. Ross," the younger nurse said again, still a little breathless from the rush in. "We had no idea—how long were you awake?

Eddie blinked up at her, the edges of the world still swimming in soft haze. He gave a faint, weary smile. "Not to worry," he said hoarsely. "Veronica was just here not long ago."

The two nurses exchanged a look.

"Veronica?" the man repeated, brows drawing together.

"There's no one here with that name, sir," the young nurse said gently, her tone careful, as if speaking to someone fragile. "You must've been dreaming."

She tucked the blanket around him, her movements practiced and kind, the way nurses do when they're used to mending more than the body. "You've been through a lot," she added softly, offering him a smile that didn't quite reach her eyes.

Eddie didn't argue. He just stared past her, toward the sunlit corner where the air still shimmered faintly, the scent of that perfume—warm, sweet, and impossible—lingering in the soft morning light.

Eddie couldn't shake it—the instinct, deep and undeniable, that what had happened was real. Not a dream. Not some morphine-soaked hallucination. It had been too perfect. The light, the faces, the voice. It all carried a weight and clarity sharper than anything he felt now. Compared to that place, this world seemed dull, like a photograph left too long in the sun.

In the days that followed, the doctors confirmed what Eddie already sensed: he had died.

Clinically dead.

Forty minutes without a heartbeat. No pulse. No brain activity.

They called it a miracle, shaking their heads as they read the charts, baffled that he'd come back at all—let alone talking, breathing, remembering. But Eddie knew better. It wasn't luck, or science, or chance.

He'd been sent back.

And whatever time he had left—this second chance—it wasn't just his anymore.

Eddie would go on and on, talking endlessly about what he'd seen on the other side. Heaven, the river of light, the people waiting for him there—Arthur, Jack, Florence, his mother. Anyone who walked through his hospital room door became an audience.

The nurses humored him at first, exchanging smiles when he launched into another story. The doctors were less subtle, their eyes flicking toward one another over their clipboards. A few whispered that maybe he'd stayed dead a little too long—forty minutes was a long time for the brain to be without oxygen. But even then, in the backs of their minds, they couldn't quite shake it. They'd seen his charts. They'd seen him flatline. And a part of them—small, buried deep—wondered if maybe he really had been to heaven.

Word of the accident spread, and eventually, Catherine and Margaret showed up. Both of them. Together. It was the first time Eddie had seen his sisters in nearly twenty years.

The reunion was awkward at first—hesitant smiles, careful questions, the soft kind of laughter people use when they're not sure what's safe to say. But soon enough, something loosened. The years seemed to fall away like old wallpaper.

They started joking, teasing him about how he looked like a mummy strung up on wires, suspended in plaster and tape.

Eddie laughed too, low and unguarded, as if the years of rust had finally shaken loose from his soul. For a little while, it was just the three of them again—kids from the South Side, finding their way through life the best they could.

And for Eddie, lying there in that hospital bed with his sisters beside him, it felt a little like heaven hadn't let go of him just yet.

Eddie knew it through and through—felt it deep, from his spirit clear down to his bones. He'd been given a second chance. And this time, he wasn't going to waste it. He sure as hell wasn't going to let God down again.

The Last Stop

When he was finally released from the hospital—six long months of recovery after the collision—Eddie moved slower, but his heart was steady. The world looked sharper now, colors more alive, sounds carrying meaning they never used to. Even the morning light through his window felt holy somehow.

The first thing he did was make a promise to himself: to set things right.

So, on a cool spring afternoon, he climbed behind the wheel of his red Dodge Ram pickup and headed west. His hands trembled a little on the steering wheel, not from nerves, but from the weight of what he was about to do.

Red's place looked spectacular: a sprawling white estate with columns out front, a wraparound porch, and a circular gravel driveway that crunched under the tires like crushed pearls. The windows gleamed, and flower boxes spilled with color beneath their frames.

It was the house they'd bought after getting married—a far cry from the south side apartment where Red used to fix things with duct tape and a hammer. Cynthia came from money, old money, and it showed in every polished inch of the place.

And yet, right in the middle of that postcard of elegance, there was Red. Same grease-stained jeans, same unruly mop of red hair. He was bent under the hood of his battered old truck, sleeves rolled up, hands black with oil. The rest of the world might've cleaned up around him, but Red was still Red.

Eddie pulled up slow and killed the engine. For a second, he just sat there. Then he smiled—a small, honest smile—and stepped out.

Red looked up, his face streaked with grease and sunlight. For a heartbeat, neither man said a thing.

It had been nearly forty years since he'd seen Red in the flesh. Back then, Red had already been a grown man, fifteen years older, all fire-colored hair and swagger. Now that red mop was thinner, washed out to a weathered copper, and the years sat broad across his shoulders.

Time had carved its story into both of them—deep lines, stiff joints, eyes that had seen too much. They'd aged a lifetime apart.

And yet, in that suspended moment, they looked at each other the way they did in the old days—not an old man and an older one, but Eddie and Red, standing in the glow of the roundhouse.

Eddie took a few steps forward, his voice rough but certain. "Hey, Red."

Red blinked, straightened, and grinned—wide, genuine, like the years between them had been erased.

Eddie started to speak, his apology already forming, but Red just shook his head.

He didn't need to hear it.

Seeing Eddie standing there was more than enough. And the way Eddie's smile trembled in return said everything words ever could.

After that day, Eddie sold nearly everything he owned—the furniture, the television, the miscellaneous items that once cluttered his small apartment. He canceled the lease, packed a single worn duffel bag, and didn't look back. No map, no plan—just faith.

For the first time in his life, Eddie Ross was traveling light.

He told himself he'd head west, let God do the steering. Wherever He wanted Eddie to end up, that's where he'd go. It wasn't about the destination anymore—it was about trust.

A quiet peace settled in him, something he hadn't felt since he was a boy lying on the floor with his carved horses, dreaming big dreams. Now, somehow, he sensed those dreams weren't dead—not anymore.

The train lurched beneath them, jerking to a halt with a metallic groan. Air hissed from the brakes, rolling through the cars like a long exhale.

Eddie leaned forward in his seat. He took off his glasses and buffed the lenses with his handkerchief, squinting at the window's reflection—at the man staring back.

"I told you, Mr. Walker," he said with a half-grin, "it was gonna be a long one."

Since we'd left Chicago, nine hours had flown by like minutes. Eddie's story—about growing up during the Great Depression and living the life of a rough-and-tumble railman—wasn't just entertaining. It was mesmerizing. The kind of story that reached out, grabbed you by the collar, and didn't let go.

It felt like we'd stepped through some kind of time machine together—one that carried us back through the cinder smoke and steel of the early 20th century, then slingshotted us forward again to the present moment, leaving us both blinking at the speed of it all.

By the time he finished—his jaw-dropping account of dying, going to hell, then heaven, and somehow being sent back again—I didn't know what to say. Words felt too small for something that big.

So I didn't speak. I just listened—to the quiet hum of the car, to the echo of his story still hanging between us—and paid attention to my intuition.

I let my gut do the talking.

He raised his eyebrows high, slow, then let them fall again, tracing the jagged pink scar in the center of his forehead.

"One hell of a ride, wouldn't you say?" he murmured,

chuckling under his breath.

I looked at him, wide-eyed, still speechless. All I could manage was, "This is me." I stood, reaching for my bag from the overhead rack.

As I stepped into the aisle, I glanced back at Eddie. He was there, calm as ever, eyes gleaming in the light that slanted through the car. And then, just like that, a thought crept into my head—one I couldn't shake.

My grandmother.

An elderly widow, who could use a helping hand.

And then Eddie—an old soul with miles behind him and the spark of something holy in his eyes, talking about second chances and destiny like they were things you could hold.

I didn't know if what he told me was true—about heaven, about meeting God, and God having a plan for your life—but deep down, something in me believed him. It wasn't logic. It was instinct, the kind that starts in the gut and rises slow.

As the air inside the car stilled and the world beyond the windows stood waiting, I recalled what Eddie had said about coincidence. That's when I realized, maybe—just maybe—God had crossed our paths for a reason.

Coincidence, or perhaps, divine alignment… I didn't know. Either way, as fate would have it, our meeting held the answer we'd both been searching for.

I needed someone to help care for my grandmother—someone patient, gentle, and strong enough to lift what time had taken from her. And Eddie… he needed his ranch, that piece of land he'd carried in his heart for a lifetime, the one God had whispered about long before he was born.

It was all right there, lined up straight as track iron—two lives crossing at just the right moment, like the switch had been thrown by something greater than either of us.

"Eddie," I said softly, my voice breaking the quiet that had settled between us. "Why don't you get off at this stop and come with me? After what you told me about Florence… I think my grandmother would love to meet you. Maybe you could help fix up that old farm of hers—turn it into the ranch you've always dreamed of."

For a moment, Eddie just sat there, silent. His eyes went distant, the way a man looks when he's listening for something beyond the world. Then, slowly, a smile began to spread across his face—steady, knowing.

"Mr. Walker," he said finally, standing with care, his joints popping like old wood. He reached up for his duffel bag, slinging it over one shoulder.

"I'd be delighted."

Source: U.S. Library of Congress, public domain image, no known restrictions.

Chicago & North Western - Proviso Roundhouse, 1942

Chicago & North Western - Worker in the Proviso Roundhouse, 1942

Chicago & North Western - Steam Engines in the Proviso Roundhouse, 1942

Source: U.S. Library of Congress, public domain image, no known restrictions.

Chicago & North Western - Workers in the Proviso Roundhouse, 1942

Chicago & North Western - Worker in the Proviso Roundhouse, 1942

Chicago Union Station – Great Hall, 1943

Source: U.S. Library of Congress, public domain image, no known restrictions.

Chicago & North Western - Worker in the Proviso Roundhouse, 1942

Source: U.S. Library of Congress, public domain image, no known restrictions.

Chicago & North Western - Proviso Yard, 1942

Source: U.S. Library of Congress, public domain image, no known restrictions.

Boys hopping a freight train during the Great Depression

CHICAGO
Jack Luken

ACKNOWLEDGEMENTS

To my wife, Christine—my rock, my sounding board, and my greatest blessing. Thank you for listening to endless hours of ideas and never losing patience.

To my parents, for raising me in the most loving and supportive home imaginable. You always encouraged me to go for my dreams and did everything you could to help me get there.

To my sister Karen, for being a motivating factor for getting the book across the finish line, and collaborating with me as we learned the world of self-publishing together.

To Atlanta First Baptist Church—the church I joined when I came to Atlanta when my spiritual journey was just starting to take off. The services enriched my soul and inspired many ideas for the book.

To the Southeastern Railway Museum, for their friendly and knowledgeable staff, whose help during my visit years ago made for invaluable real-world research.

To the U.S Library of Congress, for providing historical images of the Chicago & North Western Railroad and Proviso Roundhouse. These images, located at the end of the book, complement the story and offer vivid glimpses into the rugged beauty of life on the rails.

ABOUT THE AUTHOR

Scott Wilson's writing blends faith, nostalgia, and the rough-edged beauty of working-class America. Raised in the White Mountains of New Hampshire within earshot of the Conway Scenic Railroad, he grew up with a love for trains, storytelling, and the quiet power of redemption.

Years later, after a long career in consulting, and currently a supervisor for the U.S. Federal Government, Scott has returned to his first love—storytelling. His work explores faith, purpose, and the hidden hand of destiny in ordinary lives.

The Devil's Agenda is his debut novel.

www.ingramcontent.com/pod-product-compliance
Lightning Source LLC
LaVergne TN
LVHW100514110826
845146LV00002B/639
* 9 7 9 8 2 1 8 8 7 3 6 1 5 *